W9-AXF-772

"Farah's work is fuelled by the same compassionate rage as Solzhenitsyn's, the humanist vision outraged . . ."
– Doris Lessing, *New Society*

"An eloquent indictment of tyrannies committed both under Islamic law and in the name of Socialism."
– *The Observer*

"Nuruddin Farah has admirable poetic gifts for concision, clarity and wit."
– *London Magazine*

"In terms of vitality, compassion and the ability to take literary risks, [Farah's] talent demands recognition."
– *British Book Reviews*

"Nuruddin Farah's provocative trilogy is one of the most powerful novelistic explorations of dictatorship since Asturias' *El Señor Presidente* or Roa Bastos' *I the Supreme*. . . . He is a major writer, one of Africa's best, and this splendid and very readable trilogy is the centerpiece of his considerable accomplishments."
– Robert Coover

1992

Variations on the Theme of an African Dictatorship:

Sweet and Sour Milk

Sardines

Close Sesame

Also by Nuruddin Farah

From a Crooked Rib

A Naked Needle

Maps

N U R U D D I N   F A R A H

CLOSE SESAME

G R A Y W O L F   P R E S S

FINKELSTEIN
MEMORIAL LIBRARY
SPRING VALLEY, N.Y.

00429 5779

Copyright © 1983, 1992 by Nuruddin Farah

Close Sesame was first published 1983 by Allison and Busby Limited.

Publication of this volume is made possible in part by a grant provided by the Minnesota State Arts Board, through an appropriation by the Minnesota State Legislature, and by a grant from the National Endowment for the Arts. Additional support has been provided by the Jerome Foundation, the Northwest Area Foundation, and other generous contributions from foundations, corporations, and individuals. Graywolf Press is a member agency of United Arts, Saint Paul.

First U.S. Printing, 1992
Graywolf Press,
2402 University Avenue, Suite 203,
Saint Paul, Minnesota 55114.
All rights reserved.

9 8 7 6 5 4 3 2

Library of Congress Cataloging-in-Publication Data
Farah, Nuruddin, 1945–
Close Sesame / Nuruddin Farah.
p. cm.
ISBN 1-55597-162-8 (paper) : $12.00
I. Title.
[PR9396.9.F3C4 1992] 91-41263
823–dc20 CIP

To the martyrs of Africa

and to Koschin my son, my love

CONTENTS

PART ONE

Memory does not return
Like experience, more like imagination
How it would have been if, how it must
– Patricia Beer

One should say before sleeping, "I have
lived many lives. I have been a slave
and a prince. Many a beloved has sat
upon my knees and I have sat upon the
knees of many a beloved."
– W. B. Yeats (Quoted in Anne Sexton)

ONE

A Door in the Darkness

He was up earlier than usual. He had been asleep barely an hour when he sensed hands the size of a child's tugging at the sheets with which he had covered himself. He thought he knew those hands: small, strong, determined – and beautiful too. He had prepared something to say as he sat up, a word of welcome, something friendly, a frivolous comment, say, about the fingernails being long like a dead person's, anything by way of greeting (this person and he had not met for almost a year now). But when he opened his eyes, there was nobody there. Once awake, however, he felt there was no point trying to get back to sleep although he had closed his eyes less than an hour before.

His watch advised him that it was time to say a small prayer or two. One prayer led to another. One prostration suggested a second and a third. "O my Lord, great Thou art without a doubt, the greatest and most merciful and most compassionate; welcome us, o Lord, allow us into the enclosure Thou art in, permit us to enter Thy dwelling in tranquil peace. For Thou art a celebration and we, with every breath we receive or emit, are mere manifestations of Thy existence. And Thou art our closest neighbour, our protector; Thou art the provider of our needs and Thou art our need, our principal need; Thou art the guide of our shaky visions, the honey-guide of our dreams." And then he told his beads in peaceful communication with divine secrets.

But he stayed in bed, propped up by a pillow against the wall and reasonably comfortable. A quarter of an hour later, he heard the muezzin's call and answered it with a salvo of *Allahu-akbars* and *Alxamdulillaahs*. A little stiff, he slowly gathered himself as though he were a scatter of independent joints the years had put asunder and through the miraculous murmuring of a small prayer felt he was put together, one painful joint screwed into another, one dry bone fitted on to another; and he got up, issuing further thanks to Him who had created him some sixty-nine years earlier out of clots of blood. He looked for and finally found what his feet were groping for: his sandals. He bent double, murmuring a series of sanative phrases, breathed with lungs of gratitude and meant for the ears of his Creator.

His toes in place, his back erect, his destination clear to him: he moved in the direction of the lavatory which was on the same floor. He said *Acuudu-billaahi* as he entered the toilet which he thought of as Satan's dwelling-place, and when he came out, having taken his ablution, said *Alxamdulillah.* Then another prayer, this time of only two prostrations – the morning's *Salaatus subx!* The beads again. A litany of Koranic verses. As he counted and re-counted the ninety-nine names of Allah, as he multiplied and subtracted the number of times he had said them, he realized that the world had begun to wake up: he squinted catarrhally at the greyness outside, his ears cocked, for he thought he heard Khaliif's call and cursory noises. From where he sat, he could see Cigaal's house, Cigaal whom he always described as an "unneighbourly neighbour."

More beads. He decided he wouldn't think of neighbours and mundanities of betrayals and conspiracies; of congeries of alms paid to a traitor; of silencing fees; and of little rascals and wicked families. Nor would he think of his good friend Rooble and Elmi-Tiir; of his wife whom he loved till the day death parted them; of his daughter Zeinab and her two lovely children; of his son Mursal, Natasha his wife and their wonderful son Samawade; of Waris; of Mahad, Rooble's nephew; Yakuub, Rooble's son. He decided he wouldn't think of a madman who was not mad; of sane persons who were, in one way or another, mad; nor would he think of public justice; of vengeance, and whether this was a private matter or of public concern. He would think of God; of prayers; of the divine will which held out a hand to him whenever he felt base and inhumane; of the vision and power which enabled him to identify the enemy within and helped him get rid of it.

And then he prayed: "O Allah who art just, give us true peace, bless us with the inner tranquillity that Thou art, make us apprehend the enemy within us, deliver us, help us, o Allah, descend from the greater heights of selfishness, help us reach and be content with what we have or who we are: weak and helpless without thy guidance. The sea spits out what she cannot bury, throws up the refuse for which she has no place. Help us, o Allah, help us find peace in ourselves, in our friends, in our families and in our neighbours."

He held out his hands, rubbed them together, brought them closer to his face and spat a salivaless emission of breath and (with the prayer-beads still in the grip of the index and middle fingers) rinsed his face in his dry but blessed open palms. Then he recited a mumbled *Faatixa*. With all this done, his features cast in worshipful mould, silent, reverent, he got up, caught the prayer rug by the corner and hung it on the nail on the wall above his bed. He went and stood behind one of the windows. A little later, he pulled up a chair and sat on it crossing and recrossing his legs.

He watched dawn's metallic greyness prepare to dissolve into the morning's dust. The smile on his lips at times became a slight wince: he seemed afraid of an oncoming attack, of the paroxysms which he so hated. His asthmatic condition had made it necessary for him to be moved into this house which was equipped with the most modern system of communication: a telephone on which to call a doctor or somebody with a car if a bad attack came while Mursal and Natasha were both out. When his wife was still alive, the family had a house to which visitors of all sorts could come, callers whose main or only claim to be there was their belonging to the same clan as himself – men and women who recognized him as the Sultan of the clan. When she died, and the attacks became more frequent, he was moved to his daughter's home. His house was put on the market, despite his objections. "Now I am an old man," he said to his good friend Rooble, "an old man like yourself, dependent upon the whims of my offspring."

He was not unhappy. But he often spoke about his dependent state, about his hesitation to ask his friends over. It was not that his daughter Zeinab would have objected, no. She would have entertained anyone whom he pleased to invite; she would have slaughtered a cow to feast them or spent hours in the kitchen cooking for them. But she did not have the time. Also, through a process of elimination, through a patterned scheme of that-is-not-good-for-you and this-is-what-you-need, his children, Deeriye realized, had altered his life-style and imposed upon him a number of gentle restrictions, impressed upon him the necessity to do his exercises in the morning, go for walks in the afternoon and take his medicine regularly. And when he was finally used to it all, and had become very fond of Sheherezade and Cantar, when he had finally made friends with some of the neighbours who called, Zeinab decided to demolish half of her house and live in the untouched half. The place was in no time reduced to dust and disorder. Again he was moved – this time to his son Mursal's house.

There was no point denying that Mursal's marriage to a foreign wife did place further restriction on his movements, on his having friends in after midnight: no one dared to knock on the outside door and unannounced kick shoes off at the entrance to the living-room and engage Deeriye in one of those protracted conversations about the affairs of the nation or local politics. Mind you, neither Natasha nor Mursal ever said that his friends and others were not welcome. Indeed, if anything, she gave more care to his every move or suggestion. She washed him once or twice; she indicated that she had no intention of putting any restrictions on him, said so again and again and again; and he answered that he had heard and believed her. Did he have any complaint to make? None about his son, daughter-in-law and grandson – a wonderful, intelligent eleven-year-old – but he did not like the neighbourhood. He preferred Zeinab's to Mursal's.

As for Mursal and Natasha, nothing he said to them whether in serious or frivolous vein was ever handed over to oblivion. Immediately he made a slight comment about anything, something was done about it: anything or any person that upset him was instantly removed. When he had been in Zeinab's house, she used to supervise his meals, change his bed, help him through the difficult hours, sit by him all night if necessary, reading to him, talking about the things which interested him or playing cards with him. He was never short of company when out of detention centres. Never was he in need of someone to hear him articulate his thoughts, expound on some theory which occupied his mind. Sometimes if he went out for a promenade, total strangers, young men or women, would come up to him, walk with him part of the way, chatting with him, showing how much they admired his civil courage – he being perhaps the only man they knew who was ready to die for his principles, the only man brave enough to stand up to and challenge naked terrorism or brutal force or injustice, the only man who staunchly believed in a national rather than trivial clannish politicking; and they introduced themselves to him, these young men or women, and some would try to engage him in a passionate political discussion he was not ready for, others would walk level with him, display deference by being silent in his presence, go with him for half an hour or so as though helping to escort him out of dangerous territory and when they reached a busier roundabout or a street would take leave and go their ways.

And now that fate had consigned him to Mursal and Natasha's custody? He was not unhappy. After all, he was only a beast who managed every now and then to walk a considerable length and space and thought he had made it at last until forced to realize that the rope which tied him to the pole would not give way, nor would it snap or break. Of course, he was grateful to his daughter-in-law, who put in a lot of effort to make him happy – drove him everywhere he wanted to go, came to his room the moment she returned home from work to ask him if anything was amiss and never let him sleep without a glass of boiled milk by his bedside and a glass of cold water. He had clean linen every few days; shirts, sarongs and all other vestures a man of his age and background was fond of arraying himself in were taken away to be washed and returned warm and ironed. He was grateful to Natasha for all she had done for him. And Mursal?

Mursal was Deeriye's second son (the first having died at the age of three), born in 1943 when his father had been out of prison a year and a half. The British had released all political prisoners in the former Italian Somalia and Deeriye and his friend Rooble were among them, although Deeriye was detained again. Mursal was a healthy child, intelligent, good at anything if given a chance, ran fast just like his father and at the tender age of five and a half composed a mini-poem in praise of his mother. He took after his mother physically: his hands were small like hers, strong and determined. Intellectually he took after his father: he had a sharp curiosity and his eyes were aglitter with extraordinary intelligence. As a young boy, he preferred the company of his father to that of his mother; he loved the fables and folk tales his father told him – but he didn't like going with him to political meetings which he found very boring. But generally he loved being with his father, his small hand tucked, numb and slippery, in the tight hold of that perspiring large palm. Deeriye, who had learnt to read and write Arabic and Italian in prison, taught his son the things he had picked up, shared with him some of the experiences of detention – careful, though, not to discourage or encourage the child's mind or prejudice him against political life. When the Italians were returned to Somalia as administrators of the United Nations Mandate Territory, Deeriye was again thrown into detention. Mursal helped his mother read Deeriye's letters to her or reply to them. A year or so later, he surprised her by saying that when he grew up he would become a lawyer and defend his father and other political prisoners – gratis! When he reached university-going age, however, Mursal found that, although he still was interested in training as a lawyer, his interest lay more in research than in taking on court-cases or defending the constitution of the state. Now, after a Ph.D. on the political relevance of the Quran in an Islamic state, he had become a Professore di Diritto at the National University of Somalia, Mogadiscio.

Mursal and Deeriye took great delight in each other: they found each other's company stimulating, enlightening, the son teaching or learning from the father, the father likewise. Last night, for example, they had spoken until the small hours, their conversation following no order or logic, their colloquy about internal politics intriguing and at the same time ambiguous: jumping from a theological subject to one of no political or religious relevance and then moving on to something more pertinent – like the concept of *lex talionis,* and what it implies in a modern Islamic state; the political chaos; the political violence; and whether or how an alternative political organization could bring about any change. Their dialogue had something exploratory about it: neither Mursal nor Deeriye wished to commit himself. But they explored ideas as though they were containers in which some valuable items had been lost; neither pushed any point beyond the gentle understanding of *bonne etiquette,* neither imposed ideas upon the other. One idea reminded them of another. One topic bred a monstrous second or third, something unexpectedly off the mark, way out of the scope of their discourse. Thus they spoke of Cumer ibn Khattaab, the Second Caliph, and his having been killed by a madman; they spoke of the third Caliph Cuthmaan ibn Caffaan and his being besieged in his residence, taken hostage and killed; of Cali ibn Abii Taalib being assassinated too; of the confounded state of affairs which led to Mucaawiya's claiming the Caliphate on the strength of being a blood relation of the Prophet himself. In short, they spoke of power politics, assassinations for political ends, state and traditional politics. Deeriye at some point raised his hand, indicating that he was not interested in any further discussion when his son point-blank asked him whether or not he would consider the use of violence or condone it if one close to him were involved. Deeriye was not shocked; not taken aback. But he had asked:

"You are yourself involved in overthrowing the state? Are you?"

"I said if . . . ," and Mursal had struggled.

"Or is Mahad?"

"What makes you think Mahad is?"

"Yes or no?"

"I said if. . . . "

"Answer me straight, Mursal. Are you or is Mahad?"

"The question is, Father, whether or not there is any legal sense in finding a logical link between the aspects of traditional (i.e. private) justice and state (i.e. public) justice; and if we understand that there is, whether or not we too should work out an amalgam whose final result and aim will offer the same kind of exaction."

"I don't understand a thing you've said," had retorted Deeriye.

"Let me see. You agree – don't you? – that traditional justice is private justice in so far as the kith and kin of the aggrieved person, in order that the family or clan not be dishonoured, uses what is known as the *lex talionis* system of justice: a life for a life, an eye for an eye and that sort of thing. All right?"

"Go on."

"Embedded in public justice is that sense of an all-encompassing justice. The victim's family need not worry about taking revenge, need not worry whether they will receive a hundred or so camels in blood-money compensation for the relation killed or fifty camels for a clanswoman, for no one would accuse them of drinking the milk of the blood-wit instead of the blood of the person who had killed their relation. Embedded in public justice is the consensus of the community, their trust in public justice, hence in the constitution. It is the state which acts as the arbiter here, the state which represents this consensus or what we may call the constitution."

"Tell me, Mursal. . . ."

"Before I tell you . . . let me finish."

"But you will never finish, I know you; not once you start talking like this, hiding in the rhetoric and jargon of jurisprudence."

"Just two points. Tell me, Father, with what do you associate the names of Mucaawiya and Yaziid?"

"That is point one?"

"Point one. Yaziid and Mucaawiya," he repeated and wouldn't continue until Deeriye answered.

"The first with usurpation of the Caliphate, according to some Islamic historians anyway, I mean according to the Shi'ite interpretation of the events as we know them; the second with tyranny, Yaziid that is."

"Yaziid: you can say that name again!"

There was a brief silence in which both said the name "Yaziid" softly, with Deeriye looking alarmed when he got the meaning, the historical connection, which any Somali would get from a play on the name.

"My second but most essential point is simply this: does the state in Somalia as we know it have a traditional base in Somali thought? Does the régime of Somalia today have any Islamic legitimacy?"

Another silence in which neither challenged the other. Deeriye was for the first time in years frightened of his own reactions; afraid of being afraid; afraid of unsaying his own maxim that the shaping spirit of man is politics. But it was definitely different, wasn't it, when one was involved oneself – and not one's son or one's beloved? One knew the dangers, could skirt round these mined territories, could pick one's way through to safety and emerge all the richer with the experience. Then Deeriye remembered another conversation the two had indulged in recently; he remembered Mursal's asking him his father's views on violence. They were not alone then. Mahad had come to dine with them; Natasha and Samawade were there too. Deeriye had answered in a tone full of self-reproach that he would never make use of violent means to overthrow a tyrannical régime – not he, anyway. But, he had added, he could see himself justifying, intellectually speaking, any mind which moved in this general direction of violence. Somehow, he was able, as always, to bring a graceful end to the conversation. On that occasion he did so with a slight movement of hand and head, making wise use of the advantage old age bestowed on him by indicating signs of fatigue; he broke his jaws in a needlessly noisy yawn and everybody, save Mursal, disappeared instantly. Mursal was bent on staying on, ready to talk until he broke the back of the night and his father with exhaustion. But why had he insisted on being heard on the "theme of violence, political violence?" Why had Mahad gone into Mursal's study and called Mukhtaar so the two could wait for Mursal while they talked? What were these three up to? Or rather what were these four up to? For there was *a fourth,* a man mysterious as his voice. Deeriye never dared ask these questions. There was a good reason.

He was biologically the father of his children. But the fact that he had not contributed towards their upbringing as Elmi-Tiir and his wife had done weighed heavily upon his conscience. He was sorry he was never there when his children needed him most, sad he had not been there to wipe away the mucus of a sickly child or been close at hand when Mursal was being initiated into manhood. All the credit went elsewhere. Elmi-Tiir provided their material and spiritual needs and Nadiifa, the love that nourished them like the milk of her own breasts "as they waited for this father of theirs who had gone on a trip, sent them gifts occasionally through people; a father who wrote letters which their mother couldn't read." To Mursal's "I'm going to become a lawyer," Zeinab, feeling challenged, retorted: "And I'm going to be a doctor so that when either of them is ill, or when Uncle Elmi-Tiir is unwell, I could serve as their doctor." He: a lawyer; she: a doctor. Deeriye: asthmatic; Nadiifa: an ailing mother, weak of constitution; Elmi-Tiir: healthy. And all Deeriye could say, to account for his absence in the family album, among the images of growing-up children, was: "I was not there." He was not there when they graduated from high school; he was not there when Zeinab's children were born; he was not there when she married. A photograph once taken, he would say, could not be altered to fully satisfy artistry – unless forged; so it is within the growing mind of a child: the *absence* is indelible. Which was why they sometimes talked about him in his presence as though he were deaf or could not understand the language – similar to the way people talked about Natasha in Somali when she was there. *He was a he:* third person, masculine, singular. (Deeriye at times when speaking with Samawade would speak about himself in the third person.) "Do you think he would like to eat this?" Zeinab would say. *He! He* was not a physical person so much as an abstraction: a man whose absence was noted on the printed photograph. *He* was an idea; he was a national *notion. He* was, come to think of it, more than anything else an image; "He became what you wanted," Mahad had said; a kaleidoscope that gave one the picture one wanted; a *he*. He was also a springboard, someone on whom ideas were tried, to whom things were told, someone whose suggestions were sought. Was that why Mursal had brought up the theme of political violence?

To Elmi-Tiir's thinking, "When you approach the devil's dust, you raise your little finger and seek the protection of Allah and His saints saying, *'Acuudu billaah,'* whereas when you come and stand in Deeriye's revealed light, you recite the *Faatixa*. For he is a saint." Rooble, his friend, was perhaps the only one aside from his wife who knew Deeriye well: the two had been in prison together for a number of years and had been through hell's humiliation and shared the happiest moments with each other. Deeriye, to Rooble, was "the last life of breath after a catastrophic storm; the only pillar in place in the midst of all the rubble around."

And *he*? Or rather *he* "as Deeriye," what did he think of himself?

He was a man who attained a *modus vivendi* with his own situation. And only God knew how difficult that was. He believed, for instance, that he attained a *modus vivendi* of a different kind once before but lost it: he had just then crossed the threshold of late adolescence to manhood; and such an attainment it was. He utilized the potential of the physical in him to the full: he had been an attractive, muscular, healthy youth, ready for any challenge; an envied youth; a youth just turned man; tall and handsome; everything as easy as breathing. Then his father's asthmatic condition worsened from one day to the next and the old man died. And the council of the clan appointed him in his father's place, the council's vote more or less unanimous – although for a personal reason, a certain Haji Omer had spoken ill of Deeriye. Deeriye's firework exhibitionism and the flame of youth were suddenly replaced by the need to prove his own worth: as the inheritor of his father's title, as the continuer of the old man's political enthusiasm (the old man had been a Sayyidist all his life: he had suffered for it at the hands of the colonialists), Deeriye had had to come to terms with enormous problems. He was born in 1912. He would add for the benefit of those who did not know or might have forgotten that it was in 1912 that the first African party of resistance was formed, a party, *magac lagama miskiin maahee,* known as the African National Congress; it was also in the year 1912 that the Dervish movement of the Sayyid in Somalia defeated the British imperialists; and Corfield died in this war and the Sayyid composed Deeriye's favourite poem. Deeriye saw himself as a Pan-Somalist and a Pan-Africanist. He would immediately add that the two were not contradictory: as a matter of fact, one justified or rather complemented the other. He was Pan-Somalist, because he was a Somali nationalist and his hero and political mentor had been the Sayyid. Pan-Africanist: because he was a man who followed, with enthusiasm, all the liberation movements in Africa; a man who believed that unless the southern portion of the continent were freed from the reactionary clutch of white racism, Africa might as well consider herself a colony; but he was also a man who believed that unless the Somali dispute with both Kenya and Ethiopia were settled to the satisfaction of the Somali people (not a Somali government), there would be no lasting peace in the Horn of Africa and the years would be littered with famines, droughts, conquests and re-conquests.

Now, hours later, he was still sitting there, a little uncomfortable, and, so as to forget this physical discomfort, he began to engage the morning in a discourse of worshipful murmurs, and the prayers which the lips issued helped his mind to migrate heavenwards. Silence. He sensed someone moving about in the room below: was it Natasha preparing tea for herself and Mursal before they went to work? Or was it Samawade? The noise could now be identified: it was talking about a *he,* asking whether or not *he* would like a cup of tea in bed? Deeriye waited as though in the wings of that noise. Beneath it all: an insoluble tension in the form of a question: what will become of *him?*

• • • • • • • • • • •

The young sun had cast a net and Deeriye felt caught in it. His squint was slight, his focus a little altered (he had just re-emerged from the tunnel his catnap had led him to), his mind elsewhere. Apparently, catnaps were nowadays becoming a familiar feature of his existence. Why, he had found out now for instance while he had been enjoying his brief catnap, somebody had come in, brought in a warm cup of tea, tiptoed out – and he did not wake up. He asked himself if he could remember his last thought just before the latest catnap? Yes. Khaliif: the madman who strode out of dawn's greyness, half his face painted white and the other half dark. Dawn's veil of darkness had been light like a coat of fading paint, transparent like silk soaking in clear water. And Khaliif had come into view, with no grain of dust stirred: he had come like the allergic pain of a disorder. He stalked the neighbourhood, scoured the area: there was hardly anybody walking about at that time of morning, there was no audience to hear him proclaim himself, no crowd to cheer him on, no sympathetic listener to act as the *suggeritore* if the well of this man's mad imagination had dried up. Saying nothing, shouting no messages, speaking not a word; he moved, he behaved like a murderer on search of the evidence of his own deed returning to find out if his secret has been discovered. Yes, he looked a madman. One would conclude that he did not belong in the world of the sane. But neither did he belong in the world of the insane for he did not always behave as though he were mad. To Deeriye and many others, Khaliif was a burial mound one suspected was empty but which, out of good breeding, one never dug open. Khaliif, someone used to say, was the mystery no one was ready to solve; and such a wonderful mystery too. For mysteries are material for speculation. And Khaliif was.

Once a highly placed government civil servant, respected by all, a family man with four daughters, a son and a job that could have got him or his survivors and dependants a fat pension if . . . ! If what? Here everything became shrouded in mystery. Nobody knew what happened to him between one evening and the following morning. His wife and children saw him leave as he always had done in his car, his mood more or less jovial, his destination unknown to them. The following morning, he was mad. The house and the whole neighbourhood awoke to his screams, his profanities. No one could make him keep his clothes on long; he would begin unbuttoning his shirt or unzipping his trousers or would undo the sarong's knots the instant the helper's hands relaxed. The doctors who were consulted did not know what to suggest; one daredevil of a psychoanalyst spoke of the dangers of the haloperidol treatments and left it at that. Had Khaliif been given the treatment? No one could tell. His wife, children and the relations did what tradition prescribed: he was tied to a bed, several sheikhs were summoned and were handsomely paid to read the blessed word over him. Now Khaliif's overnight madness might never have been a mystery in itself were he not prone to making weird statements such as: "Night plots conspiracies daylight never reveals;" also his family and friends might never have questioned the hand of Providence were it not for the fact that during his lucid intervals he mentioned names, responsible names, in particular one name. But was he *majnuun?* You could say he was insane (using the term in its general sense), that he was a man who, while walking up and down the streets of Mogadiscio as ugly a sight as anyone had ever seen, spoke a language whose construction was grammatical although not all the time logical; a language which was not disjointed but whose inferential and referential senses could be questioned; and therefore a madman. Yet if you got near him, you sensed that he had washed, that his body did not smell sordid like a bedpan; neither would you associate him with the down-trodden among the urban populace who woke up before first cock-crow to attack the garbage-cans in the hope of salvaging a morsel from the tropical decay of waste. A mystery: where did he sleep? Where did he wash? Why was it that he could grind out the names and titles of those men in high government offices who were suspected of being responsible for his insanity and go unharmed? He would do this in public; the man was beyond fear. Did he believe nothing more could be done to him? He would say he would take revenge and kill. Kill whom? Was he really mad?

Some people believed he was not. They would ask: Why did he always choose to deliver his messages of condemnation before a crowd? Why did he always choose his victims well? Why did he always choose to make his cursory remarks in the presence of or within hearing distance of the new *priviligentsia?* In Mogadiscio, there were many madmen and madwomen. Some were famous and had even entered the annals of national politics. Others had become figures as renowned as the class they represented. Yet others had enriched the language as a new idiom might. Cities and towns are made more habitable by likeable characters with outstanding stories and mysterious backgrounds. However, Khaliif was a mystery half-revealed, as far as Deeriye was concerned. The charm, the charisma, the voice which made everybody stop and listen: these told his story well, these made relevant his speaking of that which others were afraid to speak; or reaching regions of thought others feared to tread. Men and women, wherever he went, assembled round him and heard him speak *for* them, on their behalf, saying what they could not have said. Every now and then some young man or young woman would make a stealthy approach with a view to putting into Khaliif's mouth words the young man or the young woman would never dare to say–for this young man or this young woman was not mad enough to speak their sane thoughts; and the young man or the young woman would be thrown into jail if these words were attributed to him or her. But Khaliif never borrowed words from anybody; he never directly spoke somebody else's lines; never–to the best of anybody's knowledge. Question: did anybody know any of his activities or contacts after he had gone mad? How much of his mysteries had been so far revealed?

It seemed Khaliif mistrusted everybody: he moved away the moment anyone came near him, man or woman, child or adult; and he would find a corner, wedge himself in where the walls met and he would launch his proclamations from there, using the space he had made for himself as a pulpit. He shunned human contact. He showed intense dislike for any violence, loathed the city's urchins because they sometimes pelted him with pebbles. He also avoided any contact with enthusiasts whose sympathies turned into pity and who arrived with gifts of food or clothing. He broke plates when presented, like a beggar, with the day's leftovers; he kicked at them, spilled their contents; he screamed, and ran off when anyone as much as touched him.

Now, sitting in the sun's brightness, Deeriye started: he could hear Khaliif's magical voice, complemented by some welcoming remarks, like a chorus, from a small crowd that had already gathered to listen. Deeriye craned forward. Khaliif did not suggest a broken man on the fringes of society; nor an alienated man whose mind buzzed with mysterious messages so far undeciphered; nor a man invalidated by or over-burdened with guilt. No; his demeanour forestalled everyone's fear, prediction or worry: he sold to everybody the very thing no one was prepared to buy, and bought from everybody the very thing no one was ready to sell. His discourse was clear, grammatical and logical:

"There are wicked houses in which live wicked men and wicked women. Truth must be owned up. We are God's children; the wicked of whom I speak are Satan's offspring. And night plots conspiracies daylight never reveals." And he held his hands together in a *namastee,* clowned a bit, entertained the younger members of the audience by doing a somersault, a karate ghost-dance, and then returned to his peaceful corner and fell quiet. Applause. He curtsied; grinning, grateful and graceful.

A number of people had come out of their houses and among them, Deeriye could see, was his own son Mursal. Others craned their necks through their windows, just like he. Most of those who came out were dressed informally: some in colourful pyjamas; others in house-clothes, *guntiinos,* or in garments thrown quickly over their bodies after a shower – their hair in disarray, uncombed, teeth unbrushed. There were, in addition, a couple of women who had interrupted breast-feeding a child or sifting grain. These looked madder than Khaliif. For he was not adorned as Deeriye had seen him when dawn had the colour of cured hide and Khaliif a face half painted white, the other black. No, he was decently arrayed in a priestly tradition (the hems of the attire a little stained from somersaulting and indulging in playful activities to entertain the younger members of his audience), he was robed all in white, his movements suggestive as a sheikh's, his voice rich, like a prophecy, with its own cadences, his proclamations saintly. Now he was silent and was facing Cigaal's house: and when the crowd turned to look in that direction, there standing in the doorway was Cigaal's grandson Yassin, who made as though to pelt Khaliif with a pebble he had picked up from the ground. Was Cigaal's the wicked house of which he spoke? The members of the audience thought so and somebody provided further notes to Khaliif's broad references. And was that why Yassin was threatening him with violence? But why had he changed his semi-rags for a sheikh's outfit?

He said, "*Mahad Allah leh;*" then he invoked Allah's names, the names of the Prophet and the major saints. He added, "Wicked,

wicked, wicked. No respect, none whatsoever. No respect for any form of divination or divinity. The word, it appears, has not reached their ears or if it has they seem not to have heard it. *Acuudu billaahi minash shaytaanir rajiimi!* Nothing is holy in their houses. They upturn traditions and know not how to create anything of harmony except something in which the devil may dwell for ever and ever. May He upset the vessel of their future; may He upturn the pitcher out of which they drink; may He break in two the containers out of which they eat: these who are *gadaal ka soo gaar!* Upstarts of the worst kind, upstarts who had upturned our sacred traditions and have begun worshipping *him* . . . would you believe it . . . worshipping *him* . . . a mortal and a fool at that in place of Him: *subxaanallaah! Fanaka cuudu billaah!*"

Without a moment's hesitation, without losing the balance of mind and logic of the sane, he flitted out of the priestly tradition into that of the actor-clown; he somersaulted, half revealing his underpants; he put his hands to his mouth, pretended to be a modest little girl, moved his head to one side, then the other and was silent.

Then a young woman singled herself out of the crowd and went into another corner and in a bold, loud voice told the now familiar story of the African dictator who, touring the country, decided to visit a hospital for the mentally ill. The patients were hurriedly assembled and those who refused to go voluntarily to hear him were frog-marched into the hall. The dictator spoke to the assembly of madmen and madwomen: no applauding, no jeering, no booing: his speech, two hours long, was listened to very attentively and he was pleased with himself. When he finished, the director of the institution called upon them to sing the praise-names of their beloved benefactor: they all sang, save one man. The dictator noticed the man's sulky silence, he saw the man's defiant smile and thought he could even hear a slight chuckle every now and then as the others sang loudly to appease his and the director's humour. But not this man. Prior to leaving the hall, the dictator asked the director who *the madman* was. The director, as though dealing with the most ordinary of questions, answered thus: "Forgive me for not introducing him to you. The man you refer to as the *madman* was actually certified sane this very morning." And the director added, speaking as though in a tandem of tension and lightheartedness: "You might say he was the only one in the room who had a certificate of sanity." The director laughed at his own joke. The dictator feigned enjoyment of it too. Then with sudden aggressiveness: "You are mad yourself," declared the dictator. To his men: "Straitjacket him, quick," he gave the order and left. The director of the institution of the mentally ill became the newest member of the community of madmen.

There was a sigh of grief from the crowd. From Khaliif this:

"Now who is mad? Down with those who kill, who humiliate and torture! Down with those who make use of unjustified methods of rule." And he burst into a guffaw of laughter which made everybody raise querying eyebrows. Scarcely had everyone relaxed than he startled them with: "Don't the Arabs say, 'Pinch the wisdom, o people, out of the mouths of madmen.'" Then a silence.

Suddenly, however, there occurred the first popping thud of a shower of pebbles and stones: Yassin, the ten-year-old grandson of Cigaal whose house Khaliif had described earlier as wicked, was collecting more pebbles and stones and indicating, with great relish, that he would pelt Khaliif if he said another word. Yassin stared stonily at all the inimical gazes trained on him. A moment later, his support came in the persons of his mother and his aunt, both, it appeared, ready to out-shout anyone, mad or sane, ready to protect their Yassin. Someone in the crowd said the women and the little boy were mad. Was this as far as they would go? Or would someone tell the young rascal not to hurt him? Mursal's voice, prompt, firm and sonorous:

"You will not throw any more stones, Yassin. You will drop the ones you have collected and behave yourself."

A pause. And a little later, at the behest of his aunt and mother, Yassin dropped the stones he had gathered.

"Now who is mad?" chanted Khaliif. "Tell me who is mad and I will tell you who is not."

Khaliif then put his hands together as a sign of resignation. He exchanged knowing smiles with those nearest him and nodded in the direction of Mursal; then he walked away, shunning any contact with violence which, he believed, would emanate from the same source as that which had robbed him of his own sanity.

• • • • • • • • • • •

Deeriye was sitting in his favourite armchair, listening with elaborate relish to his favourite litanies of the Koran being recited by his favourite sheikh: each Koranic word created crests of waves of its own, curiously rich with the wealth of the interpretation the hearer heaped on them: Deeriye's heart danced with delight. Then he heard someone enter the room – or rather he felt a pair of boots walk in; he had headphones on and therefore could not really hear anything other than the isolated Koranic litanies. And he turned quietly, slowly, with the movement of someone suffering from a painful stiff neck. Mursal, his son, was there, a radio set in one hand and a cigarette in the other; and Mursal grinned apologetically at his father and waited for him to remove his headphones before he spoke.

"I am very sorry for disturbing you," said Mursal, tottering forward, looking for the most appropriate spot to put the radio down, careful not to tread on the wires which led to Deeriye's ears.

"Please. Put it anywhere. Why don't you put it on the bedside table, which is where I usually place it anyway. Push the table-lamp and the book aside."

That done, Mursal turned round. He was thirty-eight, not quite as tall as his father, and looked like his mother.

His ears were cocked so he could hear distinctly every chord and note produced by the turbulent gale coming from beyond the ocean; a man who had the manner of using his hands effectively and well – hands which were nearly as small as a dwarf's, extensions of arms that were short as swagger-sticks, hands whose language were in total discordance with what he was saying.

"Are you unwell?" asked Mursal after a brief silence.

Deeriye knew instantly that it would be long before he returned to hearing the litanies again: so he put his headphones aside and switched off the cassette-recorder, ready to engage his son's questions.

"No, I am well, as well as I can be. Why do you ask?"

Mursal stood a little distance away in a corner, supporting his weight on his right leg and with the other inserted in an opening he had made by lifting his left shoe off the floor, he kicked at the heel of the raised shoe. The rhythmic thud was a little distracting; it put Deeriye in mind of a cow digging its hoof into the ground.

"Natasha brought you a cup of tea and called your name three or four times," Mursal said. "You seemed to be asleep but she wasn't sure. You didn't hear her, did you?"

"I may have done, but it seems I took a nap."

"So, you are not unwell?"

"I said, I am as well as I can be."

"You didn't cough, that I know, otherwise we would have heard as we always do. But is there any complaint, about, say, a tightness of the passageways or congestion, anything?"

"No. Thank you."

"But you got up early?"

"I got up to say a few prayers, that's all," he said.

Deeriye bore this interrogation with grace, with hardly a change in his tone. But the changes were clear to those for whom he was their pivotal concern; those, like Mursal and Zeinab, to whom he had been the primary and essential subject of conversation when they met: "How *is he* taking it?" had been in currency following the weeks and months when Nadiifa died; this had recently been replaced by "How is *he?*" meaning, will he survive another day, another month, another year? Cigaal's *unneighbourly* house and its frequenters spread the rumour that *he* would die any day, there was no doubt about it, they said. They even said what he would die of: a shock, an intense shock would make his heart stop, denying his respiratory organs time to recirculate the blood to the heart and the brain. But listen to Zeinab: to those who reside in Cigaal's house, the science of precision does not appeal; that of medicine, they do not understand.

"You have every comfort, as comfort goes?"

"Yes," said Deeriye. "I have every comfort a mortal requires."

"Despite the unneighbourly neighbours, despite Cigaal's house, despite all the wicked things and plots one associates with his household and those who frequent it?"

"Despite all, yes."

"It is my feeling, though, that nothing will come from them, no evil, I mean, directed at you particularly. I suspect they would if they could. I am more or less certain about that."

"But I *saw* him, I saw Yassin, that little rascal," Deeriye said, his voice slightly shaky.

"In your visions?"

"No, no. I saw him in real life, in flesh and blood, and you saw him today, you saw him throw pebbles at Khaliif the madman. Did you not? In my dreams, I see him do similar things. But we're not talking about my visionary dreams now, are we? You haven't come for that, have you?"

"No." Then after a pause, "Well."

Mursal grinned at his father to make him understand that his "Well" should not be taken as a dismissal or belittlement of the importance Deeriye attached to these visionary dreams of his. For when he talked about them, he spoke with the seriousness one associates with visions and not dreams. He talked seldom but proudly about the visits Mursal and Zeinab's mother paid him in detention, how she would come to him at night and keep him company, tell him stories, bring him news about Mursal and Zeinab, about Rooble and Mahad, about Elmi-Tiir and his children. What proof did he have that he had been in communication with her? Once when released from detention, he was brought home and upon entering the house seemed to know what each had been doing and he had talked about intimate things nobody knew other than insiders like Mursal, Zeinab and their mother Nadiifa, the three having discussed that topic only the evening before, just before going to sleep—and that less than ten hours previously. With Mursal and Zeinab seated to one side and Nadiifa the other, he recounted to them what they had said about him. He had seen them in his vision: Nadiifa, perfumed and loving, had told him all that. He could describe the *guntiino* she wore, could tell her that it was a gift from Elmi-Tiir. Another time, he told Mursal that he had fallen off a tree and broken an arm. But this had not yet happened. A few months later, Mursal did fall off a tree and broke an arm. "Well!" But that he had (or *suffered*) these visionary dreams was kept a family secret and no one spoke of them openly, not with strangers around, anyway. Others knew, however, of his deep attachment to his wife, and they teased him now and again about "this weakness of his." Nadiifa, her eyes bright with delight, was happiest listening to him build a bridge between himself and the world and using her to cross, using her as the pillar of this construction. Mursal and Zeinab wished he wasn't so obsessed, so possessed when he told them these stories. Now Mursal was standing just behind him, his hands resting on Deeriye's shoulders, and Deeriye was sitting in his favourite armchair. Both could see what was going on behind the window in front of which they were. And:

"Oh, there he is."

"Yassin?"

"Yes. The rascal."

Yassin was menacingly stalking the street below, gathering pebbles and looking for targets: a stray cat, a stray dog, a lost child, anyone or anything to hit. He looked up in the direction of Mursal and Deeriye; he could see that he was being watched, that his every movement was being followed. Deeriye had never been filled with such terror, not even in all those years of detention, not with all the tormenting dreams and tortures he had been through. He simply could not understand. He cringed at seeing Yassin. *Had he ever seen him in any of his visionary dreams? Yes, he had. Yassin had struck him on the forehead and Deeriye had bled to near death.* Everything in the vision was not clear; but there was an owl in it and there was shattering glass. Such terror, such fear. Deeriye turned away and shifted in his chair. Mursal stood further back. Fear was in Deeriye's eyes, big like a twelve-day-old moon. He felt, in a sense, that he was in a world to which Mursal was not admitted, a world whose vista had begun to narrow down to a passageway. And there was no choice but to walk that passageway, dry or wet, rain or no rain, fear or no fear, Yassin or no Yassin: alone. Mursal did not know what remedies to suggest; although, time and again, one thing had proven very helpful: Nadiifa's name. Now:

"Have you seen Nadiifa lately?"

First, Deeriye started. Then he took the sweet name thus heard into his mouth and spoke it, soft, delicious; he chewed upon it and, with great relish, held the wad of the name's syllables in one cheek. Nadiifa! A name so dear. Finally, he sent it down his gullet after he had sugared his saliva with lovely memories of her. Nadiifa: true peace.

"Have you?" repeated Mursal.

"Yes."

"How was she?"

He was sad now as he said, "I woke up too early, before she managed to say anything. I frightened her with my eyes. You see, she comes to me just before my morning prayers; she comes to me when I've rested. Today because we stayed up until late, I must have been a dreadful sight. My open, profane, red and exhausted eyes must have frightened her."

"But she did come?"

"Yes."

"And she did not say anything whatsoever?"

"She tugged at the sheets I was sleeping under and I woke up. It reminded me, in fact, of that poem of Bowdhari's in which he laments that Hodan, his love, had come when he was asleep."

"Oh, yes." This time, the "oh, yes" did sound a vulgar dismissal, a belittlement, of all that had gone before.

Deeriye looked hurt but his heart and mind took refuge in the name of his beloved Nadiifa – the mother of this young man who had been insensitively sarcastic. He remembered how most of his acquaintances, men in their late sixties or early seventies, said he was either a pervert or that the woman must have bewitched him. Many could not understand why, although he had the means, the money and the opportunity to marry as many women as he wished, and maintain two mistresses on the side, Deeriye would think of no other woman but Nadiifa. Ninety-nine per cent of his peers re-marry when their wives die or age, as at their menopause – some marry again with their wives still alive, reasoning: "But what can I do with a woman who won't give me any more children?" Rooble, his best friend, had re-married too and now had a son a few months old. So had Elmi-Tiir. And some of those whom Deeriye met occasionally at Baar Novecento spoke of how they wished he would stop his hankering after that poor woman who, they argued, had spent nearly twenty years of her life alone and longing for a man – when he was in prison, fighting for a national or personal principle. The country his vision constructed, he would say, was not peopled with materialists: men and women whose main measure was *how much one could afford and how much one was worth*. But he knew that every one of these men wore, with exhibitionistic aims in mind, the gold they had accumulated illegally, the watches their sons had brought them from trips abroad. Did he not know! And men of his own age-group? They showed off their children's worth, their offspring who maintained them plus their wives, and when they met at the terraced cafe Baar Novecento they spoke of nothing but money and women: how they were being treated badly or well by those who supplied them with the mean stipends on which they and their much younger wives survived. Mistresses of the worst kind, these! *What is Nadiifa but honour, good memory and faith in life, trust in love and friendship!* He looked up, feeling lighter having unburdened his chest, and saw Mursal standing by the radio, his hand hesitating about whether or not to switch it on. Deeriye said:

"You've been looking anxious and nervous lately. Is anything bothering you? What is on your mind? Won't you trust an old man with some of your less burdensome secrets?"

It was Mursal who started now, like a thief caught returning stolen property. He moved away from the radio which only a few seconds before had been the object of his concern.

"I am thinking thoughts, as I said last night. Just thoughts. But they are not clear to me yet."

Deeriye got up and went closer so he could look him in the eyes, see what could be seen, detect what could be detected. They were now a few inches apart; Deeriye taller and handsomer but weighed down with age and worries.

"You are not planning anything, are you?" said Deeriye, the tone of his voice casual. "I mean any . . . er . . . political violence?"

Whatever Mursal had waited for, this surely was not it. He moved back a little as if avoiding a blow. For a long time, nothing would revive the glitter in his eyes. Now he appeared a man beyond reach, his eyes in a trance – worried too. A long silence. Then he repeated, "I am thinking thoughts. That's all."

"And Mahad is thinking these same thoughts too, is he?"

"Mahad?"

"Yes. Are the two of you planning something? Are you thinking the same thoughts? . . . Use of violent means . . . say . . . public and private justice . . . taking revenge, eh?"

Mursal's hands rose and gesticulated: they opened a door with all eight fingers and two thumbs cooperating to create this effect: and they turned upon themselves, giving shape to a circle, a globe. After this mesmeric gesture, and after a long silence, he said, "I am thinking . . . , intellectual thoughts. It is possible that Mahad is thinking similar thoughts. But merely intellectual thoughts. No violence is being meditated. Not at the moment."

The sun's brightness in the room contrasted with the smiles on their faces: they understood each other well. Mursal knew that his father did not believe him; Deeriye knew his son knew that he was not speaking the precise truth. But they were gentle with each other. They wouldn't force anything. Deeriye told himself that Mursal and Mahad would never do anything of which he and Rooble would be ashamed.

"Before you go. . . ."

"Yes, Father?" said Mursal, holding the door open so he could dash out before he was asked further questions.

"Could you arrange for Rooble to come to see me here or for me to be taken to him? I haven't seen him for a couple of days and would like to speak to him."

"When?"

"When either you or Mahad can take one or the other to the place of the other. I don't know. Perhaps you can telephone Mahad at work and arrange it with him before you go to the university."

"I can't reach Mahad today. But I will bring Rooble here myself. Is there anything else you require, before I go?"

"No, thanks."

Going, Mursal said, "Peace be upon you, Father."

And Deeriye cringed.

TWO

The Devil at his Heels

"*Nabad,* Samawade," said Deeriye upon whose face broke a gentle smile. He looked at his grandson standing in the doorway, correct and well-behaved.

"*Nabad,* Grandfather. I hope I am not disturbing you?"

"No, you are not," said Deeriye, closing the Koran which had lain open on his lap. "Are you well? Is everything all right with you, Samawade?"

"Yes," he answered and moved further into the room which the sun's rays had cut in half, making the section in which Deeriye had been sitting darker than the other into which now Samawade walked. Samawade took a stool but said nothing.

And Deeriye thought that if human beings could be dismantled with a view to identifying every part of the body, Samawade's parts would pose no difficulties: you could see that he had Mursal's nose, chin, eyes and small hands; you could also note that he had his mother's hair, straight and dark; and her voice, thin and cutting. His eyes were bright like his grandfather's. "Alight," Deeriye's wife Nadiifa once said, "with the fire of uncommitted mischief, afire with the same sort of mad ambition his grandfather must have had when, aged eight, nine or was it ten, he said to his own father who had just recovered from an asthmatic seizure that he would avenge the Sayyid and kill, yes, kill those who had killed. And he repeated this two, three times, although his father's expression became insane with pain, coughing and wheezing. Samawade has the same kind of mad ambition. His gaze says that he will achieve all the things his parents Mursal and Natasha have failed to. You wait and see." She had been very fond of him, and so was he of her. When she died, he cried for days, refusing to eat, speak or go to school. Now he was attached to his grandfather, upon whom he stole every now and then when the old man was having a nap: and he would fix him with a gaze, wondering if he would die and never rouse from that nap. On occasions, he would say Deeriye's name: and the old man would wake up and say that all was well with his grandfather – speaking in the third person.

One day, when Samawade was also there, Sheherezade, Zeinab's daughter, wanted to know where her grandmother had gone. "Heaven, of course," said Deeriye. "And where is heaven?" asked Sheherezade. Samawade, ironical but half believing, said, "Somewhere far away in the sky. Where the likes of you don't go." Now Deeriye got up and walked to where Samawade had been sitting on a stool, quietly elegant, waiting, adult-like, with patience. Between them there was a formality of a sort: Samawade, because he had been trained to be considerate and correct particularly when with his grandfather; Deeriye, because he handled his grandson's growing intelligence with exaggerated skill. Now Deeriye towered above Samawade who felt uneasy and rose to his feet. Deferential, he remembered a recommendation of his father's: at no time, other than when invited, should Samawade initiate or create body-contact with his grandfather. Why? He was told that his grandfather intended to keep himself in total readiness for Allah's call and, with that uppermost in his mind, liked to be able to say a prayer or perform a humble prostration any second, any minute, any hour. Contact with an unclean, unwashed person like Samawade would frustrate this readiness: in order to perform a humble prostration, he would have to take ablutions, and this washing would require energy of which his grandfather had little. Presently, Samawade moved backwards as his grandfather approached: Samawade tried to avoid the contact Deeriye wanted to create. And Deeriye beckoned to him to stay where he was, remembering that only a few hours earlier, Yassin, younger than Samawade by a year, had pelted Khaliif with pebbles. He was glad indeed that his grandson did not have Yassin's wild look and untamed appearance. Samawade untightened the grip his grandfather had on his wrists: he turned, his eyes alight with their inventive mischief, and said, after having made a distance between him and his grandfather:

"You promised when I saw you last to tell me one of the Wiil-Waal stories. Remember, the one in which his wife tells him he is not the most intelligent and cleverest man a Somali mother has given birth to, remember?"

Deeriye stood there, his posture infirm and ancient: Samawade feared he had disturbed his mental balance by asking for a story when Deeriye was perhaps thinking of other things.

His voice apologetic, Samawade said, "You don't have to tell it to me right this minute. We can do it any other time when you have the time and you are ready to tell it."

Deeriye was silent.

"Also why was he called Wiil-Waal? Was he mad?"

The sunlight brightened the room, covering the whole of it with criss-crossing rays and hardly any shade at all.

"Was Wiil-Waal mad, did you ask?"

"Yes."

"Was the Sayyid mad? Why did the British call him the Mad Mullah?"

Samawade did not get the rhetorical nature of the question and was of two minds whether to answer it or challenge it with another question when the telephone rang downstairs in the living-room. With the suddenness of a child's enthusiasm, he dropped the mask of formality and ran down the staircase to answer the telephone. A few minutes later, he announced that it was Mahad and the message was Rooble would take a taxi and be with Deeriye in less than half an hour.

• • • • • • • • • • •

The multifarious warmth and trust between friends: Rooble and Deeriye. And the two met in the living-room of Mursal and Natasha's house and greeted each other in silence: they shook hands but fell apart at hearing Samawade's cry of enthusiasm, Samawade who ran into the livingroom to report that he had seen Mahad and Mukhtaar drive past without stopping. Neither said anything. Their eyes met Samawade's, then looked and found one another's: this made Samawade feel he was redundant. Rooble and Deeriye: the two together a tapestry whose fabric was ornamented with mutual trust, a friendship woven out of loose ends and difficult knots but the whole spread painted with clear designs – and the blood of sacrifice! For instance watch them eat, like bush-fire, the distance between them, watch them shake hands and hug, watch their robes merge and create a collage of colours: this was as powerful an image as the dust-devil, rolling heavenwards, kneading its various strands into one mighty muscle – stronger than Satan's! Nothing could ever separate them. Such emanations of trust – Deeriye! Such emanations of patience – Rooble! When they heard Samawade leave, they were silent for a while. They circled round each other, one of them stationary, the other on the move. Finally, Deeriye said:

"I've called you because something is worrying me."

Rooble sat in an armchair and having made himself as comfortable as possible said, "And how has life been treating you, Deeriye?" in a voice whose mixture of serious and unserious tones so surprised Deeriye he did not answer immediately.

Deeriye looked at Rooble, his friend, stout of patience, gentle in manners, generous, trustworthy, a good man; *a door* to Deeriye, *a door* he had used to enter and dwell in any important phase of his life, a door of symbols, yes, a good man.

"How are you, Rooble? And how is your life?" he asked.

"I am not well."

"Your stomach, is it?"

"One's stomach is one's guide."

"That is true. Your stomach does not run unless there is a reason."

"Nobody's does."

Deeriye asked, "Is Mahad the reason?"

Rooble nodded. He held his head in his hands, he pressed his forehead and mumbled that he felt dizzy as though on a vehicle that had suddenly changed direction. He got up. He wished to know where the toilet was. Deeriye pointed. While going out, Rooble passed the maid who was bringing in a tray of tea.

How would Deeriye describe his life? he asked himself when alone. A long shadow, hardly punctuated by depression, self-doubt or, for that matter, self-effacement; a shadow dark as the deepest hue of night but with a door open in that opaqueness: a door of light. Of course he would not deny that his was a life developed, like a negative, in the dark-room of isolation. He was a man who had obtained a *modus vivendi* with his body although he would never claim to have attained the same with the spirit of his imagination which was rich as the darkest of clays, inventive as the dust which was capable of entering and settling anywhere. During all the years of detention, it was true, his imagination had not suffered, as did his body, any considerable change in posture. They say that the weight of one's brain shrinks with age. He wondered how much weight his brain had lost over the years. He was sure that twelve to fourteen years' imprisonment, not forgetting all the solitary confinement and psychological torture, had done their share of damage. But he would argue that he had suffered less than many others for he had always in view "a door of light in all that darkness, a door which helped him see the outside: a door of friendship, of love, of Roobles, of Elmi-Tiirs, of Nadiifas; a lighthouse in the direction of which one moved when the storm tore into one's soul, one's lungs." There were many difficult moments when things looked very blurred like a lens out of focus; there were insurmountable obstacles in his way; there were foggy nights when he lost sight of the door altogether; nights with no visions, no dreams, no visiting Nadiifa and no door. Altogether, he remembered now, he had spent a little more than a dozen years in various political detention centres: eight of these in colonial prisons, four in post-independence jails.

The first: he was twenty-two and the year was 1934. The last, only a couple of years ago: he had been released just in time to bid farewell to his dying Nadiifa. Twelve years in dark caves, in subhuman conditions, in humiliation, chained like a beast. One thing remained framed, like a picture, in his mind: that one's conscience is the lens which helps one to see, judge and then gives one enough confidence to press the button of one's reason of being. A person without a conscience is as ridiculous as a blindman posing to be photographed can be. Twelve years in rooms dark as a photographer's, twelve years framed as one's picture of oneself or one's dearest, there for him or her to see, speak about, point at the developed print, point out the hiatus, mentioning why *he* was not there when the family portrait was taken. But that was not where it all began. His life used to be awash with the sun's brightness. He had just married a woman whom he respected (love came later when in detention, when she visited him in his visionary dreams;

love came much later when both passed the test of endurance); a woman who was also a friend; to make all this richer, he had friends with whom he had grown up and of whom he was very fond. His father, then bedridden, had been in those days the Sultan of the clan, a Sultan admired as a poet and known for his nationalistic views. And Deeriye was reared to revere Sayyid Mohamed Abdulle Hassan as the most important figure the Somali nation had ever produced; he was encouraged to learn all the Sayyid's poems by heart, which he did. His favourite was "Death of Corfield," composed and recited in 1912: the year Deeriye was born.

Twenty-two in 1934. Young, just married. Then the first political stir, like a raindrop on dusty ground. His father had been dead less than a fortnight. But what was Deeriye like in those days? He was quick as an athlete; and his elegant mind bent like rubber and offered back to him whatever form or shape he had asked for: a mind determined to serve the needs of the immediate family and those of the larger community. The first stir had nothing to do directly with Deeriye or his immediate community. The Sultan of the clan adjacent to Deeriye's, in defiance of an ordinance issued by the Italian *Residente* of the region, refused to comply with instructions to appoint stipended chieftains who would be answerable to the head of the regional administration. The Sultan, also a Sayyidist, would not condescend to receive a junior officer of a *soldato* whom the *Residente* in the nearest town had delegated. The Italian and the Somalis in his retinue, when told they would not be fed or received with hospitality, tried to force their way into one house. The young man whose hamlet this was wrestled with the Italian for possession of the gun in his grip. Half an hour later, the Italian died from a bullet in his chest. His retinue ran to save their lives and on reaching the next town reported the incident. A day later there arrived, prompt as fate, a senior officer with twice as many soldiers and retainers. This officer did not mince words; speaking through an interpreter, he gave his ultimatum: an either-or and no-questions! The Sultan's answer was another mumble of defiance. Then the Italian senior officer asked for the name of the man who had killed the Italian soldier. The Sultan wouldn't give it. Enraged, dissatisfied with the evasive responses from the Sultan, the officer had twelve elders of the clan and the Sultan rounded up and taken into police custody. Those detained, like the Sultan, refused to give the name of the man who had killed in self-defence. They all refused to admit any knowledge of the man and his whereabouts. This turned the area into a theatre of activity, an area where spies and traitors could function well. One day, an eight-year-old boy was going from Deeriye's dwelling to that of the one whose Sultan and twelve elders had been taken into detention. The boy was carrying an important message to Rooble, the son of the Sultan, when he was intercepted by an old man whom he recognized and addressed as "Uncle;" the eight-year-old told the man the gist of the message he had been asked to deliver to Rooble's community: that *the man* had been offered asylum by Deeriye's community.

Two days later, children playing outside Deeriye's dwelling saw a trail of dust materialize into a vehicle. In it were a white man, his interpreters and a couple of soldiers with machine-guns slung across their shoulders. The vehicles braked, the men got out and the most senior of the Italian officers asked to be shown the Sultan whom he mentioned by name. Deeriye's wife Nadiifa told the interpreter that the Sultan was performing his prayers and would see him immediately he had finished. Finally, Deeriye came out of the hut. With him were the elders of the clan.

He said to the most senior of the officials, "To what do we owe the visit?" his voice half-sarcastic.

"I've come to offer *peace,*" said the Italian officer.

Deeriye looked at the officer who had spoken, he looked at the others, then at the elders. He chuckled. He indicated to the other men (Elmi-Tiir was away that week) that they should flank him immediately he sat on the beautiful mat his wife had brought out. His eyes dwelled for a while on the Italian officers, each of whom had unfolded a portable seat while their Somali retainers stood rigid like wood, tense and frightened-looking.

The Italian, speaking through an interpreter, repeated what he had said. The children, aghast at these strangers with alien pigments, were told to go and play elsewhere. The atmosphere convulsed with anticipated disaster. But Deeriye was calm. He said, "You have come a long way to offer peace. A long way indeed."

"I have come to offer it. It depends on you and your people whether you take it or no."

"On behalf of my people, let me say how pleased I am to hear you say you have come to offer us peace. May I inquire how you offer that?"

"There are conditions we have stipulated, conditions on the basis of which we rule this colony. I have come to offer not peace now but the conditions for the peace."

"Peace with conditions attached is no peace and you know that, Officer. And if we refuse to accept these conditions, if. . . . "

"I would accept our conditions for peace, if I were you. Otherwise death and disaster. You know what has become of the Sultan and his councillors? Any defiance will be dealt with severely."

"You will poison our wells, will you? Before you throw us into detention?"

"Worse."

And the Italian rose and held his hips with his open hands and walked to and fro, saying no more, but looking at a small group of cattle nosing away at the near-dry grass. He nodded, as though to himself, raised his hands and clasped his fingers behind his neck; like a man suffering from a frozen shoulder although Deeriye noted no painful expression that indicated any such thing. The Italian took his revolver out of its holster. He turned, this time to face Deeriye. Everybody thought he would shoot him. The soldiers, the interpreters and the other Italians thought he would do precisely that and therefore held their guns at the ready. But no. Deeriye, however, did not blink an eyelash but stared him in the eyes as if to say, "Dare you do that and get away?" Finally, the officer spoke, nervous, tense, flinging himself at what he was saying like a man possessed. His voice indicated without any doubt that it was he who was frightened – and not Deeriye. Although it was now, at this very moment when everybody had begun to relax, that Deeriye thought the Italian might do something rash – and shoot him! He was afraid of his own fear, frightened by it. After a long pause, Deeriye said:

"Do you not think that we have somehow to come to an agreement, I mean about what it is we are being offered the *peace* for? I take it that the land has been *pacified* for years now, what with the massacres – human and cattle – what with the pacification methods employed by the second Governor-General ten to fifteen years ago . . . you know his name – de Vecchi."

Deeriye had barely raised his head to look at the Italian when he saw the man's eyes somersault with unexpected speed: Deeriye looked to see if they had fallen out: balls blind as peeled onions, inactive as dice on the dust. However, nothing fell. What Deeriye picked up, however, was an understanding much deeper than he had given thought to. The Italian talked in mumbles with the other Italians, they lapsed into some sort of high Italian which the interpreter would not understand. Having had their consultation, the Italians fell apart sharply. The senior official came forward and said:

"Answer yes or no."

Deeriye and the others were taken by surprise. There was a change of tone, a change of method in the man's approach to the discussion.

"Answer yes or no to what?" Deeriye asked.

"Are you hiding the man we are looking for? Answer yes or no!" Deeriye took care not to show sarcasm in his voice when he asked,

"How can I unless you tell me the man's name?"

"I said, answer yes or no."

"I would incriminate my community by answering yes or no to a question whose answer is much more complicated than you tend to think. You've spoken of death and disaster."

"I've come to offer *peace* and I don't think you want to accept my terms. I am warning you of the impending disaster if you do not. Answer yes or no. Have you given asylum to a man from another clan, a man whose Sultan and twelve clansmen we are holding in police custody right at this moment, *the* man who killed an Italian? Just answer yes or no and I will deal with the rest. Whether you incriminate your community is not my business. And I am getting very impatient with you. So just answer yes or no."

The silence was penetrating, a silence with a background of fears, indecision, murmurs of "What have we to do with this man or his clan?" It was during this silence that there came on the scene Deeriye's nephew, a child under three, father dead in a futile internecine tribal war, future as shaky as his gait. The child's nose was wet with mucus mixed with dirt. Deeriye opened his arms wide to the child who gurgled with glee in the warm embrace. Deeriye took time to think while drying the child's cheeks and nose. Should he fake a retreat before the advancing might of this man's government so that he would save the salavageable? But he reminded himself of what his own father used to say: that a hero must not die an anonymous death; that he must die, like the Sayyid, in the full knowledge of his actions, bearing the consequences. Deeriye made space for the child to sit beside him, since in the child the white man's presence had produced a feeling of unreality: the child pulled at the edge of his uncle's robe and pointed a hesitant finger at the white man; then with the suddenness of a tropical downpour, something diabolical leapt into the throat of the child for he burst into tears. One of the women came and took the child away.

"Yes or no?"

Deeriye remembered the meeting of the elders of the clan, he remembered their suggestion: *whoever comes and seeks asylum is offered precisely that. There is no turning back.*

"No. The answer is no."

"Then death and disaster is your lot."

The Italian, as he spoke, slapped his thigh again and again, nervous, his voice shaking like a guitar string pulled at playfully, going up and down and saying something the interpreter had difficulty following for he interrupted him two, three times until the Italian lost patience, turned and delivered a rebuke, or what Deeriye and the others thought must be a rebuke – judging from the way he spoke his words. The gist of what he said when interpreted was that the official had come to offer peace; that he warned the Sultan and elders of the clan to hand over "for beheading" the man who had killed the Italian or else the consequence would be so disastrous it would go down in the annals of the clan's history as the "Year of death and disaster."

"There is no Allah but Allah," said Deeriye.

"There is no Allah but Allah," enjoined one or two others.

An uneasy stir. A gradual relaxation, a brightened look on everybody's face as each person invoked His name. Whispers of incomplete *Faatixa*.

"You have a day in which to hand over the culprit. A day in which to bring the culprit to the nearest town in handcuffs. If you don't you will be responsible for what happens, not I and not the Italian government which I represent."

"What will you do? Kill fifty clansmen of the man who killed one

Italian in self-defence? Take some unheard-of revenge? Poison our wells? What will you do?"

"I will create a famine worse than any famine God or man has ever heard of," the Italian said, although the interpreter refused to translate this blasphemy into Somali and continued only after he had been threatened with certain death.

A salvo of *Faatixa* from Deeriye.

The Italians and their retainers lost their sense of direction and moved haphazardly, as though denied divine guidance: they turned round and round – like ants caught in frenzied fear. But the most senior of the Italians managed to say, "We will come back. I promise you we will."

An evening later Deeriye heard a pandemonium of shouts and cries. Before this died down, there came voices of appeal; then the painful moaning of cattle struggling with departing life. This made sense when he heard shots, then the thud of a target struck, a target of heads of cattle. He went down on his knees, and he prayed and prayed and prayed. He was alone. The others, including Nadiifa, had dispersed: some had run in the direction of the massacred beasts with a view to saving the meat, rendering it *xalaal* by pronouncing the *bismillah* upon the beast before the heat of life parted from it. But he was alone and he had never felt so alone. The pandemonium grew meaningless. To the shouts the women replied with harsh cries of lament, invoking the spirits of the dead and the brave, telling the living men that they should do something, anything, to save honour: avenge, kill those who had killed their cattle, kill those who had looted; to the shouts the men's immediate response was one of confusion, surprise and powerlessness: where were their guns which they hadn't used for years? Where were the shots coming from? Deeriye saw where: the shots fired from the bazooka had opened a door of flames and jehenna in the darkness of night and all one had to do to locate its source was to follow it to the gun from which it had emitted. This was the first time Deeriye had crossed the known, tactile world into one in which he could have visions, could hear prophecies, communicate with the beyond and reach out to and receive the guiding voices of other visionaries. He had been kneeling down, saying one prayer after another, when he heard a voice call to him, a male voice from somewhere outside of himself and which told him to persevere, hold on to his principle. But when he opened his eyes, he found his wife by him. He did not ask where the others had gone. He pushed away the terracotta urn in which fat burned to provide light. He performed the motions of getting up, but fell back on his knees. She helped him rise to his feet. He wished they could allow themselves a moment of frivolity, a moment in which he would quote one of Wiil-Waal's witticisms: but Nadiifa was wearing a dead-pan expression and she wouldn't have liked to participate in the joke.

And he was not alone. God had returned; Nadiifa had come to him, stood by him and they held on to each other. The rank-and-file, the elders of the clan, the rivals, the betrayers, the trouble-makers: these, he knew, would make life difficult for him. Why, they would challenge, did their clan have to pay for this so dearly when no punitive expedition was sent to the clan from which the man hailed? Why was it that their clan had to pay in blood and death, their cattle and camels, and not the clan from which the man who murdered the Italian hailed? "Whose clan is whose?" he would ask. "Aren't we all one clan, and aren't the Italians our enemy?" But the ability to reason, to provide intelligent responses to their idiotic, clannish statements, was not in him any more. All he could remember as he leaned on his wife's supporting shoulder were two lines from a poem by the Sayyid describing the Italians:

> It is you (the British) who lead to pasture these weaker infidels
> Can I distinguish between you and your livestock.

Who was the cattle now, who was the led and who the leader? Who in effect were the *weaker infidels?* Were these not the ones who couldn't see beyond the clan's interest, the ones who could never envisage the day when this nation was one? How could he distinguish between the cattle and the herdsmen if the herdsmen could not think intelligently, could not see beyond the hill, beyond the mound under which they stood? Once in his own hamlet, he lay down, his temperature high, and was unable to sleep or engage in any conversation with those who called on him. Nadiifa sat by him, a fan in hand, active and yet silent, near and yet distant, speechless and yet communicative. How much he began to respect her; how much he wished the two of them could be alone, thinking of nothing but themselves for a while at any rate; how much he felt her being near helped him greatly. He had lucid and confused moments: during the most depressive twilights, he felt alone and forgot that she was there; he also missed the presence of God in himself. *He coughed: he wheezed: he had asthma.* Then he heard that the man who had been the cause of all this had fallen victim to a stray bullet and died on the spot. He learnt much later (when he was in prison) that the man was survived by a two-month-old son: Mahad.

Then, the following morning a contingent of *soldati* came, handcuffed Deeriye and took him away and into detention. He was made to sit on a chair. A man carrying a thing with legs entered; the man hid behind a dark cloth and closed one eye, concentrating as though he were a soldier taking aim: the man took a photograph of Deeriye. Deeriye *never* could forget that day. There was a thing the white man held up in his left hand, a thing which lit like a lamp, a thing which produced a flash whose life was brief. Then came darkness in its wake. And he took another photograph. Then another. And then another.

A few days later, he met Rooble in prison.

• • • • • • • • • • •

Rooble returned, holding on to his stomach, and took the armchair opposite Deeriye's, silent. Furtive of glance; slow-paced; tardy were his reactions to anything, in particular anything which would tax his mind: he would rather put his trust in someone else and follow instructions or suggestions of those in whom he had faith; his eyes, unlike Deeriye's which were alive, vivacious, had a slumberous way of opening and closing, hinting nothing; not a minor mischief would set them ablaze and no fire of conspiracy would render them aflame. Of Rooble, Deeriye always spoke well; of Deeriye, Rooble spoke commendably well. Each paid the other compliments. Each said nice things about the other.

One positive result of their friendship was that it had brought their families together, a cementing friendship, with their children thinking of themselves as brothers and sisters, with Deeriye's brother-in-law Elmi-Tiir acting as substitute-father and guardian when Deeriye and

Rooble were in detention, paying for their children's school fees, taking care of their needs. Certainly, it was not for lack of trying that Rooble's children did not do as well at school and outside of it as Deeriye's, although, again, Mahad, the son of the man who killed the Italian in self-defence and a nephew of Rooble, did so well he was allowed to skip three years of the elementary grades. He was ten years older than Mursal and he became handy helping Mursal through the difficult years of puberty and secondary school. But Yakuub, Rooble's son, who was Mursal's peer, had no intellectual interests but followed with intense enthusiasm the international and national sports scenes: he could tell you whether Juventus had won or Manchester United; he could tell you the latest gossip about Borg, Connors and Evonne Cawley; he could give you a rundown of who was who in sports. Nor were Rooble's twin daughters interested in anything which required any thinking aside from giving birth to underweight children and marrying and remarrying – having been then married to some nine husbands. (No one knew where they were most of the time or to whom they were married. Not until they needed financial help.) Although none of this should diminish Rooble's children in anybody's eyes: for they did, within their available means, what they could for their father; and to supplement these needs, Mursal or Mahad's pockets took care of all the extra necessities. What did these necessities consist of? Rooble, at sixty-eight, was the father of a child not even a year old; his other children, eight or nine of them, could line and populate an alley to greet him if he were to pass by in a motorcade; children from women much younger than he and whom he had divorced; his present wife was not quite twenty. Deeriye disapproved of these activities which he looked upon with great scorn and he said so; but more than that, he would do nothing – in the same way he did nothing about some of the activities of his daughter or son of which he didn't approve. "You don't expect me to part for good with my friend because I disapprove of the number of women he marries. If he treats them badly, if he beats them, if he is rude to them – well, I'll speak to him," he had once said to Mahad who approached him, adding: "He is my friend and has never tried to dissuade me from holding on to my principles but has stood by them as though they were his. *Rooble is my friend.*"

Deeriye was now saying: "And how are Halima and the child?" Halima was Rooble's recently acquired young wife.

"They are well, they are well," he said, trying to hide the pain on his face. "The child is teething I think. He wakes up and cries a lot."

"How old is he?"

"He was born the day Nadiifa died. We had been at Nadiifa's burial ceremonies all day and when we returned we heard of his birth. Hence the name Nadiif. Don't you remember?" asked Rooble.

Deeriye said, "Of course, I remember."

And after a long pause:

"I've called you because there's something I don't quite understand and I thought you might be in a position to enlighten me; something to do with Mursal's strange behaviour of late."

"Mursal?" said Rooble.

"Yes, Mursal; his strange behaviour of late."

Rooble was overcome with anxiety: he looked around to see if anyone was listening. Deeriye sat back, confident that he was about to be told something highly secretive and interesting. But:

"Does Natasha know?" asked Rooble.

"Does she know what?"

"About Mursal? I mean is there another woman in his life? Is he seeing another woman?"

This threw Deeriye into a state of distaste and rage: the absurdity of Rooble's suggestion disturbed him; how could he be so distasteful as to think the world was made up of matrimonial infidelities and men who confided these secrets to one another? He spoke his mind to this effect. Rooble heard him out but remained silent, making no effort whatsoever to rise to his own defence, explaining nothing. There was an awkward pause. Then Deeriye continued, his voice gentle and apologetic:

"I was asking you if you suspected that Mahad and Mursal and their friend what's-his-name were up to something – conspiring or doing something unlawful. Do you know anything?"

"I think I do."

Deeriye sat forward, happy as a child whose newly-found toy worked to his full satisfaction: his eyes were lit with that curious intelligence and he asked, "What? What do you know?"

"I know that the three of them meet every day and go in Mahad's car with a fourth man, a man with an army officer's gait and mannerisms; I know that this army officer carries a briefcase which he never parts with; I know that Mursal, Mahad and Mukhtaar (that's the name of the what's-his-name) return to our place *without* the army officer; I know that Mukhtaar is dropped before they enter our street."

"Do you know what they do?"

"No."

"Do you know where they go?"

"No."

"Have you ever asked?"

"Yes."

The light in Deeriye's eyes dimmed: he no longer expected a satisfactory answer to his question which had gone cold, like a bed of ashes already powdery. He rephrased the question:

"When you showed curiosity, what was their reaction?"

"Nervous."

"In what way, nervous?"

"Mahad behaved strangely."

"Yes?" Deeriye's attentiveness was visibly concentrated in the way he looked at Rooble and waited.

Finally Rooble spoke:

"I asked him what they do every day – getting into that car and mysteriously disappearing and then re-appearing with one of them already not there and Mukhtaar getting out of the car before they come into view of Mukhtaar's father's house. And he said they do nothing. Nothing, really nothing, he said. I told him I didn't believe him. Then I put to Mursal the same question. He responded that they played football, did running exercises and that sort of thing. I told Mursal I didn't believe him either. He said I could go with them if I pleased."

"And did you?"

"No."

"A pity. Anyway when did these exchanges take place?"

"Four days ago."

"You should've gone with them."

"But I didn't."

"Why not?"

The power of the sun again. And the dust which it had awoken. Then the noise of children returning home from school, playing noisily and with joy in the street below. And Yassin stalking outside his father's gate, Yassin who never did what the other children did, Yassin whose mad look plunged Deeriye, at times, into an irrational fear.

"Because I suspect I know what they are up to."

The bright curiosity in Deeriye's eyes was lost in the dazzling light of the sun. He was so anxious to know, to find out, that he did not wait for Rooble to continue but asked: "What is it you suspect they are up to?"

"I saw three revolvers hidden under Mahad's mattress."

"Three revolvers?"

"I suspect they came from the briefcase the man held tightly in his nervous grip. And hand grenades. I checked and saw the revolvers were loaded, all three. I put them where they belonged."

"Have you told him?"

"No."

"When did you find the three revolvers?"

"Today. Just before he picked me up from the house. Mahad had been in the bathroom: I sneaked into his room and rummaged through his things and the revolvers were under the mattress."

"And what do you suspect they are up to?"

"I think they are up to no good."

"Mahad, Mursal, and Mukhtaar too? I understand Mahad's and Mursal's positions. What about Mukhtaar? You told me once that his father's family, unneighbourly neighbours of yours, like Cigaal's (I wonder what fate made you a neighbour of one and I the other's – Cigaal and Sheikh Ibrahim, Mukhtaar's father) just across the road, are staunch supporters of the régime. For tribal reasons. What about him? Does Mukhtaar transcend, do you think, these tribal alliances? Or is he like Haji Omer, a traitor, the worst kind of spy?"

Rooble's voice did not tremble as he said, "Rumour has it that Mukhtaar and his father fight a great deal. The same rumour has it that his father, who technically should be a guest in the house bought with his son's money, has locked him out of it a number of times. I know of one night anyway when he knocked on our door and we let him in and gave him a place to sleep; in fact, Mahad offered him his bed. I have heard it said that the major disagreements between Mukhtaar and his father have to do with ideological differences: the son does not share his father's views; the son, it is said, believes not in tribal allegiances but fully in the national interest. Also, the father disapproves of Mukhtaar's friends: Mahad and Mursal, two very close friends of his, friends long before the foundations of the new tribal allegiances which his father upholds were laid down."

"Rumour, rumour, rumour."

"There are facts I know of."

"What facts?"

"One night he hit back at his father and there was a panjandrum of cries and we managed to get into the house where we saw the father brandishing a panga saying he would kill Mukhtaar. We tied Sheikh Ibrahim with a rope as though he were mad – which he was, if you ask me. It is my feeling that the father may kill the son. If the son chooses to humiliate his authority in public."

Deeriye contained the rage the news sprung inside of him; he simply said, *"Subxaanallah wal xamdu lillaah, wa la ilaaha illa laah!"*

After a pause, Rooble said, "They are up to no good, I suspect."

"Like what?"

"Well, all three talk and talk and talk about violence. They seem to find reason to justify the use of violence against a tyrant."

"What do they say?"

"Not to me, mind you."

"Yes, yes, I understand you've overheard something. But what do they say? Can you remember any specific names, references to traditional or Islamic historical figures?"

"The names I could decipher were Mucaawiya's and Yaziid's; they talked about concepts like the *lex talionis* as deterrent and as a first step towards de-stabilizing the régime; they talked of encouraging the family of victims to take revenge – not on the weaker relations or the offspring of those who rule, but on the tyrant himself."

"Was Mukhtaar with them when they talked as openly as that?"

"All the time."

Deeriye's head buzzed with whispering prayers for a while; it seemed he was becoming aware of his chest congesting: he feared it would be a severe attack and a worsening paroxysm of coughing would follow on the heels of this. Something pulled at his inside, a pain, a terrible and dizzyingly real pain tugging at his lungs and emptying them of breath, like a punctured tyre. The first wheeze of the day, a wheeze so long that Rooble rushed down the staircase to look for help. Help came: Sunawade. He said he would telephone his aunt Zeinab. Meanwhile, he indicated to Rooble where the portable Bennet machine was.

• • • • • • • • • • •

The bronchiodilator aerosol was back in its place, hidden away in a cupboard: and Zeinab was there, Zeinab who acted as his doctor. And there they were: Samawade, Mursal, Natasha, Zeinab and Rooble, having formed a circle round his bed, standing as though somebody was taking a photograph of them, to be framed and put on the wall of history – and he lying down, flat on his back, his chest like a balloon – and out of the photographer's vision too, absent from the family portrait. Zeinab was now trying to tell everybody to leave him in peace. Why did they come back in the first place? Hadn't she told them to stay in the living-room downstairs? He couldn't tell her not to bully the people: his mouth was sticky with phlegm and whenever he moved someone stuck out a spittoon for him to use (Samawade was making himself very useful in this regard). Zeinab was insisting that he never listened to her as his doctor, that perhaps they should get a total stranger for him. Had she not told him to go for walks?

He was drinking large quantities of water. He was hungry too – this being one of the after-effects of an attack. And he was thinking: how little one knows one's body; that the lungs are larger when one is small and contract when one is older. But there they were, anyway, their manners affected (Natasha, in a kaftan, was quiet all the time, quiet like a clairvoyant, her eyes dilated with unshed tears), their minds at work and at the centre of their thoughts: a *he!* A man of whom they spoke in whispers in the third person singular, small 'h'; an old man who had lost everything over the months (they said) precisely since Nadiifa's death, had lost the passion and zeal for life; an old man whom they must keep alive for the sake of a stronger resistance movement – to Mursal; a man on whom they would perform "cosmetic political surgery" and to avenge whom they would sacrifice their lives – to Mahad;

a man who could be healthy and enjoy life if all allergens were moved out of his way and he were placed in dust- and tension-free conditions where he could pray to Allah to his heart's content – to Zeinab; a lovable man – to Natasha; a friend – to Rooble; a saint whom Satan is tempting – to Elmi-Tiir. And Deeriye? He was for his part surprised that no one so far had bothered to find out if there was any link between the emotional charge Rooble's story threw him into and the attack. Not even Zeinab. He had expected that Rooble would be cross-questioned or at least asked to say what they had talked about. But Deeriye wasn't himself sure if there was a link between the emotional attachment to Mursal and the psychological stress Rooble's information had triggered in him. Of one thing he was certain: Yassin, in effect, became an allergen – able to produce a tension which might create in him the worst disorder. When he put to himself the question of what he would do if he learnt that Mursal and Mahad "were up to no good," he did not know; most probably he wouldn't do anything; although he wouldn't stand in their way *"if they kept whatever they were doing to themselves and did not burden him with the keeping of their secrets."*

His eyes were now inflamed, his mind, as though a bed of insects, was busy and very much alive to the challenges which he would meet whatever the condition of his health, and however subdued. "My face is my lungs," he would say. "That is the seat of all my tensions. You can tell how things are with an asthmatic by the way he breathes." But no one could describe Deeriye as a plaintive old man or as a man suffering from any sort of neurosis. His attacks, thank God, were generally mild; his asthma, intermittent; and he had faith in his daughter who was his doctor; and in his son, daughter-in-law, grandchildren and his friends Rooble and Elmi-Tiir. Life's general unpleasantnesses didn't make him wheeze, nor did the stirred dust provoke an attack in him. How he hated the stuff which turned his mouth into a swamp of gluey saliva: heavy, tasteless, sperm-like in substance and thickness especially when other people were there. To rid himself of the weight on his tongue and lungs, he asked his daughter to help him drink some water.

She went round, climbed the bed with him, held his head between her hands and then placed it gently on her knees, having wedged herself between the pillow and the wall. She helped him drink.

"Pass him the spittoon, Samawade," she said. Samawade did so.

"Thanks." Then: "It makes me feel very miserable," he began to say, speaking with enormous difficulty, to his daughter, "this spitting and slobbering in the presence of all these people. Please tell them to go so I can spit freely and without inhibitions. But gently, please."

He knew she knew how to bully anyone, order anyone around: she was a drill-sergeant, born to give instructions. Whereas he was the opposite: very polite, very considerate, the kind of person who felt guilty when it was his turn at the counter if he had many questions to be answered or a number of things to buy; or if he was at the head of a queue and couldn't find the right change.

"I will. I will."

She clapped her hands and said she wished to be left alone with her patient. Mursal, who had been unduly silent and depressed-looking, seemed about to challenge her but didn't. The others shuffled out of the room, taking with them their voices, whispers, thoughts and leaving behind a silence whose chill exposed Zeinab and Samawade and Deeriye. A little later, having been assured that his help was not needed any more, Samawade got up and he too left.

Half an hour later: Deeriye was napping and Zeinab tiptoed out.

THREE

With the Portcullis Down

The following morning. Deeriye had just finished telling a story about Wiil-Waal to Samawade who now, content and quiet, was taking leave while his grandfather said to himself the most essential profession of the Islamic faith and told a few beads; when upon seeing Natasha come near the door, he leapt with delight. Natasha, tall and elegant: her perfume had entered before her, the sweet smell of her smile had heralded her arrival; Natasha, decorated with the flowery grin of her beautiful skirt, simple and yet amazingly exquisite. She moved in quietly, saying nothing at first, she walked in holding between her teeth another blossom of a smile which was, Deeriye would have said if asked to comment, tantamount to another life. She strode in, her eyes drooping in deference to him, her feet hesitant now that she had come within the domain in which he functioned best, his room where he received those who chose to call on him. He bowed as though to offer her a place, a chair on which to sit, as though to welcome her to his little abode. And yet, he knew she did not come to sit or talk to him but either to say something brief to him or her son and then depart, go away before the smile waned, before there was any need to apologize for taking leave of him. Natasha: a Jew from New York, born and bred in the upper and well-to-do parts of Manhattan; a woman whom his son, Mursal, had fallen in love with and who put Deeriye oddly in mind of his own wife every time he saw her, her voice thin and sonorous, her care ebullient – yes, his own wife, Nadiifa, whose odour of attar and touch of skin was smooth and silky, whose smile oozed with smoke-baths of prepared love, whose fingers and palms and soles were patterned with henna: Nadiifa, his wife. Natasha: light make-up, decorous, her blue eyes at times anxious, expectant – but not waiting! Finally, she said, having got hold of Samawade's hand for something to grip:

"Faccio del té per te?"

"Si, grazie. Grazie tante," he said, half bowing, half grinning and half rising.

She turned to Samawade; and because she could not endure Deeriye's eyes on the two of them, she pinched her son's cheeks and made him cry with playful pain. Another of her smiles which stirred in him and in her son a fountain of fondness and love.

"Non ti serve niente altro?' she asked.

"No, *grazie,"* he said.

And she went away, to walk the few flights of stairs down to the kitchen to make what was euphemistically known as Somali tea, spicy and precisely the way she knew he liked it.

Alone with his grandson, he took his seat again and returned to the quiet telling of the beads. He started when, coinciding with the telephone's ringing in the living-room downstairs, Samawade jumped up in a flurry of excitement and ran to answer it. Deeriye could hear Natasha speak to him in English, telling him what he would have interpreted as "be careful" or some such cautionary motherly advice. He and Natasha found they communicated with each other better in Italian than in her broken Somali and his fractured English. He spoke perfect Italian and impeccable (standard) Arabic, having learnt both while in detention. And English? He learnt a little in order to exchange a few words with the British administrators following the Italians' loss of ex-Italian Somalia to Britain. But he could not say he spoke it. It was rather like a bus ticket you hold on to until the journey for which you bought it has ended. And once that ticket is no use any more, you throw it away, of course. And why did Natasha not learn Somali? Her answer was very simple: "Somalis have not as yet developed the sensitivity to suffer, tolerate, listen to or take seriously a foreigner whose untrained tongue stumbles on the triquetral gurgles of their language. You see, your tongue trips on these very letters which the native-speaker takes for granted; at least mine does. Hurdles like the guttural, the nasal and other 'nasties' I can't think of for the moment. What annoys me is that no word ever means the same thing to two different persons, let alone two different regions of the country. Nothing is standardized, other than people's reaction when your tongue trips: they burst into uncontrolled laughter. And then speak to me in English, perfect English, flawless except for an occasional mispronunciation here and there. I, yes, I who learnt so many languages; I whose father is another polyglot and whose mother also; I, yes, I who come from a family which speaks some twenty languages all told." To communicate the two of them used Samawade when absolutely necessary and when there was no one else around; Samawade ran errands and delivered messages and carried things to and fro. At times, when speaking about complicated ideas, or things they did not want Samawade to worry about, they would use either Mursal or Zeinab. They never teased each other beyond the occasional throwaway joke; each holding back, each asking himself or herself, "What will the other think? Will the other be hurt?" Which was the reason why Deeriye preferred to stay at Zeinab's: anybody would drop in on Deeriye any time; anyone who happened to be there when dinner was served would join the others and share from the same mayida. But at Mursal's house – or, as the others called it, "Natasha's *weel*" – none of this was conceivable: after all, she was who she was. It is strange, however, that Mursal and Natasha believed that they ran an open house: believed was not the right word. They affirmed, confirmed and repeated again and again that they did precisely that. Although they had no way of convincing these friends of Deeriye's or Deeriye himself of this. When it came to a late-night or all-night card-playing session, Natasha would retire and take Samawade away, saying that it was his bedtime and that she was going to read to him; an hour or half an hour later, Mursal would say that he had a paper to write or a lecture to prepare and he too would disappear; and the others would with the passage of time become quieter and quieter and eventually would find excuses for going away. Unless – yes, unless the callers were Mahad and Mukhtaar, friends of Mursal's. Then, after dinner, night-caps would be served in the living-room with Natasha still there until midnight, and instead of vanishing justifiably into Samawade's room, she would tell him to go to bed and read the book to himself. On evenings such as this, Deeriye would retire earlier, taking leave with the explanation that he wanted to tell a few beads and the essential profession of the Holy faith.

If asked, he would say that, preferences aside, he was happy as a saint whether with Zeinab and her two lovely children or with Natasha, Mursal and Samawade; content that at Natasha's (at Mursal's, pardon!) he had more time to himself, more time for devotions, for God and for his thoughts; content at Zeinab's because his friends were at ease there, although he had found that too exhausting at times (and so had Zeinab), entertaining day and night. This was life, his own life. Prison: where he had more time for saying these devotions, more time to dedicate to God, more time for thoughts; the free enterprise of a house whose doors remained forever unclosed. No thoughts to cuddle to oneself, no light of day and no darkness of night whose hues to clutch at. His life, he would continue, was a contradiction, like a thorn pinned to a rose; Natasha: simply a float-stone in this his sea of contradictions: he loved and respected her as one would a dear friend.

Deeriye remembered when he first set eyes on Natasha. That was a few months after Samawade's birth, in New York. He had made a special trip, his first and only visit to North America. New York was hot, smoggy and humid. This sneakily brought back signs of his asthmatic condition. He couldn't breathe, couldn't eat, couldn't talk, couldn't take part in any activity without the insistent obsession that an attack would stop it all. When his antibodies had so weakened he could do nothing, he was taken to see Natasha's parents' doctors who prescribed for him a list of drugs longer than the ancestral names which he, as a child, had had to learn and recite to pay reverent reference to his clan's genealogy. As if that was all; when his medical expenses were too enormous for Mursal and Natasha's savings to meet them, Natasha's parents footed the bill. And he was made to take a trip to California where a cousin of Natasha's lent them his cottage. There he had a most marvellous time, and with him, as escorts, were Natasha's parents: the three talked, using less and less the gesticulations which characteristically accompany, as symbols, the unworded thoughts. They would sit in front of the TV set and would watch a programme together. Both Natasha's parents, professors at New York University, spoke Spanish and therefore could converse with Deeriye who, in turn, talked back in Italian. The three went for long walks; when they swam in the public pool nearby, he would sit outside the bar in the shade, sipping his orange which was glassy with ice and reading the Koran. They were Jews whose families fled the Nazi atrocities in Germany. Both were born in

Berlin. Their accents and innuendos had traces of Germanic derivation. There might have been misunderstandings between them, but never did they get on each other's nerves. In the village where they had stayed there was an Italian who ran a café-shop and he would feast Deeriye and his friends with gifts and speak about an Italy with which Deeriye was not in the least familiar. The Italo-American who owned the cafe was of the naive conviction that the Somali subjects had learnt and had benefited a great deal from their contact with the Italian colonialists. Deeriye could not make this man understand what it felt to be of the colonized millions. Anyway, not once did he suffer an attack during this period. And what a journey! What a long journey to Natasha's home, her people's world-view and their notions about Africa, et cetera. This was not because he had had to cross oceans, change planes, get into and out of different airport transit lounges. It was a long journey away from anything he had known: the portable nomadic hamlet was far from the skyscrapers of New York, the ruins of Rome, the history of Europe; nor were the material goods on display in the shop windows in these cities anywhere near what he had experienced in Mogadiscio: was it the radius of his imagination which in the end had failed him? A goat tied to a pole outside one's own dwelling-place, a friend living within calling distance, a neighbour whom one knew and whose children played with one's children; a cow scratching its ribs against one's own fence; prosperity or famine manacled to the whim of a season: if it did not rain . . . famine; if it did: *alxamdulillaah!* And in place of cow- and other-dungs: the odour of leaking oil and contaminated air everywhere; instead of camels and cows in barns: cars in car-shelters, non-dairy milk, dried milk powder and all sorts of synthetic food. Yes: the reach of one's imagination. So much money made on selling slave labour; so many people on the fringes of insanity; so many books; so many things. "New York is a mad city," Natasha's father had said. "But we love it. Perhaps we New Yorkers are mad," he had added. "The Californians think so." (Natasha's parents had said this in the context of California where Deeriye had felt so well and where Natasha's parents did not: and, on account of his unfamiliarity with the East Coast versus West Coast rivalry, Deeriye wasn't prepared to be dragged into a controversy which was purely American.

To which, sitting in Natasha's house (pardon again – Mursal's!), he now replied: "*They said the Sayyid was mad. We love him all the same. It is the mystery in the mad that one loves. They describe all unexplained mysteries and powers as signs of madness. Was the Sayyid mad? Was Wiil-Waal mad? Is New York a mad city? Is Mogadiscio? Is Khaliif a madman? Or am I mad?*"

He heard two sets of footsteps coming up the stairs; one was most likely Natasha bringing up the tray with a kettle of tea; and the other light-footed walk belonged to Samawade, half running. He had come through the door when he said, almost out of breath,

"Aunt Zeinab was on the phone. She says she is coming."

Natasha's appearance made Deeriye re-mould his inquisitive look into a flashy smile as he half got up, and half bowed, saying,

"*Grazie, grazie infinite.*"

She laid the tray down on the commedine by his side, saying, "*Non c'é di che, non c'é di che.*" There were two cups and biscuits: was she going to join him? "*No, mi dispiace. Zeinab dovrebbe venire.*" Formal, friendly, she was all smiles. She bowed. She left. Quiet as good taste.

• • • • • • • • • • •

Deeriye said to Samawade:

Once upon a time there was a king who ruled over the whole of the Somali-speaking territories and this king's name was Wiil-Waal. This king had a beautiful wife, who was also intelligent and supportive. She used to tell the king whatever she thought he should hear because many of the king's councillors were either not blessed with as rich a foresight or were afraid for their lives, afraid to tell him things which might offend his arrogance. Wiil-Waal would listen to his wife's challenges and would respond with challenges equally daring. But he loved her and he indicated this by his willingness to hear her out every time she began to tell him something, whether it was to do with a complaint which hadn't yet reached his ears, some wicked gossip, rumour or anything else she thought the king should hear. This king had one great weakness: he believed and said very often that there was not one person among his council or his populace as clever or as intelligent as he.

Every evening, upon laying his head by her pillow and just before he pronounced the professions of his faith which he said prior to his falling asleep; and every morning, upon waking up and before his lungs opened with the cries of Alxamdulilaah, *just as he was taking his ablutions, the king's wife, as though to exorcize his satanic arrogance, would remind him that there were many intelligent and clever men and women among his people but they were perhaps frightened of him, frightened of being killed if they came forward to challenge him, frightened of being humiliated in front of everybody, frightened of being castrated if they made the slightest sign of rivalling his tyrannical authority.*

One evening, she broke to him the news that she had indeed encountered a young man, perhaps in his early twenties, whose sharpness of wit, foresight and extensive knowledge of the literature of the nation impressed her immensely. She said she had never met a man like him – not even Wiil-Waal, when he courted her some ten years previously, had been as witty as this young man. The king asked her for his name. She said that she did not know. The king wanted to know if there was any way she could describe him accurately so he could track down this man and know who he was. She wouldn't promise anything other than this: she would indicate to the king when this young man came again to seduce her by cutting off the edge of his robe. The following morning, she told the king that while he had been busy with affairs of state the man had called on her. As promised, she had cut off the edge of his robe. What the king should do, she suggested, was to look for a young man robed in a go whose edge had been cut off. It shouldn't be difficult for a king who thought there was not among his people any person as intelligent as himself.

The king, when his council met that same morning, looked for the clever young man who had tried to seduce his wife – keeping in mind that the young man would have a robe with a cut-off edge. What did the king find? He found that the robes of most of the young men had their edges cut off. The king reported his find to his wife. To which she responded that it was high time he recognized there was at least a number of young men and young women who were as intelligent as he. She concluded by saying to him, "Satanic arrogance does not get anyone anywhere, my friend and husband. You must search, for there must be treasures other than that which is between your own legs." The next evening, the young man came to the king's wife and tried yet again to seduce her. The wife, to mark him out from the other men, stained the corner of his robe with red dye. And she told the king what she had done to the man's robe. Meanwhile, when he was among his companions, sitting in the clearing telling each other stories, the young man told his assembled friends that Wiil-Waal, perhaps under the mad spell of his satanic inventiveness, suggested that every able-bodied young man on the state council must paint his robe the colour of blood as a symbol of unity and brotherhood. Again, the king failed to catch the young man the following morning.

Two evenings later, when the king was busy with state affairs, the young man came to the queen and the two talked all night and parted as the muezzin awoke dawn with his cries. She told the king who to look for: a young man who was so exhausted that his head would nod with sleep. The king looked and at last found, seated in a corner, a young man whose head was nodding with drowsiness. The king interrupted the discussions of the council, pointed at the young man whose eyes were closed, and having brought this fact to the attention of all the others present shouted, saying: "Are you asleep, young Ali?" The young man responded that he was not asleep but thinking. "And what, pray, were you thinking of in your sleep?" asked the king. The young man replied that he was not sleeping but thinking whether an ostrich has two legs or four; and whether the strength of an ostrich is in her front legs or the hind legs. The king knew whom he was talking to: the intelligent young man who would one day perhaps become a king of his people. And the king said, "I will say this to you, my people: this young man here is as intelligent and as quick-witted as any you had appointed as king."

• • • • • • • • • • •

The whole house was thrown into a tantrum. Zeinab had brought Sheherezade and Cantar with her. All Deeriye's measures to make them behave failed: those two wouldn't listen to anyone especially when they were challenged by Samawade. They turned Deeriye's room into a circus of confusion. They fought, they wrestled, they chased each other out of one armchair and into the other; while Sheherezade and Cantar quarrelled over who would sit on whose lap, who would tell what to whom, Samawade, polite and correct, stood to one side and shouted to them to behave themselves or else . . . ! They were younger than he but more ferocious and wilder. Like Samawade, they were not sent to bed after eight o'clock. In short, they behaved as one-parent children generally do: obsessive with the freedom to do things not allowed, take liberties not given. It was only when they had overdone it that Zeinab's "All right, now" was heard and they would stop in mid-air, stop whatever they were doing, drop whatever they had in their hands. In this manner, they were different from other one-parent children, children who fell into whimpering depressive moods. And this occurred just two minutes after their arrival. They withdrew into a quietness you would never have thought them capable of and were silent. Zeinab fixed her father with her piercing eyes: he looked away. He knew she had a way with him too – just as she had with her own children whose inept activities ceased the moment she cried: "All right, now." With him, there was a slight variation of method: whenever they argued about something and she wanted to put him in his place, she would take hold of his wrist, count his pulse, murmur a medical secret to herself, hide in the uncoded jargon of her profession and then get on with whatever business was at hand; at times, she would stuff a thermometer into his mouth; or peel the shirt or undershift off his chest and knock on his ribs, her ears at the ready to calculate the beat of his heart. She did all this – and no one doubted it, not even him – yes, she did it "for his own good." And Mursal did all he did for his father's good. Nevertheless, Deeriye wouldn't deny that he felt pushed around a bit.

After a while: "How are you today?" she asked.

"I am well, thanks be to God."

"Did you take your pills?"

"Yes."

"And you have no complaints?"

"No."

"And the water in your legs?"

"Alxamdulilaah."

"You did not cough last night or this morning?"

"I coughed, yes."

"How bad."

"Not very."

She had his wrist in the tight grip of her hand. "Did you eat well?"

"Yes."

"Did you go for a walk?"

"No, I did not."

"Why not?"

Silence. He would tell a lie first to himself and then translate this falsehood into words which would convince her: like a smoker who hides in the lavatory, afraid that a friend or a doctor or a relation would see him draw on a cigarette.

"Why didn't you?" She flung his hand aside. When he didn't answer: "Come on. Why didn't you?"

A short pause. He thought that a lie takes a longer time to formulate, a lie which works, that is. But could he admit the truth? Dare he tell her that he was frightened: frightened that Yassin, the neighbour's son, would pelt him with pebbles? Dare he confess that he had seen that in one of his true visions? Dare he tell her this in the presence of his grandchildren? What would they think of him? An old man frightened to death of taking a walk on account of a young thing like Yassin of whom they themselves were not afraid? And what would she say? It was one thing being a small, frightened child; it was another when you were old, highly respected – and frightened!

"You haven't told me. Why didn't you go out for a walk? You used to when you lived with us."

"I just felt too lazy," he lied.

"Too lazy? Anything wrong? Blood pressure perhaps. This is why I keep saying we'll have to give you a thorough medical check-up one of these days. You haven't had one since mother's death. Your watery legs need exercise. How often must I tell you?"

"You remind me of that every time I am within your reach, Zeinab."

"A proper thorough medical check-up."

"Not a day, not a single second will either be added to or subtracted from the precise hour prescribed by Allah – whatever you or I do. How often must I tell you this?"

"And in a little while, you will be telling me that a pious Muslim dies long before his death. So does any sinner, Muslim, Christian or heathen, who doesn't take care of himself. How often do I tell you this? How often, my dearest Father?"

"Very often."

"And I will again and again."

He was silent for the good of his own mind. Now she picked up a bottle and shook the capsules in it; she counted them.

"You haven't taken the pills, have you?"

"I said I have."

"There should be sixteen. There are twenty."

"What does that mean?"

"It means you did not take the pills according to my prescription. That means you've either forgotten to take them or counted wrongly."

"Isn't it possible that you counted wrongly?"

"No. Not possible. I am a medical doctor. I've learnt to count well what counts."

Nothing was left for him to do but concede the point to her: Yes, concede, indeed. But he held no grudge and wasn't angry. He felt slightly humiliated; felt that doctors pushed him around. Not only her. Even her late husband who was also a doctor. Deeriye wondered if, when they were making love, they had gone about it with the harsh, rough way of handling each other's body: her husband who had died while serving the West Somali Liberation Front in its war against Ethiopia.

"I will make an appointment for you," she said.

"Why?"

"You need to see a doctor. Another doctor. I think that is better."

"But I see you much more regularly than any doctor ever sees a patient. You come at the first tinkle of the telephone, ready to do anything. I am all right, really."

"You are not and you know it."

"But I am."

A pause. And into his silent thinking stalked Yassin, brandishing a knife whose sharpness shone in the sun; in his other hand, Yassin clutched several pebble-stones. And out of the shade of Deeriye's memory walked Khaliif, a madman in tatters, bent double with exhaustion, his eyes red from sleeplessness. Would Yassin pelt Khaliif with the pebbles? Or would he use the knife? Now Deeriye sat in the bright portion of the room while Zeinab was in the shaded section; and he convulsed with the shock of having "thought" a vision in broad daylight, when he wasn't alone or enjoying a nap.

"Do you want to come for a walk?" she asked. "Now. I'll take you out now."

"A walk now?"

"Yes. A walk. We could go in my car to Second Lido and take a promenade there. Or if you want, we can go to Lido and have something at the bar there."

"No, thank you."

Her mind was active: thinking. "You still haven't told me why you haven't been taking your walk since you moved here. You seemed to enjoy it when you were with us; there never was a day you didn't go out. Don't you like this area? The roads here have sidewalks whereas they don't in our section of the city. Why?"

"If you want to know the truth . . . ," and he trailed off.

"Yes?"

"I am frightened."

"Frightened?"

"Yes, I am afraid of. . . . "

"Afraid of what?"

"I am. . . . "

Her palms, wide open like a door, were spread out in front of her: waiting. "Yes?"

She thought of the day he had his seizure while taking a walk; he had nearly collapsed on the road and they heard of this only when he was taken to hospital. And the story that he was unwell circulated in the whole of Mogadiscio and some (Yassin's grandfather Cigaal was one) even predicted his death before the week was over, and when this did not happen, others predicted that he would live longer than all of them for he was a saint, a martyr, a patriot—and a pious Muslim!

"Afraid that you might have an attack while walking on your own?"

"No, not really."

"What are you afraid of then?"

"You'll think I am mad if I tell you the truth. You'll say I've gone mad, I'm sure. Or weak in the head. You'll think I'm weak in the head."

"No, my dear Father, I won't think any such thing." She took his hand and pressed it tenderly and lovingly, looking him in the eyes; then kissed him on the forehead. "What? Tell me."

But he still couldn't bring himself to confess what frightened him about having moved to this neighbourhood and why he stopped going for his regular walks which she believed to be of enormous help to his health now that his legs were, like pitchers, filling with water. He was afraid of his own fear, and of speaking to anyone else about it.

"I see in my visionary dreams, and waking visions as well, that Yassin is there, with a thousand pebbles in his wicked left hand, pebblestones to pelt me with as he pelted Khaliif the madman. And I am afraid."

Zeinab stared at him in disbelieving silence, her hands were folded across her chest, no longer gesticulating – but speechless as the rest of her body and brain, numbed by the sense of shock and fear her father's words transmitted to her. Before he confessed, the map of her thoughts had been clear and studied, her confidence, her peace of mind had injected life-blood and energy into her speech and physical mannerisms. Suddenly, it seemed the roles were reversed. Deeriye was buoyant with animation: "Khaliif, because he is mad, *if he is mad, that is,* is immune to fear. But I'm not. Oh, how I envy him at times, how I envy him! He says his sane thoughts and is redeemed by them and thus becomes a living saint; because I am not endowed with the same sort of immunity, my mad thoughts turn me into a ridiculous and pitiable person such as I am, an ancient man who has reached the highest heights of political and social life but is frightened of being pelted with pebbles by a young urchin, the grandson of a neighbour who loathes me and what I represent. Do you understand what I am saying?"

She nodded and sitting down said, "I do."

"A neighbour, according to Islamic thought, is one's closest and therefore first protector. God is our neighbour. A wife is a man's neighbour. The husband, the wife's. These wicked unneighbourly neighbours: I am afraid of stepping out of the house for I see below me, lurking in the background of my reasoned out fears, an urchin waiting to pelt me with stones. If I had sinned and were stoned and thus saved, I mean if. . . ."

"Don't talk like that."

"These are my sincere thoughts. A man important enough in the public eye to command the respect of those to whom a name means anything; a man in whose direction the Head of State is looking with suspicion; a man revered for his high principles and . . . yes . . . who tells you, who confides in you, his daughter, that he is afraid of a young urchin who is less significant than the pebbles he is armed with. . . ."

"Please."

"Please what?"

"Don't talk like that," she said, her cheeks stained with running tears which she wiped away with the back of her hand. "Please, please, please. I beg you."

"Well?"

"Otherwise, I will just go and do something about him."

"What?"

"Threaten him; speak to him; strangle him!"

The tears, the choking breath of his daughter: these made him turn and see her in the same light as he had always seen her and her brother Mursal: why, they would remove any obstacle out of his way! He remembered that Mursal had talked of taking revenge and killing; and now Zeinab was going to threaten with death the urchin who had frightened him to shameful fear.

"Why threaten? Why strangle him? Why use force?"

"Or else, we'll take you away from here, I'll take you back, tell the builders to stop demolishing and reconstructing. We'll do anything. We'll rent a house for you, buy you a new one or take yours off the market."

"You will take me in, you will buy me a new house or take mine off the market. Why? Can't you think of anything but that? And threatening with death and strangling? Can't you think other than of simply *removing* obstacles out of my way and naturally out of yours too? Can't you? Why can't you use your head? Instead of employing coercion?"

"What would you like us to do?"

"I would like you to live with this reality: that your father, aged seventy, a Sayyidist who has fought for the nationalist cause all his life and would continue fighting till his ending days, is now, today, this moment, this very second, frightened to death of a stone striking him on the forehead; afraid: your father is *afraid*."

There was a brief silence; then:

"Are you afraid of death, Father?"

"No. I am not afraid of death. I am afraid of being afraid; afraid of my own fear. I am afraid of the known, not of the unknown; and the known in this particular case consists of the stone in Yassin's hand which can be activated at will by the devils that are."

"Afraid of fear? Or is there another thought behind this fear?"

"I suppose there is. For one thing, you do not stone *anybody*: you cast stones at dogs, at madmen; you pelt an adulterous woman, say, with stones; when at Mina in Mecca, you stone the pillar erected for that very purpose. In the Islamic concept in which you take refuge when you curse the devil is the keyword 'rajiim' which defines Satan as the stoned one. There is a whole lot of material on the symbolic and religious significance of stones. Idols, of stones, which were worshipped had to be discarded and they gave way to an All-present, Omni-this or-that, complemented with a sacred word and code of behaviour which still had room for stones: the Wailing Wall, the Kaaba and the making use of stones to chase Satan and his hangers-on. Madmen, with whom a saintliness of a kind is associated, are stoned by children – but not by adults; for in children, in a manner of speaking, dwells the divided and unseasoned man or woman. Nobody ever stones the object of one's love. Can you think of anyone groping in the dirt for a pebble-stone to throw at a dog when you go for a walk in Central Park in New York? Nor do you do that here, in Somalia, if it is a shepherd's dog. People are generally frightened of dogs here and thus instinctively look for a stone to throw at them and dogs feel this popular hostility and fight for survival. Nor, come to think of it, do you send a shattering stony message through a window-pane anywhere, do you? What is loved, what is expensive and what is worshipped: you do not pelt these with stones. This seems to me to be the moral, if there is one."

"And so?"

"In effect, what do you do when you see an owl?"

"I am culturally trained to stone it away."

"And when you see a crow?"

"The same," said Zeinab.

"The crow used to be worshipped once even by Somalis, I am told. Which is, Mursal tells me, where the word for prayer in Somali, *tuko,* derives from; and the reason, so Mursal tells me, why the Somali word for God is *waaq* is because it is the sound the crow makes. So to throw a stone at a crow is, for a Somali, to admit that there is an unconscious and primitive reversal of where we stand. Or so Mursal tells me."

Both paid homage to what had been said by stonily staring at each other in silence. Zeinab was proud of her father; proud that his brain was still alight with intellect; proud that he had the energy and vision to fight, struggle and hit back. He was different from most of his contemporaries, different and knowledgeable. Finally:

"This is tragic, isn't it? That I am not humble enough, sane enough to admit that I am afraid of physical pain. After all, I am the father of Mursal."

She didn't hear what he said or didn't want to. He was on his feet, he went and picked up the radio, brought it back and sat in his armchair. He seemed to lose interest in the conversation and was now ready to be fed with new information and thoughts. He switched on the radio. It was almost news time. Zeinab looked at him holding the radio in his embrace as though it were a loved child. And she remembered that the original idea behind bringing him here was to enable him to live in dust-free, tension-free conditions. Perhaps they should think things over, she and Mursal. She also recalled that in California, Deeriye hadn't suffered from any chest-congestions or complaints. Could one create "California" here for him?

"I'll come with you for a walk when you can."

"Not today; not today," was all Deeriye could think of saying.

"Tomorrow then?"

"Or the day after."

"You postpone, you postpone it till another day. Meanwhile, your legs will fill, like a pitcher, with water."

"We would postpone death if we could, wouldn't we?" he said.

She did not know what to say: she went out.

FOUR

The Key under the Mat by the Door

Two days later.

There was a noise similar to that of gurgling water. Deeriye stirred in his armchair and, like a cat which had just emerged from the furred purr of a nap, opened his eyes slightly, half winked, licked his moustache; then his hand massaged his face awake, he stretched his arms sideways and his legs forward, and yawned. He swallowed the sticky mess his salivary glands had secreted while asleep and then again wiped his mouth with his open hand. A little later, before his feline alertness could take stock of what was happening, there occurred another noise, this time threatening and irritating at the same time, not dissimilar to the noise naughty city-urchins make when they grate a corrugated zinc-wall with the rugged edges of a broken bottle. Now that he was fully awake, he wondered if he should try and identify the source and significance of this din. With this uppermost in his mind, he got up but allowed himself the luxury of yawning comfortably before tottering in the direction of the window. Then all of a sudden, a string of expletives reached him as he watched what little movement there was in the street below: a mother, in rags, sitting in the shade of a tree breast-feeding a sickly child; a donkey-waterman clucking lovingly at his beast and talking in the most endearing terms imaginable: a small girl skipping a rope and another standing by, awaiting her turn while she counted her rival's jumps. From the look and sound of it, the expletives were uttered by the breast-feeding woman. But who was that who had made the irritating din? Who made the noise of the gurgling water? The street suggested activities of a more harmonious nature, and Deeriye would not have believed that those within his view could have created such an impertinent racket. These people were too busy, he told himself, each seemed preoccupied with what he or she was doing. So who? He decided to look for another person. His eyes scoured the space within reach. And he spotted Yassin. The young rascal had something in his hand. The moment he saw that Deeriye's suspicious stare was fixed on him, he walked away, displaying signs of a nervous weakness. However, once he was sure he was standing in front of his own gate, Yassin's glance was glittery with the mocking smile of defiance and fiendishness. The poor woman, a beggar, had collected her meagre belongings and crawled away on her knees for a while, then she gathered up herself and her courage and went away, speaking further expletives and curses, dispatching the urchin and his ancestors to hell and worse. And she broke into a trot when she heard Yassin shout back, insult for insult, abuse for abuse.

A smile as fiendish as you could ever see, his movements feverish, and Yassin bent as though he were removing from the soles of his shoes a cake of mud which had cleaved to them. On closer examination, it became clearer to Deeriye that it was not a pebble that he had in his hand. He deduced this from the way Yassin chucked it gently ahead of himself, playing with it like a *boggio,* and then picked it up and tossed it again, went after it and took it again: when it hit the sand, the stone sank in, making a *chuck* sound as it severed in half the earth. Then: he made a swift about-turn, faster than a discus-thrower in action, and he prepared to fling the *xaleef* he had in his hand, as if he would hit Deeriye. But Deeriye was not frightened any more. (Here he remembered the day, forty-odd years ago, when the Italian colonial officer made the same sort of menacing gesture of shooting him; when everyone else had been frightened; and when Deeriye looked the accursed infidel in the eyes.) Yassin smiled mischievously and took a few steps towards his own gate, walking with the conscious effort of not betraying that he knew he was being watched. He knocked on the gate and waited.

The telephone rang downstairs.

It rang on and on and on. Should he go and answer it? He decided he would.

He moved towards the door, turning his back on the (open) window, afraid Yassin's *xaleef* would strike him from behind. So he walked with care, his body ready for the hit, his mind resigned. The telephone did not stop ringing despite Deeriye's taking an age going to reach it. But why was he answering it today when he had never before given its ringing further thought? Maybe he was meant to hear something; maybe he was meant to be *the medium, the receiver or the conveyor of a message.* It must be urgent, he thought as he picked up the receiver.

"Pronto?"

"This is the Mahdi," he heard.

"The who?" asked Deeriye, a little shocked.

There was silence. Then Deeriye asked again, "The who did you say? Is that Mahad? This is Deeriye, can you hear me?"

"This is Mukhtaar."

"Yes, Mukhtaar. How are you?"

"Mursal isn't at home, is he?"

"No, he is not."

"Tell him that I called. Please," said Mukhtaar, his voice nervous; but did not hang up immediately.

Deeriye waited. Then: "Any other message?" he asked.

"Yes. Tell him to listen to the midday news."

"It is nearly midday now."

"Then tell him to listen to the 2 o'clock news if he is not home for the midday bulletin. Tell him it's very important. Don't forget, eh!" said Mukhtaar and hung up unceremoniously.

As soon as he reached his room, Deeriye switched on the radio. The signature tune before the news bulletin. He turned the volume louder and placed himself comfortably in his favourite armchair from where he could see the street below. For a second, he lost interest in listening to the radio as he saw confused movement down in the street and a great deal of toing and froing: a car arrived, out came Cigaal, who rushed into his house re-emerged carrying a gun and left in a chauffeur-driven car. A second or so later, Cigaal's daughters ran out and got into a car parked outside. Meanwhile, the news came on. A failed assassination attempt on the Head of State. Nothing was very clear about whether the person or persons responsible were known or had been apprehended, although the news bulletin hinted that a suspect had been taken into custody and was being interrogated. Deeriye switched off the radio and went to stand by the open window to watch the street below, wondering whether or not its diapason of activities would offer him further hints. Only Yassin was there. Nobody else.

He sat in the armchair and closed his eyes for a second or so, relishing the sweetness of the breeze with total surrender before he asked himself the meaning of the message Mukhtaar had given him and its relevance, if any, to the failed assassination attempt. Was anyone close to him involved? Deeriye was too nervous to sit back and think. He got up and stood in front of the window. It was then that something struck him, something which the instant it hit him made his face awash with blood and the blindfold pain made him moan for help. No one was in the house. He became vertiginous and the giddy whirling of the ache lifted him to an exalted state of dizziness.

• • • • • • • • • • •

He woke up hours later, his head shrouded in bandaged pain. When he turned to see better who it was that sat by him, his forehead detonated a charge of pain so acute that fireflies of bright darkness danced before his eyes. But he bore that pain with Homeric patience. He closed his eyes and then opened them, repeating this several times. Then he saw that it was Zeinab, his daughter, who was there, Zeinab who now took one of his hands and broke his knuckles for him, massaged his feet, his thighs and wherever joints met, silent, loving, choosing a finger at a time or a particular muscle which she kneaded, gently and expertly.

"Two attempts; one succeeded, the other failed. That is a reasonable percentage, wouldn't you say? About the failed attempt on the life of the Head of State there is a news bulletin but about the successful one, none," she said.

He did not know what to say. He was too pained to, so he remained silent. His concentration was not very good because of the pain, which accounted for his inability to hear everything she said; his inability to sense the bitterness in her voice; his inability to catch the irony in her tone, or the sarcasm.

And she was saying: "No wonder Somalis say that a stone thrown at a culprit hits but the innocent."

He was furious he could not speak to make his point heard. If only he could. He remembered that he had been taken in a car to hospital; that Zeinab was there already; he remembered the smell; and the anaesthesia. But he could not remember who it was that had come first. Not Natasha, definitely; nor Mursal. One of the neighbours, whose face he was not familiar with. At the hospital: Zeinab. Apparently someone had called her, she dropped whatever she was doing and rushed to the Emergency Ward where there was no qualified doctor to attend to him. She took over. Daughter: doctor. It was wonderful to be in her company, hardly speaking, when the others were present, very professional and dealing with him as though he were someone else, not a tear shed, nor a question asked. He now remembered that he had said something like: "Mysterious devil-tossed xaleef-stones strike one, every now and then," and she was silent for a long time, only to comment when she had done the stitches: *"He is surely Satan in the flesh."*

"But I haven't told anyone," she was saying presently. "I haven't told anyone what you and I spoke about a couple of days ago and I will not. It would do nobody any good. Least of all, your reputation. In the circumstances – since it coincides with another historical event, i.e. the failed assassination attempt on the life of the Head of State – your being struck by Cigaal's grandson is laden with symbolic significance."

There! He knew his daughter and son would dwell on the pronounced ideological difference between their and Cigaal's family, a difference which was obvious to anybody who knew the background of the two fathers. Cigaal: once a collaborator of the Italians, a betrayer of his friends, some of whom were said to have died under torture later; Cigaal: whose eyebrows merged, like an alley into a road, over the bridge of his nose; Cigaal, although thrice Xaaji, a wicked man; his only son, a good-for-nothing young man who had been convicted of every imaginable felony, including rape of a minor; his daughter, the cause of a great deal of gossip. And his wife: a very noisy neighbour, a woman whose voice was rich with a language made more purple with abusive innuendos and insults. Believing the family was evil, everybody avoided contact with them. Nobody in the neighbourhood lent or borrowed anything from them. Nobody in the neighbourhood would want to be seen visiting them. But there came young eligible men from other villages of Mogadiscio to court Cigaal's daughter whose history was known to all: it was common knowledge that her Yassin was illegitimate and when the man who had made her pregnant refused to marry her, she struck him with a knife and he narrowly escaped the gaping mouth of death; no scruples and no education. The eligible men who came to court this young woman included a man whose ladder of opportunism had as many rungs as he knew Somali words: for he was a Somali born in a foreign land who expected – poor thing! – that he would be appointed an ambassador or minister if he associated himself with those who were tribally related to the Head of State. Here was the Caesar-irony of history: everybody knew he wouldn't be appointed to any important position but no one told him so. Although, again, the one to whom Cigaal's daughter's hand in marriage had been promised gave up the idea immediately he was made director-general of an autonomous government agency whose lucrative recompense was sweeter than the daily output of a sugar factory. Which made Mursal comment, "Houses or names of houses are made or unmade by those who live in them; or visit them; or associate with them; or marry into them. It was to our house that the most intelligent and most eligible of men and women came. But to Cigaal's house go the dregs of opportunism, the sediments of human feculence; these go there." He had said this to Mukhtaar. Later, his sister Zeinab pointed out that Cigaal was actually Mukhtaar's uncle and, no matter how he tried to dissociate himself from them, Mursal should not be so trusting as to believe that their friendship meant more to Mukhtaar than the blood; for blood was, in certain cases, thicker. Deeriye, silent, had been there when Mursal and Zeinab talked heatedly about ideological alliances versus tribal allegiances. But now he was dying to know whether or not Mahad was involved in the failed assassination attempt; and if not, who was the kamikaze?

He pressed his hand on the back of his head, so as to minimize the vibratory pain which escorted any speech, and very softly managed to say: "Was Mahad the kamikaze?"

She didn't hear him until he repeated his question twice. Then: "I don't know," she said.

"And where is Mursal?"

"I don't know," she answered.

He looked at his watch: in a minute or two, Natasha would walk through the door, having parked her car in the garage; and with her, Samawade. He dreaded what Samawade would do if told that Yassin had struck his grandfather. But he wouldn't think about it now. He would prepare himself for their coming. And Deeriye cringed when the door opened and when shouting and joyous Samawade rushed up the staircase to tell his grandfather something exciting and . . . he stopped; he stopped at the sight of blood on his grandfather's forehead and looked accusingly at Zeinab.

"What have you done?"

"He is all right," she said.

"Who's hit him?"

And Natasha was there, too. A heat-disfigured face – no longer the innocent beauty of smiling eyes: the maid had told her. She took Samawade by the hand, led him away to an armchair in which she sat, making room for him too. And then told him.

"I will kill him; I will strangle him," he swore.

No one said anything. Zeinab and Deeriye remembered their conversation of a couple of days earlier. They knew whom he was going to kill: Yassin. And Natasha held Samawade, his wrist in her tight grip, speechlessly staring at Deeriye who offered his hand to Zeinab who massaged it, drawing the crack of a knuckle.

Natasha ventured to say: "What obviously must be done is to take his actions very seriously; the little devil must not dare stone anyone else. He is always there, tossing a shower of pebbles as though they were God's manna."

Samawade repeated, "I will kill him; I will strangle him."

Zeinab, seemingly calm, said, "No, you will not do any such thing."

She saw that Deeriye had gradually stiffened. She asked, "Are you all right?" and did not believe him when he said he was. The pain had smartened after a little while, etching the wrinkles the years had cast on his temple: moon-shaped half-circles. She said, "Are you all right?"

Again he nodded and again she did not believe him. His eyes, however, were open: they were so still and unmoving she thought he was holding his breath, readying himself for an asthmatic attack. She motioned to Natasha to take Samawade away. And she prayed and prayed and prayed. She forgot her medical training, clean forgot who she was, what she was capable of, what power she had over him or any ailing person. And she prayed, "O God, thou art . . . ," and made a string of requests longer than any rosary, with her eyes squinting, narrow and small as beads, her gaze vague and far away. Weak and powerless, she sat by the foot of the bed, not realizing that there was no danger of him getting the attack; and she was thinking to herself, *Everything I do seems to be flawed; why, I should have taken his fear seriously and taken him away from here, moved him back to our place . . . .*

He was saying something: "A small request, Zeinab. A small favour, if you please." There was a painful look on his face. "Since you are expert at keeping disasters and my condition a family secret for as long as possible, I wonder if you will treat Yassin's striking me as a secret indulgence of our own."

"But, Father?"

"I have no evidence that it was he who struck me, for one thing. For another, the political consequences would be so great we would not be able to handle it with grace."

"You don't need evidence."

"Of course you do. And no one has it. I don't."

"We all know it. We all *know* he did it."

"Knowing is no evidence. How do you know it was he who hit me? Do you have any evidence?"

"Don't kill him; don't strangle him; don't even accuse him. And you call that a small favour, Father? Imprisoned in fear; unable to take a walk; suffocating with fright. Why, this is worse than the detention centres you spent decades in." She was Zeinab again, the Zeinab he knew: fiery!

He asked himself if he could remember anything just before he was struck, just before he closed his eyes thinking about whether or not the message Mukhtaar had requested him to deliver to Mursal had any relevance in the light of the failed assassination attempt. He recalled a pandemoniacal pain. He recalled coming to in the hospital; and the terrible pain of being stitched – his body, all this time, limp and almost lifeless and useless. A question of what is real and what is unreal: an essential question. A new-born child opens the lungs of its world with the scream of cosmic *realness* and from that second onwards, this child exists; that cry is as real as life, as a daguerreotypal reproduction of a photograph. But a child is *not present* at its own birth. It is *others* who are present at its birth, in the same way as the person who dies is *not present* at his own funeral. *In other words, is one* there, *is one* present *in these circumstances?* He was not there, was not present when he was hit but became alive to it when the pain struck him a little later, only to lose consciousness. Then:

"Another small favour, my daughter."

"What, Father?"

"Tell me, was Mahad the kamikaze of whom the radio spoke?"

She had no need to answer, she told herself, seeing that Mursal had come in. She rose, nearly as tall as her brother.

"Yes, Father," Mursal said.

And no one spoke for a long, long time.

• • • • • • • • • • •

Alone, father and son.

"It is time for the BBC Somali Section news bulletin if you want to hear it," said Mursal, holding the radio on his lap and tuning it. "Would you like to?"

Deeriye took a sip of his lemon-tea. "No, I do not want to listen to the BBC Somali Section news bulletin today, tomorrow or the day after."

"And why not?"

"Because the BBC Somali Section is no alternative to the state-run radio of Mogadiscio. It's worse, in fact."

"But you listen to the BBC Arabic Section and if you can't get it on the air as clearly as you like, you resort to the Italian Section of the BBC. Why not the Somali Section of the same BBC?"

"Neither do I listen to Radio Kulmis, a radio of disgrace to the Somali dissident movements abroad, in particular those who sought refuge in and founded a most unholy alliance with the Somali people's enemies in Addis Ababa. I don't listen to that radio station either."

"But of course."

The BBC news bulletin was on the air now; the half-hour was being allotted to the two reporters of the day: Said Farah and Idris Hassan. Deeriye lowered the volume as he heard Said read the day's headlines.

No mention of the assassination attempt on Somalia's Head of State. But he did not switch it off. The humming news served as background as Deeriye said:

"A number of times, I've been disappointed with them. On many occasions, you hear something about Somalia on the Arabic or the Italian Services but when the same commentary is used by the Somali Section, any mention in bad light of the Generalissimo is censored, cut; or interpreted in such a way that you get a different sense of the thing altogether."

"Why do they do that?"

"They who?"

"The BBC of course."

"I am told that it is all the doing of someone whom many Somalis speak ill of and whose collaboration with the Enemies of the Somali Nation they make whispery references to and who, the Somalis who speak a lot say, behaves as though he were representative of the General's tribal oligarchy in the BBC."

"This is ridiculous."

"I got this elaborate interpretation from Rooble."

"This is ridiculous. The BBC would do something about *him*."

"There are two of them. Or so says Rooble. One does the censoring; the other, I am told, is a plaintive, toothless, spineless asthmatic, perpetually sick: if not low blood pressure then rheumatoid arthritis; one week, a sinus complication, the week after that a cyst."

"Is he Somali?"

"From a highly respected family. A set of brainy brothers, he has. All this information was given me by Rooble."

"The BBC wouldn't hire two Somalis to run its Somali Section. One would have thought . . . ," began Mursal and was interrupted.

"Who said the two are Somalis? Did I?"

"I'm sorry – they are not? Forgive me."

"It is a pity that the BBC Somali Section is no alternative to Mogadiscio's state-run information bureau. Once Somalis used to receive anything the Somali Section broadcast as gospel truth but of late no. Those of us who are polyglots can switch to the Arabic, the English or the Italian. But the common man in Mogadiscio, Kismayo, Baidoa or Hargeisa has no alternative but to listen to two radio stations, one in Mogadiscio and the other in London, whose relevance to the important news and events in Somalia is minimal."

Silence. Information, Deeriye was thinking to himself, is the garden the common man in Somalia or anywhere else is not allowed to enter, sit in its shady trees, drink from its streams and eat its delicious fruits; information, or the access to that power and knowledge: power prepared to protect power; keep the populace underinformed so you can rule them; keep them apart by informing them separately; build bars of ignorance around them, imprison them with shackles of uninformedness and they are easy to govern; feed them with the wrong information, give them poisonous bits of what does not count, a piece of gossip here, a rumour there, an unconfirmed report. Keep them waiting; *let them not know;* let them not know what you are up to and where you might spring from again. As for incidents like today's, tell them the little that will misguide them, inform them wrongly, make them suspect one another so that they will tell on one another. But who would know about today's? Now he turned to Mursal:

"What do you know about Mahad?"

Mursal switched off the radio, got up and took it to the *commedine* by the window; and returned to sit down. His nervousness could not be put down to a simple preoccupation with his friend's involvement and certain execution.

"I know very little," he said.

"More than the news bulletin has given us, I hope."

"Yes."

"What?"

"I know what I've been told."

"By whom?"

"I would rather not say. You don't mind, do you?"

"I was given a message by Mukhtaar," Deeriye volunteered.

"I know."

"Yes?"

"We met . . . Mukhtaar and I . . . and the others . . . er . . . !"

"Don't speak if you mustn't," said Deeriye, undecided as always whether to ask more or be satisfied with the little he was told. Mursal could see Yassin playing with pebbles and dice, and near him, as if to keep an eye on him, the rascal's mother. There was also a woman whose protuberances of buttocks and mammalia made him ponder questions of aesthetics whenever he talked to Natasha and Mahad together. He came back, towered above his father who was sitting up, pillow cosily tucked behind his head. Mursal spoke:

"Someone told me that the General had just delivered his annual speech to the judiciary and made a great ado about justice, socialism and democracy, blaming others for the tribalistic, nepotistic allegiances people associate with his régime. Having finished his speech, he came down the protected dais to shake hands with the ministers, diplomats and jurists who were there. When he was a foot or two away from the circle in which Mahad, along with other jurists, was standing, Mahad took a step forward and (I'm quoting eye-witnesses here), possessed by an unpremeditated act of madness, grabbed the revolver from one of the General's bodyguards and tried to shoot his target. Someone, a plain-clothes security man, wrestled with him, the bullet hit the ceiling and in the chaos that followed, the Head of State managed to get away through the back door and jump into a taxi, taking with him his two most trusted bodyguards – both clansmen of his, one of whom happens to be also his son-in-law."

"Where were you then?" asked Deeriye.

"I had been invited to the annual do as usual, since I am a professor at the university, but I didn't go. I had other things to do."

"Where were you when the incident took place?"

"At the university – teaching."

"And you have witnesses that you were at the university at the precise second and minute all this took place?"

"You surprise me, Father."

"I know it is none of my business but answer my queries to set my mind at peace; for I am worried, yes, because I don't know what I'm being dragged into. Where were you at midday today?" said Deeriye, who appeared full of mad energy.

"I said I was at the university."

"With whom?"

"With my students – teaching 'Constitutional Law'."

"And Mukhtaar?"

"I can't speak for him."

Deeriye chose not to repeat, as evidence, the message Mukhtaar had given when he telephoned precisely at two minutes before midday wanting to speak to Mursal; or to say he knew Mursal was now lying.

"You were sitting by the telephone waiting for instructions from a *fourth* person, were you?"

"Is this an interrogation? And who is the fourth person?"

"I suspect his name is Jibriil Mohamed-Somali. Am I right?"

Deeriye could not have anticipated this: that Mursal would betray no signs of anxiety about someone guessing what he and his friends were up to. Deeriye was impressed at how cool Mursal remained. Then the telephone interrupted the silence. Mursal thought he would save him further embarrassment by going to answer it. But Natasha had already taken the call, and she shouted to Mursal that it was Jibriil on the line. Deeriye suggested he should tell her to ask Jibriil to call again. Mursal obliged and the message was relayed to Natasha. Deeriye said:

"Are you prepared to tell your father anything, Mursal?"

"If I said I am not prepared to tell you anything, you would understand, wouldn't you?"

"Yes."

"It involves other people's lives and I'd be breaking promises and principles if I told you anything. But I promise I'll tell you everything one day. Is that all right?"

Deeriye nodded; then:

"Mursal, Mahad, Mukhtaar and now Jibriil. What a fine set of names. And what suggestions! What a wealth of possibilities! Listen to this: the Messengers; the divine message; and the chosen one."

Deeriye's mind dwelled on the paradox and paradigmatical complications of the names. What could that mean? Mukhtaar, the chosen one, leaving a message for the messenger Mursal; and Jibriil wishing to bring forth the dawning of a new era by delivering the divine message to the messenger. Down with that infidel of a General, amen! He remembered the conversations he had had with Mursal and Mahad, their constant reference to the Islamic tradition and thought; to the Constitution of Medina; to the Khaliifas; i.e. to the law of retaliation; to Alij to Mucaawiya; to Yaziid. . . . "Four persons bamboozled with notions of power and the weighty responsibility of restoring it to the masses at whatever cost," said Zeinab.

Then the door-bell rang. They sensed nervous movement downstairs and Mursal went to the window and told his father who the visitors were: Cigaal, Yassin and the young boy's mother. Natasha let them in and led them upstairs, having called before doing so. *They will deny any deliberate knowledge or connection with what their son has done,* he thought, *and will seek to be forgiven, given pardon, from one good neighbour to another.* They came in: Cigaal first, Yassin's mother, then Yassin. Rigid formalities; hand-shaking salutations; invocations of Allah's name and the Prophet's. Seats: chairs; rearrangement of furniture so there would be a place for Mursal to sit; Natasha wouldn't come in, for she had to keep Samawade away, otherwise, he said, he might be tempted to "hit, kill or strangle and exorcize the devil out of Yassin." Cigaal gave a protracted preface to their reason for coming; he quoted proverbs, the tradition of the country about neighbourly behaviour; he apologized on behalf of himself and his family for what Yassin had done; Yassin who had been punished, corporally punished ("You can see that his eyes are red from crying all afternoon," he commented). Deeriye thought it was farcical that no one made any reference to the failed attempt on the life of the Head of State! Should Mahad, like Yassin, seek the General's pardon? And would he be forgiven? Of course not. A bullet for a bullet. Cigaal and family were asking to be pardoned in the name of Allah and the Prophet. Would the General?

Yassin was told to take Deeriye's right hand and kiss it and to say the words, "I am very sorry I have behaved irresponsibly towards you and harmed you physically." But just before the young urchin stooped to take Deeriye's hand, there arose a commotion of instructions, counter-instructions and pleas. Whereupon, Cigaal shouted that he would feel offended if he and his grandson and his daughter were not given the chance to pay deference (and eventually *xaal*) to Deeriye. All sounds lulled, everybody hushed, and the sun's lustrous presence, as witness, heightened the tense atmosphere when Yassin prostrated himself before the bed; the silence, and the brightness surrounding him joined him to receive the unringed hand of the old man whom he had struck, a hand which he kissed. That done, there followed a few worrying minutes with nobody willing to speak, and silence hovered above the heads of those present like a vulture. Deeriye, for his part, was amazed at how elegantly Yassin had shuffled through a difficult situation; Yassin was definitely a good actor. And when he returned to his place, behind his mother and grandfather, his hands behind his back, polite and innocent-looking, the action was greeted with an ejaculatory prayer of thanks – that of *Faatixa*.

Right on cue, Natasha arrived with tea, a cup a head. Deeriye and Mursal drank theirs first in order to allay any suspicion of their neighbours' that they would be poisoned. Natasha excused herself. The atmosphere appeared more relaxed. Cigaal, after obtaining assurances that things were not as bad as they seemed, said:

"And do you know what answer Yassin gave when I asked why he struck you? You won't believe it. It's to do, I think, with the logic of their generation. Absurd, very absurd. The logic of the young."

Deeriye did not ask the begged question. But Mursal did.

"You tell your uncle," said Cigaal to Yassin, pointing with his chin at Mursal, "tell your uncle what you told me. Incredible. Come on. Tell him." Yassin was gradually becoming nervous; losing all the calm which had conducted him through the most difficult phase.

Cigaal's daughter, who was Yassin's mother, made her first and most essential contribution. She suggested that Cigaal tell it. And Cigaal spoke:

"He said that he did not in the least intend to strike you. 'After all,' he said, 'Xaaji Deeriye is like my grandfather; he is not Khaliif, a madman; nor is he a beggar, nor a dog. I did not mean to strike him, I swear.'"

"Yes?"

"But listen to the logic of the young these days," said Yassin's mother.

"Yes?" Mursal's chorus.

"'I saw,' he said, 'the reflection of an owl in the window; or *thought I* had seen one,' he says. 'I meant to hit the owl which was on the roof of their house. I missed my target,' he says, 'and, by mistake, struck him.'"

"That definitely is absurd," said Mursal.

"It is, isn't it?" Cigaal agreed. "The logic of the young is."

"It certainly is," Mursal said, getting up, ready to show them out.

Cigaal got the message. He too stood up. He put his hand in his pocket, brought out his hand fisted in notes of money; he moved in the direction of the bed on which Deeriye had lain.

Mursal saw what was about to happen and so, in a hurry, intervened, saying, "No *xaal,* no payment to my father, no payment in any form, cash or kind can be accepted, Uncle Cigaal. After all, we are neighbours; neighbours in our tombs as well as under the shelters above our blessed heads. Brothers in Islam."

Cigaal turned to Mursal, saying, "But that is the tradition. A compensatory fee is paid him who is hurt. Isn't that our tradition? Besides, the hospital fees these days are too high to pay from a stipend."

"No fees have been incurred," Mursal assured him.

"Of course. Zeinab is the doctor; you, the lawyer," he said, his smile stopping at his chin, unable to spread and reach the rest of his face. He put the money back in his pocket. There was nothing to do except leave, which they did, feeling as though the victory promised by Yassin's shuffling through that tricky situation was denied them by Mursal's not accepting the traditional *xaal!*

Mursal said, as they went down the stairs unescorted, "The logic of the young these days. It is absurd." Cigaal did not answer.

• • • • • • • • • • •

Night fell with a tropical suddenness. Natasha, Samawade and Zeinab came up and chatted with Deeriye for a while; Samawade and Natasha left first; then Zeinab, having changed the dressing, said she had to go because she was on duty that night. And Mursal and Deeriye were alone. In the silence, Deeriye's mind roamed, free to graze anywhere where there was pasture for thought. And he remembered the day the Italian colonial administrator called on him, bringing peace in the neck of his long gun; he couldn't help recalling other incidents in Somali and African history wherein the colonialist imposed the methods of "pacification," a pacification of the natives through paying stipends to a few tribal chieftains and resorting to the use of the gun when this style did not work. *Pacify; bring in little in exchange for what you draw out in the form of exploitation; allow trade to flourish; create a class, an elite, and rule through them: classical methods which have worked over the years,* he was thinking.

Mursal could not bear the silence and he stood to his feet and said, "If there is nothing you need, I think I shall retire, Father. It's been a long day."

"Yes, it has been."

"Is there anything you want me to get you, before I go?"

Deeriye reflected: "Yes. Would you be so kind as to bring the cassette-player; find the Sayyid's 'Death of Koofiil'?"

"You mean *Corfield?*"

"You know who I mean. We Somalis pronounce the name that way."

"Certainly."

"Thanks."

Mursal moved about getting things ready; he went to the shelf where there was a library of cassettes, each properly labelled and neatly in order (it had been Samawade's job and idea in the first place). And as he set up a proper listening session for his father, Mursal heard:

"I would not have known how to send them away, you know. Cigaal's hand filled with his unaccepted *xaal* (it was two hundred shillings, I saw him unfold it clumsily), his heart heavy because of the unreceived compensation fee, his head full of contempt. I mean I wouldn't have known how to. But I was very glad you showed him out."

"I'm glad you approve." All this time Mursal was testing the cassette-player's buttons by pressing them a couple of times.

Deeriye was proud of the way Mursal had handled Cigaal. He was very proud of him. The two of them participated in the ending of a drama the beginnings of which Zeinab knew: to each of his children something to hold on to; to each, also, a secret. Zeinab: the fact that Deeriye had seen in his vision a Yassin striking him; Mursal: the fact that he now suspected that his father knew of Mursal's involvement with Mahad's failed effort.

"The cassette-player and the tape-recorder are both ready. All you have to do is to press the START button. The cassette will play the Sayyid's 'Corfield', the tape-recorder will play your favourite reciter of the Koran – *Surat Yassiin!* There you are. Anything else?"

Deeriye would have loved to engage Mursal in a conversation but his bandaged pain was too much to bear. He had many questions he wished he could ask: whether he would follow Mahad and drop, like him, into a black hole of madness. Deeriye would never insist on Mursal's parting with an important secret which might endanger the lives of others who also knew about Mahad's "unpremeditated" act of madness. Who would have thought that Mahad, a man who had reached the heights of his intellectual and professional ambitions, learned and intelligent and likeable, would act so irresponsibly? Why did he not plan it? Why, in heaven's name, commit this act of madness alone? And who was next, who was to follow Mahad's footsteps? He was a bachelor, had never married; he had always said he would never marry or start a family of his own until he had satisfied the twofold responsibility: the social and the political. He would marry then. He was nearly forty-seven. And he considered Rooble his father and looked up to Deeriye as one would a mentor. But why this act of madness?

"I'm going, unless you want something else, Father."

After a short pause, "Yes. I do."

"What?"

"Was Mahad's act of madness premeditated?"

"I have told you, Father."

"I am not asking how much you know or contributed towards the planning of this act of unorganized madness. But how premeditated was it?"

"I am not going to answer that question."

"And why hasn't Rooble called? Why haven't I heard from him? I am unwell, I am struck by Satan, I lie in bed and you won't answer my questions, nor will Rooble call and Mahad commits this stupid act of madness and you won't tell if it was premeditated," said Deeriye all in one breath, his voice choked on the phlegm of the tension which he felt inside.

"You're blackmailing me, Father. And you know you shouldn't. You know better than that. *It is for your own good and my own good that I say nothing.* Why does it matter whether or not it was a premeditated act so long as you refer to it as an act of madness?"

"Which it is."

"But why does it matter?"

"Then if you are taken away to be interrogated by the Security and something happens to you, I know that you, Mursal, did not contribute one brick towards the construction of a madman's edifice, that is why."

"I don't see why it matters."

"There is also another reason."

"I'm listening."

"What if the *four* of you worked out this act of collective madness to make it seem to all concerned that there was nothing planned or premeditated about it? The Head of State, while mingling with the diplomats, jurists and other dignitaries, walks in front of Mahad and this man, sane one second and insane the next, reaches for the bodyguard's revolver, manages to pull it out of its sheath and tries to shoot. What if you worked it all out beforehand?"

"I'll tell you how you can tell whether or not the General's régime interprets this as a premeditated act of madness. I'll tell you how you can decide."

"How?"

"If they suspect me of any involvement, the Security will come for me before the night is out. They'll come in the dead of night, take me away for interrogation and, if their suspicion is serious, charge me with sedition."

"And you choose not to tell me anything else?"

"Please do not make me say no." Silence.

"And why hasn't Rooble called?"

"I don't know." A pause. "Do you want me to call round and bring him here?" Mursal said.

"Don't go out. Not to Rooble's anyway. Their place must be surrounded by a million and one vultures and spies and traitors. But do you think . . . allow me to digress . . . Mukhtaar is all right? I mean, is he worthy of your trust?"

"What is this nonsense, Father?"

"It was something Rooble and Zeinab said."

There was a bitter pause. Mursal said, "I don't think you need worry about these things. You've very tired and I suggest you take a break. I'll see you in the morning, Father," and he was ready to leave.

"If you're still here; and if *they* haven't come for you."

Mursal, before going out, walked to the cassette-player and the record-player, checked if everything had been set to order. He decided to test them. Silence. Then the chorus of *Hooyaalayeey* and then the text of the poem the Sayyid composed on hearing that Corfield, under whose command had been, in 1912 when Deeriye was born, the Camel Constabulary who had died under the courageous charge of the guns of the Somali nationalist dervishes. And:

Adaa jiitayaan Koofilow	*dunida joogeen eh*
Adigaa judkii la gugu wacay	*jimic la'aaneed eh*
Jahannamo la geeyow, haddaad	*Aakhiro u jahaaddo*
Nimankii janno u kacay war bey	*jirin inshae'alliye*
Jamescooyinkii iyo haddaad	*jawaahirtii aragto*
Sida Eebbahay kuu jirrabay	*mari jawaabteeda*
Daraawiish jigraar nagama dayn	*tan iyo jeerkii dheh*
Ingriis jahyoo waxaa ku dhacay	*jac iyo baaruud dheh*
Waxay noo jajuunteenna waa	*jibasho diineed dheh*
Jigta weerar bay goor barqa ah	*nagu jiteeyeen dheh*
Aniga jirkay ila heleen	*shalay jahaadkii dheh . . . .*

Mursal switched it off. "Is there anything else you need before I go? It's been a long day and I have a longer one tomorrow. Anything? Here is a glass of water; here is a glass of milk; your tablets and mechanical accessories; your prayer-rug within reach; your Koran and your 'Corfield', Anything else?"

"No, nothing else."

"Good night then."

"Good night."

Mursal pulled the door to as he went out, leaving it slightly ajar, as one does the door to the children's room so that if they cry for help in the middle of the night one can hear them. He could hear the playback button being pressed and "Corfield" start all over as he walked down the staircase.

PART TWO

And below us in dampness,
in darkness the fish dwelled.
– Hermann Hesse

Man is the question the beast asks itself.
– George Lamming

FIVE

. . . .

History through an Unfocused Lens

On the third day: forenoon. The sun was in his eyes and he closed and opened them. But he was feeling a little better, the wound had begun to heal and the bandage had become small as the pain. He was, however, determined, against the advice of Mursal and Zeinab, to go to Baar Novecento where he knew he was likely to meet some of his peers and acquaintances (for most of whom he had little respect) with whom he would exchange Mogadiscio's latest rumour: he had decided to go to this famous tea-house in the hope of learning something about the prison Mahad was being held in; who his accomplices were supposed to be; and since he knew that Rooble was going there, he hoped their meeting would appear casual and innocuous (the two had totally severed communication when, yesterday, Mursal had been picked up by two plain-clothesmen from the university campus but released after mild questioning); he hoped he would know why Mursal was released after this mild interrogation which stopped immediately the generalities were done with and once Mursal said he had nothing to do with Mahad's incomprehensible action and knew nothing about it. Was there anything in Mursal's interpretation of why he had been released instantly: that the régime of the General was keen on denying Mahad's singular kamikaze-act national backing by treating it as though it were tribally motivated; which was the reason why so many of Mahad's kinsmen were taken in yesterday night's purge (a purge which the foreign and local media did not report)? But how would he explain why Rooble and a few others were not also swept into detention?

"The explanation is simple, Father. This is the General's expert handling of the whole affair. On a national and international level, he isolates the act, denying it a national base by showing its tribal support; on the tribal level, he is determined to isolate Mahad and (as a consequence) Rooble. Revise your who's who, Father. Who is Mahad? who is the General?"

Mahad was the son of the man whose father caused his community much pain and because of whose "mad" action the wells of his clan were poisoned by the Italians in 1934; a man who killed one Italian when wrestling for possession of the Italian's gun – in self-defence! And who was the General? What was the General, who in 1969 became virtually the unchallenged leader of Somalia, doing in 1934? Could it be that the General was one of the soldiers the Italians took with them during that raid first on Rooble's community and later Deeriye's?

"You exaggerate sometimes, Mursal," said Deeriye.

Deeriye was depressed today; he was plaintive; he complained constantly about everything. *He has become the old man and the asthmatic he was,* said Zeinab. She and Mursal believed he worked himself up into an attack when they suggested he did not go to Baar Novecento; thought himself into a fit like a child crying himself to sleep. He relaxed and suffered no more chest congestions when Mursal said he or Natasha would take him there. *His face: his lungs!* He was a man in much distress. The nights had been rough, so rough that Zeinab and Mursal stayed by him one night. Then came the ominous news which so disturbed Deeriye (he had been having a nap when she began telling the story): he woke and his chest burst into an asthmatic explosion immediately. Zeinab (who didn't like Mukhtaar right from the start) had repeated upon his request that people were circulating a cursory remark to the effect that Mukhtaar had betrayed Mahad. But Mursal would insist to his last day that Mukhtaar would *never* betray a friend – although, "Come to think of it, Mahad couldn't be betrayed: how could he be when he acted in the full view of the public gaze? These wicked rumours help discredit Mahad and Mukhtaar; they paint all underground dissident movements in unfavourable colours; and someone like Zeinab shouldn't listen to this nonsense." Whereupon, Zeinab said that Mursal "should never use the word *never* when speaking of matters such as this."

"I think he is right," had intervened Deeriye. "I think Mursal is right in saying that a person who commits an act in the full view of the public cannot be betrayed. The question is: do people say that Mukhtaar betrayed the names of accomplices, men and women who were supposed to have been behind him in one way or another, whether in the planning of the act or in preparing escape-routes or maps if the attempt failed and he got away? So do you know of any suspects, names of accomplices mentioned?" he asked Zeinab.

She shook her head: no.

"Then don't give credibility to these wicked rumours by speaking them in our presence," Deeriye requested.

After a brief pause, he spoke and touched on aspects of betrayal and spoke of known historical precedents already documented such as the constabulary *Ilaalo* who, having sold his gun to the Sayyid for four camels, reported to his British masters that the Sayyid had "stolen his rifle;" then he touched on another traitor, Haji Abdullahi Shaxaari (a name to note), who, in exchange for a meagre sum, produced a false letter which he claimed had been penned by no less than the mentor of the Sayyid, a letter in which the founder of the Salixiyya Religious Movement, to which the Sayyid belonged, was supposed to have dissociated himself from his disciple's irreligious wicked motives; a third traitor to whom he made reference was the man who helped the Italians to intercept and confiscate the correspondence between the Sultan of the Kingdom of Obbia and that of Mujeertenya, the only two Somali kingdoms which had remained independent until the 1930s: Deeriye wondered what turns Somalia's history might have taken if Cesare Maria de Vecchi, *il Gran' Pacificatore,* had not found the weak traitor to serve his purpose: and Mursal doubted very much, as did Zeinab, that the European nations would have made any fuss or even polite gestures, as they had done when Abyssinia was invaded by Italy only two years after the complete pacification of these two kingdoms, had the Sultanates appealed for international help. And Deeriye had said, "In almost all cases, the betrayed is one who has absolute faith in the one who betrays him. Somalis say: 'O Lord, protect me from my friends; I know how to deal with my own foes.'" Lastly, he alluded to the part of his own history which involved a traitor by the name of Haji Omer, the man who exploited the innocent trust of the eight-year-old

Waris, a young boy carrying a message of great importance to be delivered from Deeriye's community to Rooble's and on which depended the lives of hundreds of people and cattle. What makes traitors betray? He had asked the question and heard Zeinab and Mursal dwell for long on the psychology of traitors and what made them behave the way they did. It would make Deeriye all the more sad if Mukhtaar betrayed because he knew that Mursal was somehow party to the failed conspiracy.

Now. He moved away from the sun and waited for either Mursal or Natasha to come and tell him who would give him a lift to Baar Novecento in the afternoon. He knew they were both there. The movements on the ground floor suggested a jitteriness of a kind he always associated with nervousness; the typewriter had been silent for half an hour but the turntable was playing some European music. Deeriye did not know precisely what since it all sounded alike to him: he wished someone would play some of those jazz records and the Spirituals which moved him to tears although he could never decipher the words, nor tell one note of music from another. But Samawade was not there. Nor was the maid – for she had brought him breakfast before going to the market for the day's groceries. Occasionally, he would hear Natasha and Mursal mention his name and a little later that of Rooble or Mahad or Yassin would be mentioned. Why could he not stay in since he was not feeling very well? Why did he have to insist on finding out for himself what people were saying? What information would these old cronies give him? Nothing but rumour. Mursal had suggested that Deeriye stay home, having offered to bring anyone to whom he wished to speak to where he was. "To go out means to expose yourself to all kinds of violence, for Mogadiscio is a violent city; to queries about Cigaal's grandson Yassin and the wound he has inflicted upon you; to young men and young women who seem to wait on corners to tell you how much they respect you – the same men and women who have a habit of putting suggestive words into the mouth of Khaliif the madman." But Deeriye wouldn't be dissuaded from going and meeting "the old cronies" who perhaps would talk to him upon his paying for as many cups of tea as there were persons seated at the table.

Mogadiscio? "The city of Mogadiscio," Deeriye would say, "has aged before it teethed; it is no city for the elderly or the very small. It is a violent city, in which only the strong among the young are able to survive; if not strong and young, you have to be collected like a shattered glass into the caring hands of somebody with a car, for there are no taxis which you can take with the comfort and civility the old and the very young need. The old, if they go into the city after seven in the evening, run the risk of being mugged or simply pushed aside like an inconvenient idea when the taxi they flagged down brakes in front of them. Buses? These go on straight lines, mapped, as it were, to be driven by the sightless who sit behind the wheels and move on until they hear the bells ring. Buses, blue as the sky, blue as the flag of the nation, as rare to come by as are the Virgini constellations." And they talked about old men whom they both knew and who had been mugged; or children who were in no position to defend themselves against the violence meted out to them; but definitely the city's urchins needed less sympathy than their victims: the elderly, the weak and the very small. Of course, Deeriye went on, not everyone was as lucky as he in having a daughter-in-law who would drop everything to escort him somewhere, or a son who would re-arrange his teaching schedule in order to take him somewhere else, or a daughter who could call another friend to do her father a favour if she herself were not available for the task. So why was Deeriye making all this fuss? Was he not grateful? "Certainly. But these are favours my children and their friends lavish on me and spoil me with – not my rights. Rights. I am a Mogadiscian, have been a Mogadiscian the past thirty years or so, and as a Mogadiscian I am entitled to certain rights. Transport, water, electricity, personal safety, not to forget all the other civil amenities that a person who lives in a major city anywhere in the world gets. Who should I get these from? The government. No infrastructure, no intrastructure, no superstructure: nonsense. Weak excuses. No good. What about all these unnecessary showpiece trips abroad and vanity-of-the-nation dos at which they spend millions of dollars: these should cease. Do you know who gets something out of a government like ours? Foreign journalists and scholars who specialize in Somali affairs; these make the occasional trip and praise them in their papers. Some hundred and eighty of them were invited last year to Mogadiscio, tickets paid both ways, hotel bills settled. Why? Somali Studies Congress whose first meeting coincided with the tenth anniversary of the revolution. Coincided? It was deliberately arranged. That's it. See what we have done."

"In many countries, one hasn't any rights; but neither does one really have them in Western Europe or North America although one is made to believe one does. Governments decide how best to rule masses; and to the elites of these countries are guaranteed some rights. That is more or less the situation," said Zeinab.

"Someone was telling me the other day, I think it was Natasha," Deeriye said, "that if it is known that you are a declared communist in the Federal Republic of Germany, you are not offered a job in any of the government services. And when you are taken into the employ of the state, you are made to swear that you will not join the Communist Party. Now what democracy is that?"

"Democracy is the instrument with which the elites whip the masses anywhere; it enables the ruling elite to detain some, impoverish others, and makes them the sole proprietors of power. Who knows what is good for the people? Who knows whom the people love most? Who knows best what the people need? Go to Moscow; go to Zaire; go to Bonn; go to Cairo; or come to Mogadiscio. The self-declared leaders will tell you."

"The Somali Republic became the Somali *Democratic* Republic when the General came to power. The 'Democratic' portion of the name is decorative, to say the least, an embellishment of the worst kind. For what is *democratic* about rigged elections? What is *democratic* about painting one ballot box with the flag of the nation and writing on the other a notice 'that only an enemy of the nation need use this'? And then what is *democratic* about putting the 'No' ballot-box so conspicuously far away from the 'Yes' ballot-box so as to enable the Security who loiter near the 'No' ballot-box to follow the dissenters? And they have one box into which all the 'No-votes' are dropped and another for the 'Yes-votes'? Of course you know what will happen to the box which contains the 'No' ballots. And you call that 'democratic elections'? You would reach for your gun when the word 'peace' or the concept 'pacification' is employed? I do just that when concepts like 'popular democracies' are used."

"Rights, I am talking of rights!"

"Rights, yes. Rights."

"Rights, not favours."

"Yes, yes, rights not favours. I understand."

"It is like when somebody wants a birth-certificate and is told that he either has to know some official there or pay a bribe to get it issued – then I go mad. Why can't we simply insist on our rights, and the rest be damned? If we are not allowed our rights, we have to go to prison for them. I am fed up with all these apologetics. Workers with no right to go on strike, despite the inflationary prices shooting upwards of 150 per cent. We Africans did not struggle against the white colonialists only to be colonized yet again by black nincompoops. Rights! Let's talk of rights – my rights, your rights and *their* rights."

Then they spoke of the fact that the first threats to the democratic institutions came from the colonial governments which imposed unconstitutional and untraditional dictatorships on the African or the non-European peoples. With informed tolerance and scientific detachment, they talked of the two forms of government the colonial powers employed: one for their own people, the other for the sub-human African.

"And when Africa attained its political independence, black apes took over and aped the monkeys who trained them," said Deeriye.

Zeinab yawned.

"I'm going to stay up," he said. "You are tired and since you must go to Sheherezade and Cantar, perhaps you should go now. I am all right, really I am."

But she wouldn't go until she made sure that he took all the tablets she had herself prescribed: she supervised him, like a child through his toilet rites, she watched him wince as he swallowed the pills, his face making long and bitter grins.

"You would be a dictator, you act like one, you are a prisoner of your obstinacy, insisting on being right all the time. Which is what dictators do," he said teasingly as she took the cup out of which he had drunk the water. "*We become in the end that we hate most.* That is how best we express our hate."

"You wouldn't be a dictator if you were the head of a government?"

she asked him. She continued after a while: "Are you telling me, Father, that you would not imprison traitors like Haji Omer, the betrayers of the national cause, those who've sold their soul to the enemy?"

"There is a difference between myself and a potential dictator."

"What?"

He swallowed his bitter saliva and with it the last tablet.

"Every African head of state carves a mask of national ideology, one which fits only the head that has carved it. Can you see Zaire's Mobuto's mask on Numeiri? Or Arap Moi's mask being worn by Gadafi? The likes and the dislikes, the humour and personality of the leader: these are the essential deciding factors of the size and shape of the mask."

"And you wouldn't be a dictator if you were head of state of an African nation, are you telling me that?" she asked.

"I am not a black ape imitating the monkeys who trained me. For no man trained me, I did not learn what I know from a white man whose ways I hold sacred."

She went and kissed him on the head. And she made him promise one thing: that he would refuse to take part in any negotiation between the elders of the tribes and the General. "These negotiations are designed to discredit the principles we stand for." And she left, having kissed him again on the scaly spot of the forehead.

That was last night. Now, it was nearly one o'clock, and Mursal shouted from downstairs that Natasha would take him to Baar Novecento once they had eaten lunch. Was that all right by him?

"Yes, yes," he said.

• • • • • • • • • • •

They drove in silence. Time was an echo of a purring, revving engine, a change of gear, the ticking of two wrist-watches, the speedometer, the car-clock; time was the dust which trailed behind them; time was the sun which lay ensconced behind the clouds; time was the travel, the journey each undertook so that *another* arrived, because each would eventually reach his or her destination having become *another*. Time: a city within a city, with some roads paved, some walked, some so far unused; with alley-cats, street-Arabs, urchins, chanting beggars, stray dogs suffering from rabies, open sewers, uncollected donkey corpses, unclaimed children left at strangers' doorsteps, children wrapped in towels which smelled of urine and vomit. Time was also the abyss with the open door; it was human for it had hands: one for seconds to give the minute and another for minutes to tell the hour, fingers praying deferentially to the God who created the hands that are in motion, like a clock's, losing, gaining time; eyes of quartz in the darkness of a room; ears of ticking time, adding a second only to take the same from the life of those who have experienced it, who have lived through it. Time was also the rest of sleep, a cat-nap, the night-cap, the uncounted heads of cattle chewing the cud in peace and quiet, the prayerless screams, the absent father-husband and the loved wife. Time was the photograph whose future print would read like an illuminated manuscript: rather like a negative with which depressions and dark spots, something reminiscent of an X-rayed lung while coughing, while wheezing: one person's conditioned asthma. Time was history: and history consisted of these illuminated prints – not truths; history was the Sayyid's struggling movements; and Osman Mohamoud's refusal to accept de Vecchi's "pacification" policies aimed at bringing under Italian control the eastern portion of the country which was the last to fall; and the unpacifiable Omar Samater, a *Naayib* who, almost single-handedly, recaptured the fort of Ceel-Buur that had been lost to de Vecchi's men; history composed of betrayals and Omar Samater's finally escaping to Shilaabo now as always in the Ogaden, now but not always under Ethiopian administration; history was as much about the movements of tribal peoples with no technological know-how as it was about the conquest of territories, of "protections," of "pacificatory" methods and of created famines whether in Vietnam or in the Ogaden. Time was history: and history was a shy little thing hiding in the folds of its robe a giant: i.e. a little boy of eight years of age, a little boy named Waris, burdened with a message heavier than his years and who in innocent trust opened his heart and therefore his secret and Deeriye's to a traitor whom he, the little boy, referred to as "Uncle Haji Omer;" and history was a congeries of half-truths: of the so-called peace-loving nations who are *progressive;* and the so-called free nations who are *democratic;* and of hemispheric Balkanization, with Africa as much re-divided as in the Berlin days of the African Scramble. History was a string of intolerable nonsense: of dominations that were called civilizing missions; of "pacifying" expeditionary forces which looted and raped and robbed while they misdescribed these "mass killings" as the ennoblement of the savage: turned countries into colonies, the colonies into (peaceful) commercial centres; pacify a 30,000 population of indigenous extraction so that the 300 Italians could live as masters (in 1930, there were 300 Italians in Mogadiscio of whom 40 were women, 230 men and 30 children; of these 84 worked for private businesses; 70 in the army; and 78 in the civil service; the Somalis of Mogadiscio: 30,000). History (in the 1920s, the years of fascist rule) gave to Mogadiscio *"tre buoni ristoranti e tre alberghi cosí cosí; tre circoli con ampie sale da ballo,"* two cafes, one cinema hall and six hundred motor-cars. Since statistics are what governments love and live for, what has the present régime given to Mogadiscio? Deeriye asked himself. "So many roads, so many buildings, so many revolutionary showpieces and so many modern architectural wonders. . . .

Natasha was saying, a smile spreading generously across her face: *"Mursal mi ha detto che verrá lui a prenderti. Va bene?"*

He nodded to say that he had understood that Mursal would collect him from Baar Novecento later in the afternoon, but added that if he was not at Baar Novecento he would probably be at Rooble's. *"Va bene?"* And she nodded in the affirmative and was silent and so was he.

He found himself thinking now that Mogadiscio, like every city anywhere, is an expression of its residents' notion of good living, an answer to the question every dweller asks himself or herself. Its nights, its days, its politics, its life: these indicate of what clay the residents are made, what grain, how serious and how wealthy. He remembered his granddaughter Sheherezade once asked him what he would have liked to be if he had the chance to train as anything and he answered, "either an urbanist or a photographer." And there was also that famous and often-quoted panel of urbanists and the city's Major of a Mayor. The Mayor, a young major just appointed, talked of Mogadiscio metaphorically as a body when he was asked why the suburban villages of the city could not be reached by public transport or why the city services and amenities were not extended to Medina and Wadajir. To which during question-time Deeriye added, making an observation from the floor, that only children or the very old could not reach all parts of their bodies: the old generally obtain a *modus vivendi* with their own situation, and the very young never tire. What was the Mayor's answer to this? Embarrassed silence.

The Raqay Shopping Centre. The one-way circuit which one could easily drive into but had enormous difficulty coming out of. Natasha avoided colliding with a mad motorist hooting playfully and showily: Deeriye told her that it was one of those young upstarts, and to make her appreciate a connection pointed out that the young man at the wheel of the expensive vehicle was Mukhtaar's cousin, as a matter of fact: a Mercedes, brand new, and with him three young ladies and the young man, barely twenty, was carelessly driving against the oncoming traffic, deliberately breaking the law. She stopped. To their left, Ufficio Governo; to their right, the shops and a stream of humanity meandering out and into tributaries of afternoon shoppers; behind all this: constructions, some half mud, some half stone; a thatch-hut with mud coating and metal roofing; the Xamari's stone-houses, old as the nine hundred years they had lived through, depicting all the interpretations of cultural influences which Mogadiscio received: from the Turks, the Persians, the Middle East, Europe and Africa too.

Now she unfastened her seat-belt. Would he mind getting down there, for it was impossible to drive through the mess and crowd? No, of course, he did not. She then bowed, saying nothing. He too bowed, saying "Mahadsanid & grazie." Then she caught the glitter of his eye and held it there in her smiling pupil. And she drove off.

• • • • • • • • • • •

In the wake of his arrival at Baar Novecento: movements, small but precise. Chairs were surrendered to him; faces brightened – some with the smile of honesty, others with that of hypocrisy; the men who had been there before him began to anew tease one another as though Deeriye's coming brought them a fresh sense of relaxation. He remained standing for a few minutes, giving the impression that he was undecided as to which chair he would accept and next to whom he would sit. He stood there, clearly a giant among midgets, tall among men who, although they might never have said it openly, talked about him with envy. One of them, now standing behind one chair removed, namely Gheedi, had once said that Deeriye "was draped with arrogance and we, mortals that we are, have a glimpse of him through the openings in his saintly clothing." For many of his acquaintances and some who would say they were his friends (although he might not have accepted them as such) Deeriye, in a way, served to make meaningful their own understanding of public and private myths. Of course, there were those who thought he was mad, because he did not receive with gratitude all the gifts providence had bestowed upon him. What did Deeriye think about this category of men?

"They are the ones who would have called the Sayyid mad," he would say. "They are the kind of men who would describe as mad any person who tries to effect an improvement in the lives of his or her fellows; any revolutionary and visionary would have frightened them to death. No, they are not the kind of men I want to associate myself with. They are the *Bringers-about-of peace,* as the General's euphemism has it, but all they stand for are the principles of others – *and only if they are paid something, if they are made stipended tribal chieftains,* traitors that they are. To these lazy men – because they never tax their brains – all is very simple: I can *afford* to hold on to my principles and keep them: I am wealthy; my son is well-placed and is married to an American: my daughter is a medical doctor. They give thought not to pressing nationalist questions but to whether or not one can *afford* this or that principle. The acoustics which echo their fears, their suspicions, their allegiances, their hopes and the position they take: materialism; the blood which runs through them: material- and compensation-fees. They deliberately do not wish to have any dealing with ideas and national principles because they believe these are of no immediate concern to them, only whether or not the clan they are spokesman of is getting the share the government has promised (it doesn't matter whether the government is national or colonial, democratic or fascist: nothing matters so long as they are made content); they make do with scrapings and breadcrumbs or, worse, hand-me-down gifts from anyone; beyond that, they are busy litigating with their offspring so that they and their younger wives and their newly born children are taken care of by young men and young women in their early thirties who cannot themselves marry because they have to support these crones, their new spouses and their children. How very inconsiderate of them! How very shameful! He believed they were naive as the reductionist philosophies they upheld: they couldn't understand how Deeriye could approve of his son's marriage to a Jew when he said he was a pious Muslim – to which accusation he responded: "All Jews are not Israelis and even then all Israelis are not Zionists: I oppose racialist-Zionist policies, not Jews. I do not oppose a person because of his or her race or religion; I oppose a person because of his or her principles. How can I love my son's wife when I know she is Jewish? Don't Somalis say 'You love the dog of the person you earnestly love'?" And behind his back, they speculated on how much money the American wife must have brought with her. Afrah, the one who dealt most in gossip, reported that it was Daahir who had said this. And Deeriye: "Let them serve whom they serve: a fascist Italian or a fascist Somali; let them be the peace-makers. Did they know what the name of the bar meant? *Baar Novecento.* Would they know that it was named after the century of the scramble for Africa, the century of partitioning of the peoples of Africa?" Deeriye doubted very much if they did. How could these be his friends? *"Friendship is a very complicated organizational concept of self- and group-definition: and I would define myself out of this lot; any day."*

"Shall we sit down, then?" somebody shouted. When Deeriye looked, he was greeted with a smile much friendlier than the voice had suggested. It was Gheedi, and he was saying, "Let us sit down and have some tea. Deeriye will pay."

Silence. Deeriye's gaze was slow, one might even say deliberate. Six men: grey and stooping with age, all experienced with the art of litigation at clan gatherings, now in the country's major city's *localissimo* terraced tea-house; and the twelve eyes waiting, patient and calculating. To his left, Daahir; to his right, Gheedi; the others spread themselves so that they would be able to hear what was being said from where they were. Gheedi:

"How is your head?"

"It hurts very little, thank you."

"That was a daredevil action, that boy's," commented Gheedi and a chorus of voices repeated the same thing in different forms. "A daredevil action."

"He is only a small boy," said Deeriye, his voice plain.

"And Cigaal?" It was Gheedi again.

"What about him?"

"How are things between Cigaal and yourself?"

Deeriye told himself he should be careful. He was likely to be misquoted and that wouldn't do anybody any good. Gheedi wouldn't misquote him deliberately; he was above that. But Daahir might. He had the look of someone waiting for something to drop from Deeriye's mouth, something worth reporting to Mukhtaar's father or Cigaal for that matter since Daahir's son, to be made first secretary at an embassy somewhere in Europe, married a girl from that family.

"All is well between Cigaal and myself," Deeriye said. "He came and paid me a generous visit and I am content. Besides, he and I have no reason to go to war over what a little boy like Yassin had done while playing."

A brief silence. Then Daahir asked, "But we've been made to understand that Cigaal called on you, carrying with him a recompense gift which you refused to accept."

"I did nothing of the kind."

"Mursal showed him out. That's what we were told. Gheedi, don't you remember somebody telling us that Mursal had shown Cigaal out? It was Afrah, wasn't it, the person who told us? Where is Afrah?" They looked around but Afrah, a friend of theirs, was not there.

"I haven't been informed of that," Deeriye lied.

Gheedi. Daahir. And now Soofe, further to the left, wanted to say something, but changed his mind: three, four, five voices rose above the clamour in the street, voices urgent with heartfelt messages, urgent like mediocre pupils jumping the gun because they think they know the answer to *this* question the teacher is asking. As a result, there occurred a collision of noises, none of which made any sense even to those who uttered them. A pause followed. And the waiter came on cue, as though to save the situation. He arrived, holding forth a smile which was not at first received with welcome: he indicated that he had brought them tea. There was, however, a hesitant movement on the part of Daahir and Soofe for they were not certain, since they did not have the money, if Deeriye would stand them afternoon tea after the nasty things each had intended to say about the incident involving Mursal's showing out Cigaal. Deeriye showed his willingness by communicating furtively with the waiter to place the cups of tea on the rickety table between them.

"Welcome," said the waiter, a man in his late forties who was from the River People. "Welcome back among the walking corpses who are heavier than their unpaid bills. And thanks for coming since we are now sure whom I will claim the money from."

For a few minutes, there ensued an argument between the waiter and two of the men, Daahir and Haji Jama. The waiter insisted they hadn't paid him for their tea yesterday and the day before and the day before that and that he would present his bill to Deeriye. Daahir and Haji Jama denied this meekly. Then Deeriye said he would settle it. The waiter, bestowing his blessings upon Deeriye, touched him on the head, and then kissed the forefingers of the hand which he used. The others looked at one another but made no comment. Before leaving, however, the waiter brought ruin on the house ("no need mentioning wicked names") which had caused physical inconvenience to "the benefactor of our benefactors." And he was gone.

But the tea was not drunk until Allah's name was praised, until a string of His names were said, until a rosary of the Prophet's chanting names were sung. The tea was warm, white, sugary and in glasses; the fresh milk with which it was made enhanced its taste: milk bought from dust-laden women; milk brought in containers pasteurized in smoke-wood so it wouldn't go bad for a day or two despite the tropical heat and despite there not being fridges. And they drank in silence. After a while:

"I've come into town, although I am not feeling well, because I would like to know if you know anything about where Mahad is being held, and what rumours are being circulated by the government or by any other factions – underground or not. Do you know anything? Has anybody heard anything?" He addressed nobody in particular but hoped that each would think he was being asked.

Silence. They sipped their tea – saying nothing. What did he expect? They were suspicious of one another: that he knew. Then why did he think they would share the secret information they had gathered from the crumbs of rumours abundant as bread at a lavish feast? He was sure that none of them would risk a day's incarceration for a principle they did not hold close to their hearts. They would not go to prison: they could not *afford* to. And they were not his friends really – and wouldn't care to trust him. Nor would he trust them. Their principles and his seemed at variance with one another. He viewed friendship as *a very complicated organizational concept of self- and group-definition.* Don't Somalis say: "Tell me who your friends are and I will tell you who you are!"

Now he looked at Gheedi, a man who was definitely informed by the richest imagination. He wasn't saying anything. Nor were any of the others willing to speak. Daahir, Haji Jama and Gheedi went to elaborate lengths to show their enjoyment of the tea; and the minor puppets who were also present but whose names were hardly mentioned by anybody anywhere, even if they were present, were sucking their sweetened tongues in fulfilled surrender.

When they were joined a while later by Afrah, no one rose to greet him, no one as much as acknowledged his arrival. (One would've thought either Gheedi or Haji Jama would ask him to repeat what Cigaal had said to him: that Mursal had shown him out. But neither did.) He pulled up a chair and sat next to Deeriye and, after placing his order with the waiter, opened up: he was a flood, a river with a broken bank; he said a lot of things. A sample:

"Mahad is being held at Laanta Buur and has refused to speak although he has been tortured, although the Security has used its expert torturer (you know who I mean? The one who makes everybody speak). The questions they put to him and which he refused to answer: who are your accomplices? What part have Rooble and other clansmen of yours played in all this? Who are the others? He was given names of possible or probable accomplices chosen from his own clansmen. He said he had no accomplices: he had acted on the spur of the instant. No accomplices; no premeditated plans.

"It is becoming more and more obvious that the Security men believe he was not alone in planning the kamikaze effort. And rumour has already been circulated by government sources that others assisted in obtaining information for Mahad. One person is said to be Mukhtaar."

Yet another sample:

"Not Rooble; not Mursal, his best friend and your son; and not yourself; but Mukhtaar, a cousin of the General himself. That is one reason why no arrests have been made. What do you drink if you choke on water? Difficult to decide, eh? Well, *they've* choked on water and *they* cannot send it down by drinking more water, can they? Mukhtaar is the water the General's own clan has choked on. And do you know what one person has proposed? Shocking, very shocking."

"What? What have they proposed?"

"Blood and death. Mukhtaar's father, Xaaji Ibrahim, *must* take steps to correct this, they say. There is no other way. You think I am talking nonsense? Wait and see. All these sitting here and who've probably refused to speak to you were present when we were told this. It is all over town. Look at them, with their dead-pan expressions, pretending they know nothing, have heard nothing. If I were you, Deeriye, my friend, I would go and look for Rooble: I think they are coming for him, too. I am not afraid to speak up. I am no tribal chieftain; am not stipended; and won't be bribed with a monthly pittance. I have nothing to lose."

"Of course," said Deeriye.

A sad note, indeed. There were sniggers, soft-spoken asides, chuckles here and there: these were meant to discredit him, make Afrah look and sound ridiculous, naive and stupid. True, there were two things which made him bitter: one of his sons had been taken into detention for another son's part in organizing a demonstration in front of the Somali Embassy in Rome; and he himself had been fired and replaced with another tribal chieftain. Deeriye was glad these men sitting here never made part of the life he had invented for himself. They hadn't the sensitivity to understand the subtlety of this statement: that confinement in prison opened to Deeriye a vista of a wider, larger world: detention compelled him to think of the history and contradictions which the neo-colonial person lives in; detention forced him to see himself not only as a spokesman of a clan, but made it obvious to him that he was a member of the world's oppressed; detention painted for him a different picture. He need not have invented these men as he had invented his own history, the date of birth astraddle two important events in the history of Africa, or a future worthy of a visionary: these men existed on their own, they were real as pain: they were the product of a neo-colonial system. You found the likes of them all over Africa, the Middle East and Asia: old men who employed the power of tradition and the trust of their own people in order to support and justify a non-traditional authoritarian head of state; the same men who served the colonial governments were now serving these dictatorships or authoritarian régimes.

Now the question: what was Deeriye to make of the information Afrah gave him? He was incapable of responding to it with the warmth expected from him. *How on earth could a man be asked for either the head of his son or his acceptance of the policies of the "Father of the Nation, the Patriarch of Patriarchs?"* Paraphrasing the ideas of a philosopher whose name eluded him (Mursal had given him the quote: he was sure), he said to himself: *In the figure of the chieftain, the authoritarian state has its representative in every clan or tribe so the elders of the clan become its most important instrument of power.* He reminded himself that tribal chieftaincy was the invention of Egyptian viceroys who were the absentee landlords of Somalia. As an institution, it probably could be dated as an eighteenth-century form of rule, a delegating of power the Egyptians themselves had learnt from the Turkish Empire days. However, the term which denoted the importance of this institution changed with every new colonial government but the office and powers thereof remained unaltered. The original words "Caaqil," Arabic for "a wise person," i.e. an elder who is a spokesperson of the community; from "Caaqil to Jawaabdhaar" in the former British Somaliland; from "Caaqil to Capo Cabiila" in the former Italian Somaliland; and finally the General's *Nabad doon:* Peace-maker. Men (never women) who used to be chosen for their oratory and leadership would be awarded titular political power and a stipend and made responsible to the state authority, be it a governor or a district commissioner to whose representatives they would report. (They are these days chosen for their lack of gut and leadership.) Deeriye doubted very much if they knew the background and history of their profession. They didn't know what Novecento meant; they did not know the history of the institution they served.

"Awoowe Deeriye," he heard but dared not turn for he was frightened by the fragility of the little voice, that of a small boy or girl, which called him "Grandfather Deeriye." If it was Samawade or one of Zeinab's children: disaster. He felt himself being touched and the little voice gnawing at him. He finally turned and found one of Rooble's grandsons. Everything seemed silent and expectant: Gheedi, Soofe, Daahir, Afrah and the nameless ones sat waiting.

"Yes?"

"I've been asked to come and see you here."

"Who has sent you here, my son?"

The little boy's voice grew faint the moment he realized all these eyes were focused on him: for eyes which could *hear* frightened him; eyes which could register the movement of lips; eyes which could betray; sell information they deciphered. A young boy of eight carrying an important message: a history to be relived through: Waris again; Deeriye again; politics again.

"My father."

"Yakuub?"

"Yes."

"I understand."

"He says . . . ," he began and trailed off.

"I will come after the evening prayer."

"He. . . .

"Don't say anything. I understand."

"Yes?"

"Run along now, my son. I will come after I've said the evening prayer. And don't say anything to anybody on your way home. Don't speak to a living soul. Do you hear me?"

"Yes."

"Run along. And God bless."

The boy (perhaps disappointed he wasn't allowed to speak) ran off and disappeared into the dust he had stirred. A minute or so later: movements, chairs emptying, Daahir leaving, having thought of an excuse; Gheedi going too and the others following suit. Afrah and Deeriye were the only two who stayed; but neither had anything to say. The din of street-noises; Tilly lamps coming on in the tin kiosks down the road in the direction of the Afar Iridood. Behind him were seated a couple of men, each talking in turn to a man who was writing letters for them; and behind the scribe, there was the pseudo-sheikh who was involved, rumour had it, in several handshake agreements as lucrative as any businessman anywhere in the world would envy. At Deeriye's behest, the waiter took away the empty cups: after which he was paid a handsome tip. But Deeriye asked him to ask if Afrah would like another something before his evening prayer, a cup of tea, a lemonade or something else. Afrah shook his head: no. The waiter walked away, balancing the tray evenly and gracefully, teasing this or that person.

"Tell me, Afrah," said Deeriye. "Has there been any mention of Mukhtaar's betraying Mahad or the names of the others who are supposed to have helped him in his failed kamikaze attempt? Now that we are alone, tell me."

"No mention of betrayal."

"Are you sure?"

"That is why I said that the General's clan has choked on water and doesn't know what to drink to send it down. Nobody knows who created this rumour: that Mukhtaar has talked. This rumour about Mukhtaar's betraying Mahad is the doing of one of the underground dissident factions. The meaning isn't clear. Unless they mean to create tension within the ruling tribal oligarchy itself."

"Thanks, thanks very much."

The muezzin's voice came on cue this time. Both men got up, each politely asking the other to lead the way to the House of Goodness. In silence, they walked the fifty metres to the Holy House of Allah, turned left and entered in reverent silence.

• • • • • • • • • • •

He walked in the direction of Via Roma, with Mirwaas Mosque to his left and Super Cinema and the Indian-owned shops to the right. He wanted to cross the road and then walk further up three to four flights of a stone staircase, rather a roughly cemented landing; but he stopped to give way to those seemingly in a hurry. He found himself at that dangerous T-junction, out of which poured a number of cars which had made illegal U-turns in order to avoid oncoming traffic from the one-way in the Raqay District of Hamar Weyne. Every time he walked there, he believed he would be run over by a vehicle, bought second-hand, salvaged from ending up in a cemetery of useless junk in the Federal Republic of Germany or elsewhere in Italy; a vehicle for which its owner had not paid the yearly insurance fee; a vehicle which in Europe or Northern America would definitely have been relegated to the graveyard – but in which would sit, here in Mogadiscio, there in Cairo or in New Delhi or Tunis, yes, there would sit behind the wheel a half-wit of an exhibitionist, honking away and terrorizing the pedestrians; a driver who would take any red light by surprise; a vehicle which was not worthy of travel, just as its driver was not worthy of coming into contact with thinking humans.

"I am sorry," he mumbled, for he had collided with somebody as he backed away from the rushing crowds.

"It is me, Xaaji Deeriye," said Afrah grinning. "Are you going to Rooble's place?" he asked.

Deeriye was silent for a second or two: his mind explored the depth of the pause; it occurred to him only then that perhaps Afrah was being used to misinform or deliberately over-inform Deeriye about Mukhtaar, or for that matter Mahad. But he did not trust him; he was not someone whom he could take into his confidence. Therefore Deeriye would not allow Afrah to betray him in the same way as Mukhtaar might have informed on Mahad, in the same way as Haji Omer might have betrayed young Waris and consequently Deeriye and Rooble. A traitor can betray only the one who trusts him!

"I do not actually know where I am going," he said. "I want to get to the other side of the road, to begin with, and then I will decide whether to go to Rooble's or call my son or daughter-in-law to come and take me home. So, my friend, may God be with you," said Deeriye sounding formal, his decision to be left alone final.

"My best wishes and may God be with you," said Afrah, making it very obvious that he was offended as he walked away to join the rushing crowd. Cars moved hull to hull, while out of the mosque still flowed a stream of men, most of whom were wet from their ablutions before their prayers; some holding their shoes, others having had to stop in order to stumble into them as they fell into the human tributaries. Deeriye looked at his watch: just after six twenty-five. He remembered he had prayed less than attentively and had misquoted a verse: to atone for this regrettable slip, he would have to make a special prostration once he got to Rooble's or once he reached home. And where was Afrah? He was no longer there. So, as soon as there was a small opening in the road, Deeriye took it, half running. A narrow escape: *Alxamdulil-*

laah! He walked in the direction of Rooble's, his lips ashiver with the shibboleths of the pious, thanking Allah for the loan of breath, life and soul; praying that Allah, the Prophets and the Saints would stay by him during these most tempting hours. And, thank God, he did not suffer an attack while at the bar.

He was markedly calmer now that he found his own pace; alone, he could relax, let his mind lead on a leash the rest of his body. And before he knew it, he was on to his favourite topic: friendship. "Friends are the landmarks of one's own growth," he said to himself. "They are the landmark of one's moods. There are three major categories of friendship: conventional, carnal and spiritual. The conventional is formed with persons one has been in touch with or known for a long time although there may never be any deep understanding or close relationship between these people and oneself. The carnal: with those one is related to by blood, marriage or through other contractual ties. The spiritual: the kind of friendship which enlists one's interest and devotion to a common spiritual union, which ties one to those to whom one feels closest: between Rooble and myself; between Mahad, Mukhtaar (let's hope) and Mursal; between Elmi-Tiir and myself; and even between Nadiifa and myself – why not!" He turned slightly right, walked by a petrol station, saw a young couple kiss with passion, a young couple whose straying hands pressed the klaxon: this wild activity so frightened Deeriye, he felt his heart miss a beat. Then he heard:

"*Nabad,* Xaaji Deeriye," and this threw him into another fright.

"*Nabad,*" he said to a young man in his early twenties. He did not know the young man but waited for him to speak. "Yes?"

"I am sorry. I hope I have not disturbed you."

"No, no, you've not."

Something told Deeriye that there was no need to worry, that the young man was as innocuous as he looked. So he resumed walking and the young man kept level with him.

He was saying, "You don't know me but I know you . . . and I would like to say this to you. . . . " He trailed off, appearing intimidated by Deeriye's fierce look.

Deeriye stopped and said, "Is there anything I can do for you?"

"Not really. No. Not really."

"If you have something to say, please say it, for I am in a hurry."

Silence. The young man's smile was dry, his mouth stained with the salivating juice of *qaat,* wads of which he was still chewing.

"I just wanted you to know something," he said.

"What? What is it you want me to know?"

"I just wanted you to know that . . . oh, well . . . perhaps no matter."

"Is there anything troubling you?"

"I am the spokesman of a group and when you listen to my voice or look at my face which appears frightened, it is a real shame," said the young man, inarticulate with tension, and he looked over his shoulder at a group of young men having tea and a chat at Baar Rooma. "Very shameful. I've been asked by them to come and say something."

"I don't understand."

"We were sitting there, several friends of mine and I, and you walked past and someone pointed out who you were, so we decided we would send somebody to you, one of us to let you know how much we respect you and what you stand for. That's all."

"Thanks; thanks very much."

"We hold your name in high respect."

"Thank you."

"And we mean it."

"Very kind of you."

"We'll do anything we can for you."

"Thank you."

"There is nothing to worry about. It won't require anything to get rid of somebody like Cigaal or his little rascal of a grandson. We were sorry to hear of your being hurt."

Suddenly, the young man flowered into an orator of a politician: the tree of his imagination branched into numerous directions and it struck root. Deeriye remembered other scenes, other encounters with young men and women who had displayed their admiration: it embarrassed him greatly that there were many who would stay by him, willing to listen to him – quiet in the wings of his shade. But it gave him delight too; gave him delight that he was worth something; although the sense of embarrassment was generally greater when he realized that he had not done a quarter of what he could have done; he was also delighted, bccause he was not afraid of the loneliness of old age, what with these young people who came up to show their support by escorting him, like a presidential plane, out of the territorial space of their villages.

Night had fallen – silent and reverential.

• • • • • • • • • • •

Upon seeing Deeriye enter, because the outside door was open, the woman rose to her feet – rather, her body shot upwards, quick and clothed, like a parasol whose button had been pressed open: then her eyes dropped in becoming modesty: and she smiled. She then covered her head properly, her teeth holding the edge of her *guntiino*-robe in place so that it wrapped itself elegantly and smoothly round her young cheeks. Her smile appeared affected, like that of a person weak of constitution. And yet she was young, certainly younger than thirty, definitely younger than Yakuub's wife who now rushed out to half-bow, smile and greet him. The first woman upon whom he came and whom he had surprised was Rooble's third wife; the second was Yakuub's; although Deeriye could not tell apart the children who began to chatter noisily once the preliminaries of welcoming Deeriye, they thought, were over.

"*Nabad,*" came their chorus.

"*Nabad,*" he said.

He stood there as Yakuub's wife went to get a chair for him, while Rooble's wife entered Mahad's bedroom to rearrange it so he could wait there in complete comfort. He took the chair which Yakuub's wife had placed right under the burning light: and he heard above his head the movement of moths and the *mayooka,* heard the occasional mosquito buzz a poisonous message into his ears.

"We do not know where Rooble is: he went out yesterday saying he would find out what he could about Mahad. That was early yesterday morning. It seems he was going to meet somebody. He left right after arranging to be picked up by Yakuub from Baar Novecento in the afternoon. But we haven't heard from him."

"And Yakuub?" he asked.

Yakuub's wife was silent for a second; Rooble's wife now re-emerged from the room, called to one of the boys, unrolled a shilling from the folds of her *guntiino*-robe and whispered something in the boy's ear.

The boy, perhaps Yakuub's, or maybe Rooble's, ran out: he would buy a bottle of soda from the village general store, which sold ice-cold soda for nearly a third more than normal to customers who didn't have a fridge.

"Yakuub went first just across the road. Apparently Mukhtaar had called him; he returned and then rushed out saying nothing but looking very agitated. I dared not ask him why."

"Mukhtaar shouted to him, you said?"

"We heard a noise and the children later said they saw Mukhtaar and his father wrestle for possession of a club. The children think there was a fist fight. But I don't know for sure."

"Very many inexplicable things are happening," said Deeriye.

"Too many in such a short time," she agreed.

A brief silence. Yakuub's wife, unlike Rooble's third wife whom he had imported from the countryside, was a proper Mogadiscian, had been to school and had trained as an elementary school teacher. When talking to Rooble's wife, Deeriye had a tendency to choose his words with explanatory care; whereas Yakuub's wife, although she showed him as much respect as Rooble's, tended to hold in a healthy tension the conversation they had: sometimes, she improved on the information he had given, leading him into unexplored territories. A person is made of the relationships he or she has with such persons, he thought now, sitting down on the chair provided while she remained standing. Then they talked fleetingly of the *peace* Cigaal had brought; of the *owl* about which he spoke; of the *gift* which was not received; and of the conspiracy plots whose main aim was to *destabilize* things in order to rule; of the *stability* for which régimes paid plenty of money and poured lots of blood into. Yakuub's wife was an enlightened person, at times much more so than Yakuub or Rooble.

"Has anybody come to see him since the *incident?*" asked Deeriye.

She reflected. "Many tribal elders of the clan called," she said. "There was to be a gathering of the clan. I don't know whether or not that took place yesterday."

Their eyes scoured the view in front of them: the courtyard, moonlit and beautiful and clamour-filled with children chasing one another, opened on to the four or five rooms, crescent-shaped and harmonious. Mahad had bought the house and made a gift of it to Rooble and

Yakuub since neither could afford to pay rent and raise a set of healthy children and maintain wives; Mahad who had not himself married but who had his private life, a private life which had room for affairs, conspiracies, a life outside the martyrdom, the sacrifice of which his existence and history were part. Meanwhile, the boy had returned with a soda bottle which he presented to Deeriye. Yakuub's wife asked the young boy if he remembered seeing someone visit his grandfather yesterday morning before he went out. The young boy described three old men who had called on his grandfather. The description fitted three tribal chieftains Deeriye knew.

"Thank you. Thank you."

No one was sure whether the "Thank you" was for the soda bottle or for the information about the visit; or whether it was simply addressed to Yakuub's wife because Deeriye wanted to be left alone.

S I X

Come Home, My Loveliest

There was no sign of Rooble. But his son and grandchildren all came and, with absolute warmth, greeted Deeriye, some referring to him as "Father" or "Grandfather," an indication of full trust and respect. He was given a mat to sit on the floor in Mahad's room. Once he had said his prayers, there came a stream of visitors, young boys and young girls, timid, quiet, a finger in a mouth, a pigtail or a *dhoor*-hairdo; or the boys (most probably Yakuub's), between five and six, who pushed each other, telling each other to behave themselves in Grandfather's presence; one of them overdid the pushing, and when they were out of sight, they were blind with play as they wrestled, pitted themselves against their mother who lost her balance and nearly fell forwards. A smile: that was all anyone could get from Deeriye, no comment whatsoever; and a silence which was punctuated with the furtive drop of his counted beads. Rooble's wife was in the furthest corner, her head and face wrapped in her shawl of modesty. If he were alone, he would have bent and risen and prostrated before his Creator, to atone for the slip he had made while thinking about mundanities and politics; he now remembered he had misread God's message and misquoted it as though he were a careless pupil exploiting his teacher's absence. At last, the room emptied in less time than it took Yakuub to take off his shoes at the entrance, tiptoe to and plant a kiss on the hand Deeriye had intended to be shaken but hadn't the sense to withdraw in time. Deeriye readjusted the pillow which had been tucked under his elbow, wedged into the triangle of a corner where two walls met.

"So, what news have you brought?"

"Not much," Yakuub said, sitting down. He tried several positions, all of which he found uncomfortable. Deeriye commented that sitting on a mat gracefully is an art like eating with one's fingers: you have to know to do it well, otherwise you are awkward and clumsy. By comparison, Deeriye's composure was majestic, his posture was a comfort to the eye. Yakuub finally got up and went and sat on a chair which he pulled closer, placing it on the edge of the mat. And to think he was once a sportsman. Now he was a referee, fat and heavy on the waist and accused often of not running enough to be present when players fouled on each other.

"Where did you go?" said Deeriye.

Yakuub shook his head. It was obvious from the way he looked that he had seen something terrible. Deeriye hoped that it was not anything to do with Rooble.

"I drove Mukhtaar's sister to hospital," Yakuub said.

"To hospital? What's wrong?"

"It is unbelievable."

"What's unbelievable?"

"There was a fight, it seems, in which they were hurt."

"Who fought whom? What happened? What's all this?"

Yakuub was the least articulate of the family; he began his story, paused, began again and told Deeriye that, as far as he could tell, Mukhtaar and his father had been involved in a fist fight; then Mukhtaar's father grabbed a club and threatened to beat his son with it; Mukhtaar, it seemed, simply wanted to be allowed to indulge in the pleasures of the friendship he had made on his own, to indulge in the satiation of the ideology he believed in, "Mahad is my friend, has been my friend all these years and will remain my friend for the rest of my life, whether you like or not." Mukhtaar was saying this when Yakuub, having been called by a young girl, entered and saw the ugly scene and the blood, heard the scream. In the wake of his arrival, everything froze: nobody, apparently had expected a stranger to be allowed in, a stranger who would see, report and judge. Mukhtaar now had the club in his grip; his father lay on the floor, shirt in rags, sarong undone; one of Mukhtaar's sisters was holding her nose which had bled from the blow and the other held her bleeding forehead, unable to say who or what had struck her.

"And so I drove them to hospital," Yakuub concluded.

"And what about Rooble?" Deeriye asked.

"We know very little."

One of the young girls entered, bringing a radio-cassette player which she placed within Deeriye's reach: they knew he liked to hear the news and it was nearly time. The young girl went out. She came back in less than five minutes, this time carrying a flask of tea and two cups. She poured two cups and left. The door remained open on to the courtyard which, in its turn, was open to the starry sky. The night was bright with moonlight and whispery with the soft voices of Yakuub's and Rooble's wives and children who sat outside, waiting, like understudies backstage. Every now and then, Deeriye would hear one of the women tell a child to stay quiet, to do this or that, get this or that from the kitchen or to play outside. A little later, one of the children would be sent in to find out if Deeriye and Yakuub needed anything. Now Deeriye asked Yakuub a number of questions.

Again in the most confusing manner, Yakuub told Deeriye how Rooble and a couple of tribal elders had been deceived by a man who brought them the news that the General wanted them to have a gathering of the clan to meet and discuss the "Mahad affair": they should take a position either associating with or dissociating themselves from his unlawful activities. The man said that a meeting had been called and Rooble was to go with him to the venue. At the meeting, scarcely had the first speaker painted the floor offered to him with the beautiful colours of his elegant rhetoric than there emerged from the closet, as it were, five security officials who, in the frenzy which followed, told the beguiled gathering that they were under arrest for breaking the law which forbade the assembly of more than five citizens in one house unless in the House of God or to celebrate the great names of the General. Twenty-five of Mahad's clansmen, including Rooble, were accused of conspiring with intent to commit sabotage.

"May I ask how you came by this information?" said Deeriye.

"Rumour."

"I see." A long pause. "Do you know where he is being held? Are Rooble and Mahad in the same prison?"

"I don't know precisely but I know from what others told me that Afrah came here and told Rooble that Mahad was being held prisoner at Giardino Police Station."

"Giardino Police Station?" asked Deeriye, slightly irritated at another frustrating digression. "Mahad at Giardino Police Station?"

"That was what Afrah said. Where Father is we have no idea."

"But dangerous political prisoners are never kept there; Giardino is where common criminals are detained, and tortured until they confess: the thieves, the one-night-stand prostitutes. How could you believe that?"

"I don't know. When I went to Giardino myself, the constable I spoke to, somebody I know, said that Rooble had come, asked a few questions and then left. He could not tell me more than that. I know the constable because he plays forward in the Police Football Team and he would have told me the truth."

"What time did Rooble leave the station?"

"Yesterday before lunch."

"That's as much as you've been able to gather?"

"So far, only that. I am afraid I don't know any more."

There you are, Deeriye said to himself. Rooble ever trusting, going where he is told, doing what he is told. Someone whom he trusted dug a trap for him and Rooble fell into it immediately. *Why can he never see the obvious? Why can he never read the signs? Rooble is a threat to himself, a threat posed at making disintegrate the notion of innocence.* How over-simplistic! Why, when one's relation is detained and held in Giardino, it is not the state which feeds the prisoner but those closest to him or her; it is never the tax-payer's money which keeps the body and mind of the thug together but those from whom he or she has hailed. And Deeriye wondered if Rooble had taken a basket of fruit (Mahad was near vegetarian and would be content with an assortment of the tropical fruits one could once have got for almost nothing). But what would Afrah get out of it all? Perhaps he had been promised a review of his status; perhaps he had been promised re-instatement as the stipended tribal chieftain. Deeriye said:

"I saw Afrah at Baar Novecento."

"Did you?"

Deeriye looked at Yakuub, whose inarticulacy put him in mind of Afrah's, although the result of different pressures: Yakuub's because he was too lazy to bother to make himself understood; Afrah's, because he suffered from an inferiority complex and believed no one trusted him: and therefore on occasion spoke and spoke.

"He tried his best to feed me with misinformation."

"Misinformation? What kind of misinformation?"

Deeriye reflected. After a long while, he said: "I think he was the messenger-boy from somewhere high up and was telling me things I could not understand then but think I do now."

"What specifically did he talk about?"

"A lot of things. For instance, that Mahad was alone in this; that Mukhtaar definitely did not play any part in planning the kamikaze effort; that Mursal, although his closest friend, was not on the list of suspects; but Rooble's clansmen were on this drawn-up list."

"Maybe you were not misinformed by Afrah after all."

"If I understood correctly (and this is not the first time somebody talks about Mukhtaar's father's régime of rigid rules and patriarchical authoritarianism) Mukhtaar, Afrah said, will meet with death. How, he did not care to tell me."

"Blood, yes, I saw plenty of that this afternoon."

"And death? Death is waiting at the door and it shall enter."

Yakuub was called out; his wife wanted to know if they were ready to eat and Deeriye declined. Yakuub went out. Alone, Deeriye remembered that it was Elmi-Tiir who described Yakuub's priorities in life and preoccupations as "cheap as a modern disposable one buys to use only to be thrown into another plastic disposal which in turn will be discarded." He sat quietly and unthinkingly, unable to improvise a prayer, unable to get up for his legs seemed filled with water. He said and made the motions of a prayer and immediately began wondering if Mahad's action brought home any message: that tyranny should be fought with counter-tyranny. He wondered if the action's unplanned nature was to dislodge, disorient and send everybody off the track of a (movement's?) calculated logic. Mahad's soul would perhaps live in another: if not a Somali, then perhaps a Zulu struggling against the tyranny of apartheid, a Palestinian fighting for the principles of human justice. Life was made of encounters and departures: the living dead meet the spiritually dead when both dwell in a tyrannical state. Was Deeriye beginning to see the *raison d'être* of Mahad and Mursal's use of violent methods? One thing of which he did not approve was an indiscriminate scattering of deadly fragments and explosives. It was ironic that whereas Yassin's stone hit its target, Mahad's missed. How ironic! Young men and women at the height of their power: Mursal, Mahad, Mukhtaar and Jibriil Somali; Medina and Zeinab and Sagal and Ladan. Mukhtaar: a tree tender as a plant – or rather a mere sprout; and an old man's withered hand had no right to pluck it out just like that. Yakuub had, in the meantime, returned.

A silence. Deeriye said a hasty prayer. He told himself that one reason why he did not see "blood and death" was because neither his visions nor his dreams spoke of any such thing. He closed his eyes.

Someone said, "*Ciao,* old man." Deeriye looked up. It was Mursal. Standing, Mursal hung before him like a portrait which he, alone, could appreciate in silence. No one said anything for a minute or two. Then Deeriye's face spoke the message his lungs wished transmitted. He coughed and coughed and coughed. Then his chest wheezed.

Zeinab was called. Deeriye was told to spend the night at Rooble's.

• • • • • • • • • • •

When he was feeling a bit better, Yakuub brought out two decks of cards and they sat down to play Scala. Zeinab, as Natasha would have done, became a member of the male community by virtue of her background and was never excluded from taking part in any activity because she was a woman. But Yakuub's and Rooble's wives withdrew into the kitchen when strangers were present; on occasion, when the company was young, Yakuub's wife entered into dialogue with one of them. Three men and a woman, the cards were dealt, the conversation was amicable but never vulgar enough to exclude either Deeriye or Zeinab. They teased one another as they scored points, with Deeriye winning more points than any two persons put together, and saying that it was because they did not know how to sit on the mat on the floor. "Just look at them, clumsy and uncomfortable." They played on, however, with their ears half listening, their minds half waiting for news from Rooble or from Mukhtaar – not really knowing what to do, whether to knock on Mukhtaar's door to ask how things were with him, or to leave things as they were until tomorrow morning and hope for the best. They knew for one thing that Rooble would not walk through the door kept open for the purpose that night or probably another night in the future. People had strange ways of disappearing into the prison-bowels of the Somali security system; and those who tried to find the missing at times disappeared into another hole just as black. Rooble must have dropped into a compartment different from the one Mahad had been pushed into: one *dropped* in like the ball in a billiards game; the other was forcefully *pushed* into a compartment with a deeper infernal hole just like the *Alam Bagga* of Haile Selassie fame.

"It's your turn, Father," said Zeinab.

"How many points have I?" he asked.

"Two hundred and ninety, I think," she said.

"One more hand and I will have won," he declared, but did not play instantly.

For something strange had occurred: Mukhtaar had walked in through the open door, strode in, looking wasted, dishevelled – a great mess. Those in the yard had reacted negatively (although unjustifiably) to Mukhtaar's arrival: the children, like frightened chicks, ran for cover; Rooble's wife had risen from her shambles of silence to exclaim fearfully something like, "Oh, but, Mukhtaar, are you still with us and alive?" Mukhtaar seemed a person who claimed no attention, wanted none: nor would he say anything. He stalked, tall, once handsome, eyes mad with the mystery of the unsaid – or so thought Deeriye, who indicated that he wished no one to speak to Mukhtaar, no one to ask him anything; and he also motioned to the two boys who, out of curiosity, stood in the doorway to leave. Yakuub, however, got up, and went to Mukhtaar and, when Mukhtaar's wild eyes did not recognize him, grabbed him and shook him like a fruity branch of a tree in the hope that something would eventually drop. Deeriye, his voice firm, instructed Yakuub to let go. Mukhtaar's face appeared pained now that he was left alone and he displayed a sense of helplessness: he stuck his hands in his trouser pockets and stared at Mursal without showing the least sign of having met him before. On Mursal's part, the anxiety to speak and be spoken to was so great his father beckoned to him to stay put.

Deeriye remembered what they said about Khaliif the madman. Did they not make one understand that Khaliif had gone mad between one sane evening and one mysterious morning? What was it that made these sensible men disintegrate? Why is it that they hear *voices* from their unrecognizable selves, voices which originate from deep down in their victimized existences? A mind so overcrowded with ideas and things, a mind made into the symbol of disorder and indecision by the powers that be, a mind rendered useless because it cannot decipher these symbols, cannot tell apart the good shadows from the bad, cannot distinguish between the virtuous and the wicked. Mukhtaar–mad. Yes! That was a painful reality that one would have to live with. For where there is harmony, the régime brings about disharmony; where there is fraternity, the régime brings about death, disorder and disaster, thought Deeriye. An instant later, Mukhtaar's eyes melted into tiny spots of sightlessness. Saying nothing, he stormed out of the room.

A very long silence. Then there was a stir of confused movement: Yakuub's and Rooble's wives; the boys and one of the girls; Yakuub himself; Zeinab and Mursal both got up, each having dropped their cards on the floor. In other words, it took a long time for the disorder to die down. This occurred when the infiltrators to the inner coterie returned to their courtyard. And Deeriye sucked his teeth noisily and was silent. Yakuub, however, said he would deal the cards and suggested that anyone interested in continuing the game should sit down. Zeinab and Mursal looked at their father, speechless.

"I think he has gone mad," Yakuub said. "Did you see how his eyes looked–as though he were sightless. Khaliif, a few years ago. And Mukhtaar now. The exception proves the rule in Somalia today."

One could have drawn, with a pencil, the details of the silence which followed Yakuub's speech; one could sketch and trace, with precision, the darker fringes where the frontiers of silence ended and spoken thoughts began. There was the enfeebled echo of Zeinab's shuffling the cards purposelessly. Finally, Mursal spoke, what he said sounding like the continuation of an unfinished sentence:

"A father can beat his son to madness in full public view and the son is expected not to raise a hand but to receive the beating in total silence. The son is not allowed to question the wisdom of his parent's statements, must never answer back, never raise his voice or head. A daughter is not, of course, expected to refuse or challenge her material worth: she is worth as much dowry as she can obtain for her parents – not more or less than that. As for public justice being confused with private justice, what would happen if Mukhtaar were to receive a fatal blow on the head and die? Nothing. Nothing would happen to avenge Mukhtaar's life and his father would not be submitted to questioning: after all, it is the prerogative of a parent what to do with the life and property of an offspring, in the same way as it is the prerogative of the husband what to do with the life and property of a wife for whom he has paid the necessary dowry."

"What do you make of all this?" Zeinab said, speaking to no one in particular.

Deeriye said: "This madness is becoming wearisomely common."

"And you, Mursal, what do you think?" she asked.

He mumbled something about "friendship."

"I don't understand, Mursal," she said.

"The man is expressing the outrage of the insane, that's all," Mursal said.

Deeriye signalled to Zeinab to leave her brother alone.

They all surrendered again to their wandering thoughts. Deeriye was thinking: *Friendship is an organizational concept of self-definition; family is an organizational concept of being defined by blood. One is (mentally?) more like one's friends than one's family. You define your activities by the associations and relationships you make of your own accord, whereas you never choose your family. And yet Mursal dare not just walk into Mukhtaar's house, grab him by the wrist and bring him out unstopped, unhindered. Blood is heavier. This clan-based society would not care about Mukhtaar and Mursal's friendship. Mursal could not save his friend from getting into trouble with the law, with tradition and with the clan by challenging the authority of Sheikh Ibrahim.* In a way Deeriye, for his own conscience, was happy Mukhtaar was not a traitor – as rumourmongers had alleged.

Was this not the basis of his fight with his father? A most sensible man, Mukhtaar. Man: wedged between a breath and the dust which finally settles and dissipates; between a drop of (white?) sperm and the clots of (red?) blood which forms between the lung-opening (dark?) cry of life and the last (grey?) groan. The madman is an intensely lonely person; friendless in so far as we define this concept, the madman seeks no one but his own company. Which meant that Mukhtaar had crossed the frontier Khaliif had crossed before him, a frontier Deeriye hadn't as yet gone beyond, or the Sayyid or Wiil-Waal, for that matter.

• • • • • • • • • • •

"Come, Uncle, come to the window," Yakuub was saying.

"What is there?" he asked, seeing that Zeinab and Mursal had joined Yakuub who was still waving to him, and he added: "These unneighbourly neighbours frighten me to death."

"Come."

"What is there to see at this time of night? Madmen and Khaliifs and rootless night-wanderers. What is there? Tell me!" he said.

"Come and see," said Zeinab.

He could not remain impervious to their comments. So he too went and watched the toing and froing of men and women, some standing in corners whispering to one another, some in civilian clothes and yet others in military uniforms: they either entered or came out of Sheikh Ibrahim's. Yakuub, Zeinab and Mursal took turns in naming those who came into view: almost all them of the same clan, the General's, every one of them – including Ahmed-Wellie and the pedimanous pseudo-sheikh. Then an ambulance arrived with no singing siren, silent and creeping like death. No one came out of the ambulance. The engine was switched off, however; the light too. The gate to Sheikh Ibrahim's was flung open and Deeriye and the others could see a woman being tied with a rope, her mouth gagged, a woman being held back. Mukhtaar's younger sister. And what was she doing? Struggling to free herself, as far as the onlookers could tell. And there was another woman (Yakuub explained that she was Mukhtaar's step-mother) trying to do the same. Things were in an agitated state. There was, as a matter of fact, something exhibitionist about the sinister movements. Then the gate closed, and they could see nothing more.

"We're witnessing a world gone mad," said Zeinab.

"What do you think is happening?" said Yakuub to Deeriye.

"My forte has never been the language of the mad. I don't know what all this is about, don't know whether I am seeing visions or dreaming.

Will someone kindly tell me what all this is about when the sane are separated from the mad?"

"I will tell you what I think," said Mursal. "Somebody has been hurt; and hurt badly too."

"How can you tell that?"

"The ambulance; the women being gagged; the arrival of Ahmed-Wellie himself, although now Minister of Information, a medical doctor. Maybe one of them is dead; maybe they've had it out in the end. Something Mukhtaar knew would happen one day, sooner or later."

With self-abandon characteristic of his family, something the Deeriyes lacked, Yakuub said, "I'll go and find out. Somebody, I am sure, will tell me something." And he went out. The door once opened told Deeriye that Yakuub's and Rooble's wives and children had gone into their rooms but were not asleep.

Deeriye wished he could say that what he was seeing belonged in the world of a symbolic dream and was not real; he wished he could analyse these events quietly and understand them. Now he remembered the absurd encounter Mursal and he had with Cigaal, whose interpretation of Yassin's behaviour was more absurd than anyone could have expected. One explanation which came to him presently was the attempt by Mukhtaar (Yassin?) and Khaliif to attain the autonomy their families, their society, their jobs and contacts had denied them; the same autonomy he himself had sought thirty-odd years before: a going-out-of-hand, as it were, a losing-control of the clan-ideology or the narrow-minded "family first" ideology. Ideology? Yes. This was a commodity he had never denied his own children; which was why he never really wanted to be told what plots Mursal had been involved in. Now he heard Zeinab ask a question, not addressed to him in particular but one which she hoped he would answer. He pretended he had not heard her. He watched from behind the window Yakuub go from one man to another, putting to them queries which evidently made the men uneasy, for they walked away, shaking their heads. One of them made "I know nothing" motions with his hands, and another made similar gestures with his shoulders. Finally, it seemed Yakuub met somebody whom he knew: their communication appeared to proceed in an amicable manner. Then Deeriye turned to Mursal and Zeinab and the two were arguing heatedly about what Mursal's position should be, about mutual trust; about whether or not Mursal should tell them (Deeriye and Zeinab) how involved he had been in these mad activities (that is Mahad's and Mukhtaar's) and how he had contributed towards the failed attempt on the General's life.

"Please calm down," said Deeriye.

Mursal and Zeinab calmed down.

"He doesn't trust me," said Zeinab. "Mursal doesn't trust you either; he thinks it is none of my business and none of yours, and says he doesn't wish to say anything lest he betrays or is betrayed."

"I said no such thing!" shouted Mursal.

A pause. They kicked into each other's court the blame for this or that: they behaved as though they were children fighting over the ownership of a toy or something else. Strangely, however, it gave Deeriye pleasure, at least for an instant, to see them fight like children: for he could then say that he was there when they fought as children, that he was not absent or in prison; and he could utter the parental words of wisdom which would make them stop quarrelling, make them behave themselves in the presence of adults. But a parent takes sides, he thought to himself. And he did not want to do that.

"And why should he trust anybody?" he asked, in the end.

"I am not speaking about others, Father. I am talking of you and me. Why should he not trust us? Why should he not tell us if he has something on his mind, something that is bothering him? Probably we can help. Who knows!"

When Zeinab's torrent of words dried up, Deeriye continued, doing precisely what he hadn't intended to: taking sides.

"A political secret is a burdensome thing and, come to think of it, I wouldn't wish to be burdened with Mursal, Mahad or Mukhtaar's secrets, neither would you if you knew how heavy political secrets are. You constantly wonder when something dreadful might happen to the one whose conspiracies you are party to. I feel it is a sign of maturity on the part of Mahad, Mukhtaar and Mursal and Jibriil that they can work in total ignorance of the motives and actions of one another although, I hope, they are working for a common purpose; I'm sorry I tried to insist on his telling me something. I'm glad he decided not to. So please let's ask no questions."

"What if something happens to him?"

Mursal's face put on the lustre of a triumphant grin and he said sarcastically: "What do you think will happen to me?"

"You may get hurt in this."

"Hurt? How do you mean, hurt?"

"Killed. You just tell us, me and Deeriye, whether you are party to these attempts and let us talk it over. Maybe we will join you, you never know. And what about Natasha, this poor foreign wife whom you'll leave behind as a widow, what will become of her? Will she be able to live in Somalia once you're dead or in prison?"

Natasha's name lay heavily on their consciences for a long while; then:

"I am no child, Zeinab. I know my responsibilities."

"And neither am I. My husband died serving a nationalist cause. Not a tear dropped."

"What do you think I'm doing? Going for a promenade on a sunny afternoon?" Mursal challenged her.

Time to blow the whistle again; but gentle; metaphysical; something which would not indicate which side he was on; something wise. *Quick, think,* Deeriye told himself. He said:

"Tombs are dug before the dead are buried in them. There are precautions which the living must take. Does the digger know who will use the tombs he digs? Which reminds me: isn't the worst curse on the head of any Somali the malediction: *May your tomb never dig!* I am certain Mursal's reticence on this topic is justified; I'm also certain Zeinab's worries are justified. So please."

After a while, "Look," said Zeinab.

The ambulance's doors opened. A stretcher; two men in white uniforms. The gate opened. Toing and froing; and Yakuub, going from person to person, like a beggar in a busy street, insistent, unashamedly asking everybody for a ten-cent coin or anything for that matter; and a fresh group of men arrived. And Deeriye's thoughts wandered in the deserted streets of the familiar world and he was saying to himself, "He came – Mukhtaar, I mean; he could have said something if he wished to be saved; he could have dropped a hint. Friendship is a concept of group definition – but it is also one of self-denial, taking upon oneself the responsibility for the others, one of self-sacrifice. Did he know

Mursal would be there? To be autonomous (and blameless) within the self-defined group: that's the essence of a healthy friendship. And I respect that. Maybe he would have spoken if he hadn't seen Mursal? Or perhaps I don't understand a thing."

The silence which descended upon the place was frightening when Yakuub entered. What news did he bring? He wouldn't speak for a long time. He looked for cigarettes; when he found them, he looked for matches; then he lit himself one.

"Things have got out of hand. I do not know how to describe it. But it seems Mukhtaar and Sheikh Ibrahim, his father, were both wounded in the fight. Sheikh Ibrahim has survived; but Mukhtaar no."

"He is dead?" asked Zeinab.

"God bless his soul," said Yakuub.

"Amen," was all Deeriye could manage to say.

• • • • • • • • • • •

Hedged in with soft whispers and the weak, reassuring light from the lamp, Deeriye woke. He saw Mursal and Zeinab; the setting had changed (they were in Mursal's house) and Yakuub was not there. Was he dreaming? Had he seen all this in a dream? Had his nap turned into a long sleep in which he had dreamt about Mukhtaar's death? What was real? And what time was it? Was it dusk? Or dawn? What day was it? What date? He was tormented by the suspicion that Satan had played a trick on him; he had decided long ago that his was a life dominated by landmarks of *absences:* children who grew up without him; photographs taken with him missing; and now that he was here, it seemed, Mursal had decreed him *absent* by not consulting him. And Zeinab was saying, no longer whispering but speaking normally, her voice hard:

"Have you all gone mad? What is all this?"

Deeriye's fingers, in the unchallenged quietness, worked plaits out of loose thread on the hem of a robe with which someone had covered him after helping him into the bed. He sat up: pillow in position, head up, eyes wide open and grinning.

"Mad? No, we are not mad," said Mursal.

"If you are not mad, I don't know anyone who is."

Mursal looked at Deeriye, but Deeriye looked away, not ready to get involved: first, he would find the "setting" and only then would he say anything. Mursal:

"Each of us, woman or man, adult or child, is grabbing what he or she can; and doing it his or her way. The road is lonely, the journey tedious and long, the ideology flimsy and badly defined. But we're not mad. We may be said to be badly organized. But not mad."

"Showing no care: Natasha. Samawade. Your father. Us. Do you care?"

"Each of us is doing it the lonely way, all the way, towards a healthy autonomy, Zeinab; one of self-definition or self-destruction; and away from familial (tribal) dependence. Are we mad? We're exacting the precise price and vengeance. But we're not mad. *Lex talionis! Justice.*"

"Do you know what this sounds like? This seems to be a very laborious way of justifying the madness in which we dwell, the kind of madness we've witnessed in this country and many countries in Africa, Asia and Latin America. And you know how I define it? Mass madness."

"That's a beautiful phrase, I grant you."

"Which is what dictatorships are, or create. Mass madness. Mass euphoria."

Deeriye felt his chest prepare to explode: he held his breath and waited, anxious, his face pained. He was becoming more or less certain that he hadn't dreamt the death of Mukhtaar, and that somehow he had a few hours whose "absence" would perhaps dominate this eventful night. But he dared not ask anyone to account for the "hole" in the sieve of his memory. What had happened? Had he suffered a severe attack?

"How are you feeling now?" asked Zeinab.

Deeriye was now certain that he must have suffered an asthmatic attack. Otherwise, why the question – and why was he in Mursal's not in Rooble's house? Or had he dreamt all this? The saddest thing was that the voice and vision which kept him company and came to his rescue every time he was unsure of things were not there; nor was Nadiifa. Should he tell his daughter that? Finally, he just nodded: meaning that he was well; and she seemed content with that.

He pulled the radio towards himself. The volume low, he switched it on, wondering if he would be able to find a station awake at this time of night (he had already consulted the clock and knew what the time was), a station which would provide him with a service of the Holy Message whose company, he believed, might invite back to him the voices and visions. He stole a furtive glance in Mursal and Zeinab's direction and saw they were both silent and waiting. He tuned it and the undecided needle of the radio came upon a station, speaking Arabic and preaching the message of peace, talking about the peace-loving nations of this bloc and ill-describing the war-mongers of the other bloc. This made his mind travel back to 1934; and to the Italian colonial officer who had brought him "peace" and, in the end, created "famine": did peace from a superpower always mean that they would sweep clean your national resources and make you live on the dry sticks of famine and total economic and political dependence? The news-reader gave Deeriye the impression of being overtly self-conscious, as though telling his listeners they should know that someone else had tampered with the news content; as though he were chuckling to himself. What station was this – Radio Moscow or Voice of America? Or was it the radio station of the Vatican? Or Libya's? *Let anyone who wishes to take pleasure in this self-flagellation do what they please,* he said to himself. *Masocho-sadists, self-conscious arrogance, and peace offered on poisonous platters: we say, no.* And he switched off the radio. He turned to Mursal and Zeinab and said,

"What are the two of you talking about?"

"We are talking about mass madness," said Zeinab.

"She has been a nuisance. Insistent. Social blackmail. Reminding me of my duties as a brother, a father and a husband to Natasha. And a son to you. And then talks of mass madness."

"How you distort things, Mursal," retorted Zeinab.

"And she blames me for Mukhtaar's death and what she calls Mahad's madness."

So Mukhtaar *was* dead. It had not been a vision or a dream. How sad! No one said anything for a long time. Then he said, seeing that both were curious as to what he was thinking: "I'm thinking of *absences!* Isn't that strange? Not of death. But of absences."

"What absences, Father?" asked Zeinab.

"My life is landmarked by *absences* I cannot account for: naps; daydreams; and just before the seizures, there are the few seconds during which I cross into a world whose logic is unknown to any living soul. How else can I describe the hole in my memory tonight?"

"But we can tell you what happened between the instant we heard about Mukhtaar's tragic death and now," offered Zeinab. "We can fill some of these absences for you. No?"

His reason choked on the unwise words uttered by his daughter, and he coughed; like the cough which is every now and again produced by the faulty tuning of a wireless set.

"Maybe he doesn't want you to fill these *absences* for him," Mursal said.

"I am sorry," said Zeinab.

"To go back to what we were talking about," began Mursal.

"Yes, let's," said Deeriye, as though participating in a conspiracy.

Zeinab felt excluded. She went to the window and reported that she had seen someone who looked like Khaliif materialize out of the metallic greyness of dawn. The news was given time to register.

"What's he doing?" asked Deeriye.

"Gesticulating."

"Is he speaking?"

"I can't hear him," said Zeinab.

Deeriye took a solid hold of his rosary and counted his beads. Whereupon, Zeinab reported that Khaliif was saying something. She could hear the word "Peace" occur several times in his speech. What else? He was saying that "a moth never asks itself what amorous pleasure it receives from its mad dance round the light of the lamp, does it?" Deeriye was readying himself to get up, to see and hear Khaliif's prophecies, when he was told that Khaliif had gone away.

"Yes, Mursal. Please. Continue," he said.

Mursal showed no displeasure at having been interrupted: "The mad do it the lonely way, I was saying, and it seems there is enough evidence; just look at Khaliif, he provides it. But then so do the very old and the very small: they keep sane by constantly *naming* the objects and things they come into contact with lest they lose touch with the reality they know. The young are mad or sane as their deeds or thoughts. But when people like Mahad or Mukhtaar wish to have little or nothing to do with the family or the clan, when they try to define themselves *outside* the boundaries which the clan or family had delineated for them, when these men or women define themselves as individuals with likes and dislikes of their own, each a person capable of changing single-handedly the destiny and a history of a nation . . . well?"

"What happens?"

"Zeinab speaks of madness. Or rather mass madness, as my sister refers to it. It is only when the person so called proves to be right, when history is on his or her side, it is only then that one hears a different position taken: that the person in question has been a visionary all along and the masses do not understand him."

"Yes?"

"Which is the history of great men; which is your own history, dear Father, when the massacre occurred and everybody defined your defiance of Italian colonial power as madness; or when the British described the Sayyid as mad. But if and when one succeeds, if Mahad were to achieve what he set out to do: then he would become *a hero.* I am addressing myself to that *brand of madness* as opposed to the one Zeinab refers to; or you for that matter."

"It is not a condition then – I mean the one you're talking about?" said Deeriye. "I don't think it is . . . er . . . madness if success or failure of one's activities in the end determine it. Do you?"

Zeinab re-entered the scene by putting to her father a question which made him hold himself in check, think and then try to answer: "What did you think of Mukhtaar, Father?"

He reflected for a long time, and: "He had something fresh about him. Yes. That's how best I can describe him. He had something fresh about him, that young man. I didn't know him well."

"Fresh?"

"Yes. That was how I felt when I was first introduced to him by Mahad. Clean and fresh, I said. Natural."

"I still don't understand," said Zeinab. "Please explain."

"He had something fresh about him like a tree in full bloom, which could suffer the loss of a branch or two but would stay green and comforting to the eye; a tree which would remain whole too. I remember saying that to Rooble once. 'That young man,' I said, 'does he not put you in mind of a tree fully grown to its natural height and size?' And do you know what Rooble said?"

"No. Tell me."

"'Don't say these things,' he said. 'Otherwise, an evil person will come upon this tree-in-full-bloom and pull it down, roots, branches, leaves and all.' I said, 'Nonsense.' And now? What a tragedy!"

Mursal, his voice troubled and shaky, said: "You make it sound as though Sheikh Ibrahim, Mukhtaar's father, being himself the man who planted and watered the tree in question, remains now the unchallengeable farmer: if a farm is yours, what you do with your trees is primarily your business and no one else's. Is that what you mean?"

"I certainly did not mean to say that. The thought never crossed my mind," said Deeriye.

"How you distort things," said Zeinab to Mursal.

"Please, please."

Mursal was steadfastly gaining more confidence and could maintain ground; he said: "Remember a few days ago, you and I talked about public and private justice; about *lex talionis?* Remember? Well? Now we have a problem. When and if a father kills the very son whom he would either avenge or compromisingly accept compensatory blood for and the state power is behind this father, what is the position of traditional and public justice?"

"You are asking me?" said Deeriye. "Well. According to traditional . . . I'm sorry, private justice, as you call it . . mind you, I do not like the use of these phrases . . . although I don't know what else to call them."

"Just 'private and public justice'."

"According to private justice, if a father kills his own son: first he is not killed; second, all he has to do is to take leave of absence, from his community, disappear for a few weeks or months, until the heat cools. The same, I suspect, would apply if the son were to kill his father."

"Right. Leave of absence, as it were. But he needn't take leave of absence if he were to kill his wife because all he would have to do would be to pay the blood compensation of fifty camels; the same if he killed his daughter for refusing to marry the man from whose hand he received a generous present of a dowry. Right?"

"I suspect that is right, traditionally speaking."

"Naturally, if the state power is in complete agreement with the father who has killed his son because the son is a political dissident, then we don't expect any legal complications to arise, do we?"

"His leave of absence is undeniably justified since Sheikh Ibrahim is in hospital," joined in Zeinab.

"A justifiable reason will be published in the morning's paper, a reason that does away neatly and justifiably and medically with the death of Mukhtaar. This is what I mean when I speak of Mukhtaar as a political dissident," said Mursal.

"Oh!" Deeriye said, apparently shocked.

They heard Zeinab's half drowsy voice: "Madness!"

All fell silent. Deeriye remembered several conversations with Mursal who warned him again and again that a confrontation between Mukhtaar and his father would take place. Now why could son and father not disagree and live together in harmony, knowing that they disagree ideologically? And why could he not have seen all this in his visions? Why was it that lately the visions and dreams ceased to call on him? And why had Nadiifa? Was all this due to the "omitted" word from the scripture when he once said his prayer inattentively?

"The son must accomplish what the father cannot," said Mursal.

Zeinab, quick to correct, said: "That's masculinist."

"I am sorry; I meant the child must do what the parent cannot."

"That's better." There was a brief silence. Then, "And why do you not help one another?"

"Help one another – who?"

"You; Mahad; Mukhtaar and what's the name of the other one?"

"Jibriil," said Zeinab. "Jibriil Mohamed-Somali."

Mursal did not speak for a while. "We are helping one another. In accordance with the covenants of a binding contract, that of a movement's."

"You are hunted down separately, one after the other. First, Mahad; then Mukhtaar. Just tell me," said Zeinab. "Whose is the next move?"

"Don't rise to her challenge, Mursal," said Deeriye. "You've already given way more than I would if I were you."

Zeinab, indifferent, continued. "You must have taken an oath in terms of precedence. First this, then this other person, then the other one and so on and so forth," said Zeinab, sounding too exhausted and half yawning. "Now that Mahad and Mukhtaar have both been eliminated, whose turn is next? Yours or Jibriil's?"

Deeriye intercepted: "Do as I said, Mursal. For your own good and ours too. Do not answer. Please."

A sigh of relief from Mursal and a "Thank you" too.

Then the muezzin called the name of the Creator of Dawn, reminding those who had not awoken that it was time they did so. "Awaken to your responsibilities and duties of the Muslim," shouted the muezzin. And Deeriye, without pointing out to either of his offspring that they too had to wake up to their Islamic responsibilities, asked teasingly if either would like to join him, glad there was a good reason to disband. Neither volunteered. He said a few small prayers, said loudly the standard formula professing the Islamic faith, then prepared to get out of bed to take the ablution and say the morning's prayer with a few more prostrations. He wondered if, having atoned for all his lapses, the visions, the dreams and Nadiifa would call upon him again. He was feeling lonely; and cold, too.

Mursal and Zeinab left him alone, alone with his Allah.

SEVEN

The Possible Outlets

It was seven in the morning. And Samawade was saying to Deeriye: "I saw an owl crash into the window-pane, I saw it fall on to the floor, bloodless and motionless, not issuing a single mournful cry. When I went and touched it, it had already died."

"That's an awful dream," said Deeriye wrapped in the same sheet as his grandson whose hair, straight as his mother's, he ruffled now and then. "An awful dream indeed."

"Yes. And I was frightened."

"You could've come here."

"My parents' bedroom is locked. That's very unusual, because I used to get into bed with them whenever I was frightened. I called to them; I knocked on the door, but it wouldn't open."

"Maybe they're still asleep."

"Or they are gone?"

"Gone? Where? Where do you think they've gone?" asked Deeriye.

"I don't know."

"Mursal was with me until morning. So perhaps he went to sleep."

"And Natasha?"

"Maybe she is with him; asleep too."

"You're sure I'm not disturbing you?"

"I am sure. Are you comfortable?"

"Yes. Hold me for a few more minutes and I will be all right."

He hushed him. He was happy Samawade could come to him and draw out of him the parental warmth neither Mursal nor Zeinab received from him: because he had been *absent*, was not there when they needed him most; he was not present to comfort them when they were frightened in their dreams.

"It crashed into the window as though it were a stone flung by a human hand; and I saw the human hand, too, as it withdrew."

"A man or a woman?"

"I saw a one-armed man in rags; as though he were *pretending* to be a beggar."

"Had you ever seen the thrower before?"

"No."

"It was a grown man? It wasn't Yassin? Or his grandfather Cigaal?"

"No. I had never seen the man before."

"Not Khaliif?"

"No. I would have recognized him."

They were silent for a while. Then suddenly like a chest which unblocked he could breathe, could feel that something had cleared: *the visions* (maybe because he himself had sinned), *the dreams had now come back to him through his grandson who spoke his words, who saw them and who became his voice,* he told himself; and he could see signs which indicated that from now on his visions, dreams would return to him; his Nadiifa too. Dreams which while one was seeing them impressed upon one's mind the truth of their message; like photographs which one "replaced" with the real and took as real: and one spoke about the hour or defined the date and day on which these photographs were taken; *absences* from a family album – whether justified or not; whether one said "Deeriye had been in prison then" or not. The clearing of the chest, however, brought along a voice which was not Nadiifa's (she came only when he was alone or lonely, or when he called her; she came to keep him company or give him warmth). The voice was Khaliif's. Deeriye and Samawade pulled the armchair they were sharing a little closer to the window so they could see and hear better. The crowd had already begun to assemble, a crowd which had become familiar by now although among them there was nobody from Cigaal's family, no Yassin gathering pebble-stones. Cigaal's gate was closed: no movement. What seemed absurd was that Khaliif had his back to that gate and was addressing the cursing motions in the direction of Mursal's (Deeriye's?) house. Samawade slipped out of his grandfather's embrace, listening anxiously, his hand under his chin, his face pressed to the window-pane.

"Cursed are those who *betray,*" Khaliif was saying. "Cursed are those who exchange the safety of what they know for principles they no longer believe in. Curse them! Curse the traitor who betrays when in the tight grip of his vicious impulses! Cursed are those whose villainy trespasses on the territory of the weak, the mindless weak! Curse those who break them! *Lacnatul laahi calayhim!* Forgive those, o God, who succumb because they know no other way; forgive them if they tremble while they stand under the baton of the powerful; forgive them and turn their descent into ascent! Turn the stones of their fresh graves into rings, their rings into voices of Solomonic wisdom, make their trees flower and blossom, show their followers the way, show the betrayed young man the way to Yourself, o God, and when Munkar and Nakiir visit him today, when he is buried, remember he's died serving a cause, Your cause. Help the weak, o God! Show them their weaknesses. Curse them," Khaliif shouted, making it apparent to those present which house he was cursing: Mursal's. "Curse them when you pray communally or in private; curse them with me: the wife, the wife who is not and never has been one of us and will never be; the father too; and the son. Curse them; curse them for they've betrayed a friend. But let's pray for the soul of the old man who has never betrayed. Amen!"

The crowd became smaller; many who might have stayed did not when they saw, from a distance, the burning eyes of Deeriye; but some stayed; more silent than normal – with no one cheering him on. *Were they disappointed in hearing the news from the mouth of the mad prophet that Deeriye's family had betrayed?*

"He is looking in this direction all the time, Grandfather," said Samawade, having turned round. "Why is he doing that? He used to cast his curse in the direction of Yassin's house. No?"

"I do not know."

"Have you done something?"

"Not that I know of."

"Has Mursal?"

"Not that I know of."

"And he has insulted my mother."

"I didn't hear her name mentioned, did you?"

"But it was obvious whom he meant: 'the wife who is not and has never been one of us and will never be'. Who else can that be, tell me? The man is mad."

In the silence which followed, Samawade left the window and began to gather things: he would pick up something, say, a book, feel its weight, then choose another in preference to the one he replaced. Finally, it seemed he made his choice. Deeriye watched him go to the window clutching a book in one hand and a cassette in the other.

"What are you going to do, Samawade?" asked Deeriye.

"Chase the madman. What else?"

"How will you do that, pray?"

"Throw things at him. Just like Yassin used to."

"What things?"

"Things. Anything I can get."

"Do you know what that book you are holding is?"

"I didn't look."

"Why don't you?" Samawade did so. "What is it?" asked Deeriye.

"It is an edited collection of the Prophet's tradition," said Deeriye when Samawade confessed he couldn't read it. "Do you think you should throw that at him?"

"I'm sorry, I didn't look."

"And the cassette? Are you going to throw the cassette at him? Please check the title on the cassette."

Samawade could read this. "It is the Sayyid's 'Death of Corfield'."

"My favourite poem of the Sayyid's. You shouldn't throw things at persons whether they are mad or not," said Deeriye.

"But when they curse you, what do you do?"

"Don't do the thing for which you are being cursed."

"I won't throw anything at him, I promise," he said, returning the things to their appropriate places.

"That's good," said Deeriye.

But when they looked again, Khaliif was talking to Yassin: the two seemed in agreement with each other: and Khaliif was teasing him about something, pinching him on the cheek.

"You will forgive me, won't you, Grandfather?" said Samawade.

"Forgive you?" asked Deeriye absentmindedly. "Forgive you for what?"

"For being naughty and for wanting to throw the Prophet's Tradition and your favourite cassette out of the window at Khaliif. You will forgive me, won't you? I promise I won't do it again."

"Yes, yes, of course."

Samawade had seated himself comfortably on his grandfather's knees, had taken his grandfather's right hand and begun to play with it; he kissed it, then touched Deeriye on the knees and with the same hand tapped his own temple.

"Come, Samawade, rise. What's all this?"

"I'm sorry."

"Up, up. Come on up and on your feet."

Samawade obeyed.

They looked: Khaliif was gone.

"If you've forgiven me . . . or rather to show that you have . . . ," started Samawade but trailed off, looking at the street below where Khaliif had been. "Will you tell me a story, Grandfather?"

"I can't think of any, to be honest."

"Please, Grandfather."

Deeriye thought hard. He decided not to disappoint his grandson; he decided to build, on the framework of a proverb he had just remembered, a story. So:

• • • • • • • • • • •

Wiil-Waal, the King of the Somalis a thousand or so years ago, one day, a month after his wife had died, called a meeting of his state council and told the men present (women were not invited to such meetings) that he wanted each participant to go home and bring to the next day's gathering that part of the slaughtered sheep which makes or unmakes friendship between men, makes them friends or enemies. He would give no further explanation.

That evening, there were consultations among the men. Many did not know what to do. Word went round that it was one of their King's mad whims and they suspected there was a trick behind this. Also the King had not said whether the piece to be brought should have been cooked and how and in what spices; or whether it should be raw. The rich among the populace had little to worry about: having chosen the part, many decided to bring their choices in both cooked and uncooked states. But the poor encountered a difficulty: not only could they not afford an expensive joke of a King's whims, but they did not know whether if they failed they would be fined or, worse still, made to slaughter more.

There was one such worried poor man. This man owned no more than the hut in which he and his only daughter lived and five sheep. But he was a saintly man and a man with a great deal of foresight, for he had believed in the Prophet's tradition that "he who educates a young boy for future and for Islam educates a man-in-the future; and he who educates a girl for future and for Islam educates – symbolically speaking – a larger community": and had cared for his daughter in the way other men pampered their boys; and he educated her by paying from his meagre wealth the little that would make a Koranic teacher pass on to her all the essentials. That evening when he went back to his hamlet, he wouldn't eat nor would he say what ailed him or worried him. After a lot of questioning, he told her what the King had said. She said she did not understand why her father should be worried; he should let her deal with it.

"But, my daughter, this is a grave matter," he said .

"I know, I know," she said. "Eat your soor *and we'll deal with it. The King's whims are cheap once you think about them the way I do. Leave these things to me."*

"And you will slaughter the sheep yourself?"

"Why need we slaughter a sheep? We only have five."

"But that's what the King said."

"I do not think that the King said specifically *to slaughter a sheep – but that every man should bring that part of the meat he thinks will make other men his friends or his foes."*

"I don't understand," said the girl's father, unable to eat the food she placed before him.

"The slaughtering is least important. It is what you take to him," she said.

"And we needn't slaughter a sheep?"

"No, we needn't."

"You're not making a fool out of me, are you?"

"Have I ever, Father?"

"No. You never have. Truth must be owned. You've always been good and wise – just like your mother – may God bless her soul, amen!"

"Eat your supper in peace. I will be back in a moment," she said.

The girl went out. The dwelling was busy and noisy, what with the move-

ment and the excitement the slaughtering of the sheep had created; what with men gathered in clearings talking about what the King would do if they failed him. The girl went to the home of a wealthy man who had half a dozen sheep killed. The meat was being sorted. The girl stood among the women, spotted what she wanted and asked the butcher if his mistress had a need for a part of the animal he had thrown away. When the butcher and the wife of the wealthy man saw what it was, the wife said, "We don't. Take it away." They knew the girl and her father were poor and thought they probably wanted that piece for their meal.

When the young girl entered the hut again, her father, having still not touched his food, said, his voice worried, "What have you brought with you?"

He looked at what she gave him and shouted, shocked beyond belief:

"A gullet! What will I do with a sheep's gullet?"

"Take it to the King" she said.

"Are you mad? You want to make a fool out of me."

"Have I ever, Father?"

He said again, "You never have."

"Take the sheep's gullet and you will see," she said.

The following morning, every man went to the gathering, carrying choice parts of meat. No one showed his chosen part to another. They walked to the tree where the meeting usually took place and the King was already there, waiting. The men walked past him, each depositing or naming the part of the sheep he had chosen: a leg, a liver, a thigh, ribs or other parts of the meat which could be eaten by other men, with no one presenting the King with the portions of a sheep's meat meant for women and not men. Finally, the poor man's turn came. Hesitantly he walked to the King and speaking softly and shamefacedly with his eyes down he named the part which he had taken to the King, the part which, according to him, could make men friends or enemies. The King asked the poor man to repeat loudly what he had said.

After much hesitation the poor man said, "A sheep's gullet, my King."

There was a shocked murmur in the crowd. Some even laughed; others shouted at the poor man, accusing him of insulting the gathering and the King too. Then the King's face opened like a door and his eyes shone like two lamps.

And the King said to the gathering, "I see you have only one wise man among you, my friends. Only one other wise man, since I mustn't forget myself like the man with the ten donkeys to sell at the market who forgot to count the donkey he had been riding every time he rode one. And this," he pointed at the poor man, "is the only wise man among you."

The poor man stared at the King in total amazement. The King saw this and said to the man, "If it wasn't you who thought this out, can you tell me whose idea it was?"

"My daughter," said the poor man, this time with pride.

"Your daughter?" said the King unbelievingly.

"Yes, my daughter."

Then the King stood to his feet and said, "My councillors, my friends, my kinsmen and my clansmen. I did not ask you to bring meat but I asked you to bring that part of the beast which makes men either friends or foes. The symbolic significance is something, I am afraid, that has escaped the grasp of all of you save this man's daughter. And why a sheep's gullet, you may ask? The gullet is the receiver of food, and it is the distribution of food and wealth which makes men either friends or foes."

A great number of heads nodded in total agreement with what the King had said. When the clamour had died down, the King said, "Of you, I ask your daughter's hand in marriage, for she is worthy of a King. I promise you I will love her and care for her."

And the King and the poor man's daughter became husband and wife.

• • • • • • • • • • •

Deeriye refused to let Mursal wash his feet in warm salted water; he refused to be tucked into bed or given a massage. He would have loved to do these things himself, he said, while the two of them talked about the politics of betrayal and friendship. He was grateful for the kindness shown; but no. He told Mursal about Khaliif and what he had said that morning. Mursal looked disturbed by the news.

"What do you know about it?" said Deeriye.

"You mean, have I talked? Father, are you asking me if I have betrayed? The answer, Father, is no, I have not."

"Someone must have."

"Do you say this on the strength of Khaliif's cursory accusations?"

"I believe in the *truth* of what Khaliif says. And again how do you know, for instance, that Mahad was not made to talk, having been broken? That's very possible. It happens all the time. It is also possible that Mukhtaar might have said something unbecoming of him during a heated discussion."

"I do not think so."

"Can you tell me how you know that Mukhtaar did not do that?"

"The paper tells me he did not."

He pulled himself together before he asked: "What does the paper say?"

"Suicide. It says he not only committed suicide but that Sheikh Ibrahim was hurt while trying to prevent it."

"Does it say who was there when this madness took place?"

"The paper doesn't go into details."

"When are they burying him? Does the paper say that at least?"

"This afternoon."

"No post-mortem obviously."

"Obviously."

"A tree that was cut down before it greened into full bloom. Trees are an essential commodity in arid areas like ours. May Allah water Mukhtaar's with His blessing," prayed Deeriye.

Mursal was silent. And the sun, Deeriye could see through the window, had erected a scaffolding of rays whose framework, platform and poles, suggested the hanging-place of a culprit; the clouds, however, had constructed a protective ring around the scaffolding and no one, it seemed, could get to it. Deeriye wondered how long this cloudy enclosure would stay unbroken.

"One by one, a process of elimination if you want to call it that. And they will come to you. I know you haven't said anything to me and I don't want you to. Is there anything you wish taken care of, aside of course from your family, Natasha and Samawade?" Deeriye asked.

Mursal shook his head.

"There is nobody you owe anything, no debts or favours to repay, nothing by way of material compensation that you want looked after?"

Mursal again shook his head.

"Any requests?"

Mursal now nodded. "I want you to go with Zeinab to Hargeisa, Father. I want you out of the way until all this is clear. Do me that favour. It will unburden my conscience a great deal."

Scarcely had Mursal finished pronouncing his request than Deeriye realized that it had been prepared beforehand and was why Mursal had come in the first place. *("Wash his feet in warm water then put it gently to him!")* And to say that Deeriye was shocked by what he heard would be an understatement. So he took time to gather his shattered thoughts, time to piece them together.

"Why is Zeinab going to Hargeisa?" he asked, primarily to gain time in which to handle this very delicate situation.

"She is going on government business."

"How long will she be there in Hargeisa?"

"Long enough for us to know what is happening."

"Days, weeks, months or years?"

"A week, or two weeks maximum."

"And her children? What about her children?"

"They will move in with us when she is gone."

The sun had gone into hiding; the scaffolding had melted, the protective ring too. But the clouds had thickened considerably; thick and dark. Deeriye wondered if it would rain.

"Have you consulted them?" he asked.

"Who?"

"The children. Have you consulted the children?"

"They are too young to be consulted on complicated matters like politics," responded Mursal.

Deeriye looked at his son with suspicion; was he being directly accused of having never consulted Mursal and Zeinab as children, when he got more and more involved in the policies of the country?

"But you, have you consulted Natasha?" said Deeriye.

"No, I haven't as yet. But I will."

"Don't you think you should have?"

"I don't think she really minds. She loves Zeinab's children and will be pleased to have them here. There is no problem about space either. We can move things around a bit."

"Move people around as though they were pieces of furniture? Don't you think you should consult Natasha at least on everything you do, tell her something, give her hints?"

"She wouldn't understand fully."

"And yet she is your wife. And you are the most essential bridge which connects her with this country."

Silence. Deeriye then said:

"You would be dishonest if you didn't tell her *something*. And it would be immensely difficult for me to deal with her if something were to happen to you."

"This morning I told her enough to warn her."

"What's her feeling?"

"Confused."

"Does she know what she wants to do once you're no longer with us – dead or in prison?"

"No. But she understands. Her parents lived through the Nazi holocaust in Nazi Germany because they are Jews. So she understands that aspect of sacrifice. What she is confused about is whether to leave now or later. She believes her being here might burden me."

Deeriye needed to clear his head of the thought which clogged it so he asked: "Just tell me. Are you the third or the fourth?"

Mursal's was a miraculously put-together face, thought Deeriye as he watched him debate with himself how best to tackle an inquisitive father. There was no point withdrawing the question. Mursal's reticence was certainly something he would respect.

"To get back to the point, Father. You will go with Zeinab to Hargeisa and will be away during the stormy week in which anything is likely to happen; she has instructions what to do."

"Instructions?"

"We have agreed, she and I, about certain things."

"May I know what these are? Or am I like Zeinab's children or Natasha, not deserving to be consulted on these matters?"

"You will come back when all is at peace."

Something made his hackles rise: was it the word *peace*? Here was that word again being used by a man who had a gun hidden somewhere and was planning to kill, in order to bring about peace: peace for his and other minds; peace small as the bullet which would make a hole of death in someone's head or chest. "*You will come back when all is at peace.*" It was *peace* that everybody wanted, that most expensive of commodities, which could be got only through the mouth of the gun. Deeriye's voice was enraged:

"You don't have to answer this – in fact you mustn't – but allow me to clear my chest by asking: Are you going to blow yourself up or are you going to make a bullet hole in the head of the Head of State to bring about this peace to which I can return from Hargeisa?"

When Mursal looked he saw his father's face was half in light and half in shadow. Mursal, unwilling to be taken in by his father's anger, grinned. He reminded himself not to get his father excited or agitated lest the cursed attack exploded in his chest. Whereas Deeriye, to while away the silence, contemplated, while he unwound, the arabesques and bars of light and shade the sun's brightness had cast around him. He said to himself *"Alxamdulillaah;"* and to Mursal:

"What do you and Zeinab plan for me after a week in the city of Hargeisa? I doubt very much if this is as far as your plot extends. Enlighten me."

"Actually. . . . "

"Remember: Hargeisa is within the General's régime's reach. The Head of State, if not struck, can telephone the regional authorities there and have me thrown into jail. He can organize purges even in Hargeisa. Which reminds me that the General has taken the wind out of Mahad's ideologically motivated assassination attempt by making it appear tribalistically motivated. He did this by purging his tribesmen; which is why, although suspected, you have been allowed to roam around freely. I am saying all this so you know what I think."

A gentle smile broke on Mursal's lips and spread in all directions, like the beams of a searchlight, until his whole face was lined with the defeated amusement of a good loser. And:

"After Hargeisa, Djebouti for you."

"All details have been dealt with, I take it? Means of transport, passport, date of entry into the Republic of Djebouti, place to stay, the guarantor in Djebouti, eh?"

"Yes."

"Anything else?"

"We have booked you on a plane to Kismayo. Someone is going to take that. Using the name of the person who is using your ticket to Kismayo, we've booked a seat on the flight to Hargeisa but you won't take that either. You will take a military plane to Hargeisa. That they will never suspect. I mean the Security."

"I'm impressed. But who's arranged a military plane for me?"

"A friend."

"Jibriil?" asked Deeriye; but Mursal wouldn't confirm or deny.

Finally: "Well," said Deeriye. "What is there to say?"

"That you will go with Zeinab on that military aircraft."

Now Deeriye's face opened: it rolled up with deliberate slowness like a sail: it indicated where there had been deep furrows or darker wrinkles and stains. Mursal's mind was at sea, thinking out other alternatives to other possible queries. Then Deeriye said, his tone determined:

"No. I will not go. I have other things to do here; I too have responsibilities and duties to perform."

And that was that.

• • • • • • • • • • •

An hour later.

Deeriye's hard stare softened when he saw Samawade come in with a tray on which were two cups of tea. Samawade put the tray down then passed one cup to his grandfather.

"Aren't you drinking the other yourself?" asked Deeriye.

"No."

"Who is the other cup for then?"

"Mursal asked me to bring two cups up."

"Is he coming himself?"

"I don't think so. I've taken him his: he is in the study."

"And where is Natasha?"

"With Aunt Medina in the bedroom. I think, crying."

"Crying?"

"Crying and arranging and re-arranging things."

"Why do you think she is crying?"

"I think Medina has brought her some sad news. They read the paper together when I was there."

"And?"

"Somebody has committed suicide, they said. But I didn't ask."

"Who is the man with Mursal?"

"Promise to tell me a good story and I will go down and bring him. Promise you'll tell me the one about the blind man again?"

"But there is no time for that. Who is he?"

"You promise you'll forgive me for what I did this morning."

"I promise."

"He is a very likeable old man and he comes from Kismayo. I'll go and tell him he's expected. I'll also bring you biscuits and some more sugar." And Samawade was gone.

Deeriye, apprehending the visitor, made extraordinarily generous rhapsodic movements, half-bowing, half-rising (as though he were praying), scrambling to his feet and knees as he tried to get up and exchange a warm handshake and embrace with the visitor. Deeriye's knees appeared trapped in the folds of the tunic with the ornate margins (the one Natasha had brought back from Morocco when she went there last year on her way back from the States): and for that brief period, Deeriye looked a cairn of clothing wrapped in reverence. And who was this man whom he paid this extensive, expansive respect?

"Welcome, Elmi. Welcome."

"Alxamdulillaah!" said Elmi-Tiir, his gesture reverent, the tips of his fingers, having curved his hand into the shape of a crescent, resting on the spot between the breasts.

"Come on in and welcome."

"Thank you."

"And when did you arrive?"

"This morning."

Deeriye's face glowed in total joy at seeing his friend and brother-in-law Elmi-Tiir, who, in turn, demonstrated that he, too, was as efficient in the communicative skill – but outreaching as well: the two rather like wild game at the approach of a fellow animal in whose odour they recognize themselves. With Natasha, Deeriye was a prince of smiles; with Rooble, he was a door that had just been pushed ajar: his friend could roam in and out, the pleasure of doing that his and his only; but with Elmi-Tiir, he was the residence of man's ragged spirit – and humility. He would stoop, as though in prayer, to the superior intelligence and abundant generosity of Elmi-Tiir's soul. Elmi-Tiir was five or so years older than he, stouter and healthier. Deeriye could be himself with him; he could show his weaknesses, trust him with his secrets, trust him much more than he could trust Rooble or his own children. He could take to Elmi-Tiir his complaints: the way a child goes to a parent with a broken toy. He could tell him how Zeinab and Mursal had reduced him to the state of a pauper, a houseless vagabond, reduced him to the state of a man in need: in need of the machines and medicines they provided him with; in need of being taken care of. He could complain to Elmi-Tiir how he had been reduced to more or less a political anomaly: a man whose house had been sold, moved here and there; and now they were sending him out of the country to the Republic of Djebouti, until *peace* reigned again. Peace at what price? Complaints, pains, disappointments, displeasures: Deeriye was the pupil who took the unsolvable obstacles to the teacher with the clear head and foresight: and Elmi, confident and warm as his voice, dealt with these matters as though they were not worth the cost of buying an aspirin. He was good looking, hair all white, beard full and painted with henna, skin smooth, elegantly robed in the simplest of garments: he was a man you would look at twice even if you did not know who he was. But he wasn't known; he was less known than Khaliif the madman; less known than Deeriye. He was the maker of men in the way mentors were the shapers of the ideas their disciples constructed.

"And how did you come?" said Deeriye having served him the tea and biscuits Samawade had brought and offered the most comfortable armchair.

"I came by plane. Military plane."

"Oh!"

"Why oh?"

"Someone else spoke about military planes this morning."

"In connection with your going to Hargeisa?"

"You are well informed."

"We've talked a little, he and I."

"I can see that."

"And you are not going?"

"I am not."

"Neither would I."

"Thank you."

"Mursal told me about Mukhtaar too. Tragic."

"Yes," said Deeriye. Then he asked, "Why a military plane?"

"Transport is transport."

"Yes, yes. Of course. But not your own choosing, I meant?"

"No."

"Is something up?"

"Yes. We have an ultimatum to deal with."

"An ultimatum?" asked Deeriye, surprised.

"Yes. An ultimatum from the General. A tribal council has been summoned so *we* can deal with that."

"At the General's behest?"

"Strict instructions."

"And you've been brought to Mogadiscio in a military plane?"

"Yes."

"What's the General after?"

"He wants to isolate you. Or imprison us all for having broken the no-right-of-assembly law. . . . "

"So you've heard about Rooble?"

"And thus he wants Mahad's attempt on his life to seem one which has tribal support and no ideological backing. Maybe I am wrong but this is how I was made to see things. According to Mursal, anyway," said Elmi-Tiir.

"All the clan's peace-makers are going to be there, then?"

"Yes."

"This tribal council to which all the clan's peace-makers have been invited will put on trial my history, my background, my ideology, my friendship with Rooble. Am I right?"

"You are."

"Do you remember the historical trial of the elders and clan leaders the Sayyid was invited to in 1897?" said Deeriye.

"Why?"

"Because this colloquium reminds me of that."

"But the Sayyid was at the beginning of his political career. And you are not."

"Never mind. I am on trial for my principles, my belief, my friendship with Rooble, Mahad's failed attempt on the life of the General. I am on trial by a tribal council for my ideological stand vis-a-vis state-power. A national government, not colonial. Imagine!"

"That is why I am here."

"To be on my side during my hour of need?"

"You need Allah for that, not me."

"But you are here, all the same."

"And there is another thing."

"What?"

"Have you been thinking of going to Mukhtaar's burial?"

"I haven't thought of it or spoken to Mursal about it. He is *his* friend and if *he* thinks I should go, I will. Why do you ask?"

"A suicide is, according to Islamic tradition, to be denied ceremonial burials, the communal escort to the burial ground, the full participation."

"Now what does that mean?"

"It means he will be buried like a dog without purifying ceremonies and Islamic sanctions; it means that he will be buried without anyone praying the *jinaaza* over him or saying a special prayer for him."

"But he did not commit suicide."

"There, now. How do you know?"

"Who told you all this, Elmi-Tiir?"

"Xaaji Cigaal, who was on the plane with us from Kismayo."

"*Us?* How many were you?"

"Twelve altogether. There was the pedimanous sheikh (I don't know his name), there was a Minister of State, a young man – I think his name is Ahmed-Wellie – Xaaji Cigaal, myself and a number of women."

"Cigaal and Sheikh Ibrahim: my unneighbourly temptations."

"That is where it all began?"

Deeriye nodded. These unneighbourly neighbours: a world stood on its head, he reflected, a world whose inhabitants live, like ants, in societies of total exclusiveness from one another, busy eating away at one another's foundation: may they be struck by the Creator's curse, Amen! Traditionally, one had but the best welcome for one's neighbours. It was your neighbours who were first intimated of your ill health; it was your neighbours whose fire lit your hearth; it was your fire's ember which hid the secrets of your neighbour's cold fears when you buried it at night, just before you went to sleep. And one referred to as one's neighbour anyone, man, woman or child, whose dwelling fell within a forty-house radius of yours – in all seven directions. One played cards with them; one shared a few whispers of gossip with them. But then one's neighbour was generally one's relation: hence Somalis use the terms of address "brother" or "sister" or "cousin," because those one met often were one of these or something like an uncle, an aunt; a relation, at any rate. It seemed that the Somali rationalism nowadays shared space with the materialistic cynicism of the urban citizenry anywhere: a materialistic cynicism based in fear of one another and suspicion. When Somalis meet, their encounters are tinged with false smiles which alter the emphasis of their unspoken thoughts. Neighbours spying on one another. God forbid!

Elmi-Tiir sipped his tea in silence: thinking about the same things, more or less. Now he asked:

"How badly were you hurt by Cigaal's grandson?"

"Did he tell you that himself?"

"He put the blame squarely on the incomprehensible generation. How badly were you hurt?"

"What explanation did he give for his grandson's striking me senseless? Or didn't he?"

Elmi-Tiir admitted that he was confused about the explanation given: something to do with *an owl which Yassin aimed at and whose shadow he struck;* but Elmi-Tiir confessed he did not understand.

"Neither did we."

"Is that where it all began?"

"Technically speaking, no."

"Where did it all begin?"

"I suspect it all began with my being moved here."

"Why was that found to be necessary?"

"Zeinab wanted to add an extension of a wing for me in her house. Being allergic to dust, my condition being what it is, it was suggested I move in here, having been moved from my house originally for the same reason and having had it put on the market."

"And?"

Here Deeriye hesitated; beyond this point was his private life, so private he wouldn't share it with anyone; well, not exactly that, but he would hold on to it for as long as he could. Also, he did not want to expose himself to all sorts of exploitation and questioning: for beyond this was his private life which consisted of the visions he saw, his encounters with Nadiifa. Not that these facts were not known to Elmi-Tiir, not that these were not public knowledge; but it pained him to speak of them. Did he not, however, think of Elmi-Tiir as the one person to whom he could take his complaints, show, like a child to a parent, the boil which wouldn't break? Why could he not tell him? If Elmi-Tiir had come during the brief tempting period when Nadiifa and the visions were not showing themselves to him directly or through Samawade, then Deeriye might have said to him: "Please speak to your sister and ask her to come and see me." Not now. The visions had returned; so had Nadiifa. And there was no need exposing oneself to being teased.

"You had no intimation whatsoever of what Mahad was planning?" asked Elmi-Tiir.

"Indirectly, yes."

"How do you mean?"

"Mursal and Mahad came to me and talked day in day out of what they referred to as public and private justice. They explained justifiably, to me at any rate, that a clansman whose brother is executed in public because he has broken one of those laws decreed by the General's régime can traditionally, instead of exacting blood compensation for the dead brother from government pension schemes, take the law into his hands, *lex talionis,* kill: kill the General. Or something like that."

"But Mahad did not tell you anything himself?"

"No."

"Nor did Rooble know, as far as you can tell?"

"No."

"What about this extraordinary information that you have about Mukhtaar? You say he did not commit suicide. How did you come by that information?"

Apparently the inquisition had already started and Deeriye thought he would answer all the questions put to him as best as he could, and trust the faith he had in Elmi-Tiir.

"Mursal, Zeinab and I were at Rooble's when it occurred."

"Last night?"

"Yes."

"He's told me. What else do you know?"

Deeriye spoke of Afrah and the information this man had provided; he spoke of Mukhtaar's mysterious calling on them when the four of them were playing cards; he spoke of all the things he would never have bothered talking about were it not for the fact that he wished to convince Elmi-Tiir of the *suspicions, not knowledge,* that Mukhtaar did not commit suicide.

"It is extraordinary, isn't it? – the names these four young men have? As though they were invented as part of one's burning need to change the destiny and history of a nation."

"Yes. It is."

"Just listen. Mursal. Mahad. Mukhtaar. And Jibriil Mohamed-Somali."

"And how do you know about Jibriil?"

"Zeinab told me."

"Oh," said Deeriye. A pause. Then: "All carriers of *the message,*" he added.

"The message of the Lord; the message of the revolution; the message of a future happier than the present we live in; the message of brotherhood and true peace."

"Messages that aren't delivered change the history of a people."

"So do messages that are distorted; lies that are fabricated to serve the vicious need to be wicked, such as the camel-constabulary's lie that the Sayyid stole the gun, when he paid for it with four camels."

"Four, was it?"

"I think so."

"Messages that are intercepted change the history of a man, too."

"Of course. Waris."

There was a brief pause.

"Haji Omer's son is coming to the meeting."

"He is, is he?"

"So is Waris."

"Curse the traitors! Forgive the innocent! O Lord!"

Then after a protracted silence, Deeriye took the opportunity to relate to Elmi-Tiir all that had happened since Khaliif's first appearance that dawn so many days ago; to him, he also took the complaint about the madman's prophetically frightening message: that they (Mursal and Deeriye) had betrayed. He reviewed in haste all that had taken place. A change of neighbours. His fears. His dreams. His life. His asthma. The water in his legs. His need to go for walks. Zeinab and Mursal's cosmetic politics. Unneighbourly neighbours. A madman out of dawn. The shadow of an owl: or rather being hit because the owl was the target of a stone thrown (he went into details, giving the religious and the irreligious implications of being stoned, et cetera); the discussions of public and private justice with Mursal and Mahad; the failure of Mahad's attempt to assassinate the General; Rooble's visit before that; Cigaal's calling on the stricken old man and Mursal's turning away the compensation present from him; the misleading information that Mukhtaar had betrayed so as to discredit Mahad; Afrah's volunteering of information about Mukhtaar's imminent death; Deeriye's appointment with Rooble; Rooble's not turning up for the appointment; Yakuub's son and the message he gave to Deeriye in the presence of Afrah; Deeriye's *omission* of one significant word of a Koranic verse; the visions which deserted him; Nadiifa who refused to come to him; his agony over that; and Mukhtaar dead, but not before making a mysterious appearance before him, Mursal and Zeinab; and Khaliif the madman again, Khaliif who had earlier in the week pointed an accusing finger in the direction of the Cigaals and described them as wicked; and who, as a result, was pelted with pebbles by Yassin; but who, this morning, pointed the same finger at Deeriye and Mursal, naming names, striking directly at the core of the matter: and who, were it not for Deeriye's being there, might have been struck with a book containing the Prophet's tradition and a cassette containing the Sayyid's "Death of Corfield," which Samawade had intended to throw at him to chase him away.

"A tribal council whose job is to inquire into the sanity of your choices, your decisions, your friendships, the validity of your arguments," said Elmi-Tiir. "This is a mad world."

"And let me not forget something else."

"What?"

"Moving, removing and re-moving."

"What is that?"

"Mursal came this morning to me with the idea that I should go with Zeinab by military plane to Hargeisa so that I would be away until everything returns to normal. And you come by plane, perhaps the one that is supposed to take us tomorrow to Hargeisa."

"He told me."

"Has he also told you about Djebouti?"

"He told me that you refused to be moved around like furniture. Yes, he told me that. What he didn't tell me, though, is how important a part he played in Mahad's conspiracy."

"He hasn't told me that either. You know I prefer that he doesn't burden me with his secrets. I don't pester them with my worries; neither did Nadiifa ever, bless her soul. If I don't know, I don't worry, you see my point."

There was a great deal of movement downstairs. It transpired that Medina was leaving and was willing to give Elmi-Tiir a lift to Zeinab's place. Did he want to go with her?

Before Elmi-Tiir accepted the lift Medina had offered him, he managed to say that Deeriye had nothing to fear, nothing to worry about. In any case, he did not believe that the General would dare sweep those who attend the meeting into prison since that would achieve the opposite of what he intended: to isolate Rooble's clan – which was a way of saying that the clan was behind Mahad's failed kamikaze assassination attempt. He also assured Deeriye that he, Elmi-Tiir, would be in the chair and wouldn't allow anything to get out of hand; although he made it obvious that he was suspicious about the wisdom of Deeriye's total refusal to know what Mursal was up to. However, in the final analysis, Elmi-Tiir said that he too would be of a mind to support Deeriye's acceptance not to challenge Mursal's moratorium on his underground activities.

"Till tomorrow then, my friend," he said after they had tied all the loose ends gracefully but in haste. Elmi-Tiir said that his daughter Dahaba and grandchildren would come on the morrow.

And then he was gone.

PART THREE

Curse, bless, me now with your fierce tears, I pray.
Do not go gentle into that good night.
Rage, rage against the dying of the light.
–Dylan Thomas

Experience is the name so many people give
their mistakes.
–Oscar Wilde

Vague memories, nothing but vague memories.
–W. B. Yeats

EIGHT

A Paltry Thing

The morning made a gift of itself to Deeriye. He decided to open it with studied care and tenderness.

He stayed in bed and held the gift unopened for the best part of an hour, held it close to his heart as though it were his re-discovered love, held it in his head as though it were a thought, held it in his mouth, tasting and re-tasting its sweetness. And he remembered: he remembered Nadiifa who had come to him a few hours earlier – after he had said the solemnest prayer and several extra prostrations; after Khaliif had appeared out of dawn and disappeared into its greyness. She called when he had been having a quiet cat-nap. He remembered Nadiifa's stare as peaceful, her smile fresh; he remembered her mild reproval for his *principled ways,* her gentle voice reminding him of things she said he had chosen to forget: "Do you remember that you said," she had told him when he saw her, "that you wouldn't discourage or encourage Zeinab or Mursal's involvement in politics? Why don't you challenge Mursal's moratorium on his political activities if you suspect they are harmful and dangerous?" He defended himself as best he could although this did create, for the first time, an atmosphere of general disquiet. She said, talking about the unchallenged Mursal: "Politics is not only a war of left-wing and right-wing principles. It is also the making of choices – personal and political. I plead with you: please let them make their own choices. But guide them gently."

And what a gift: the morning!

The sun's rays, intertwining like strands of hemp, stretched flat and combed – like Nadiifa's plaited hair after she had taken a smoke-bath of *cuud,* had washed in that perfumed soap he so much loved and painted her palms and soles with Egyptian privet. How she smelt well! How smooth her body felt: like silk! And they would make love: long and beautiful and wonderful. With her menopausal complications, they found out they could be at it longer – a little dolorous, she would admit, but nice. She counted her days in accordance with the solar year. Six months of a dry season, each month containing thirty days; and the *todoba-dirir:* a sub-period of seven headings whose occurrence coincided with Virgini's total concealment from the human naked eye. The smoke-bath of *cuud,* the *xinna* patterns on the palms of her hand – and that tea which she made, sweet as her smell and rich as the suggestions of her eyelashes. . . .

Now the sun was, after the early morning shower, almost too cheery: Deeriye thought that the sun behaved as though she would collect herself together, beat the rays of dust off her bright garment, put on her goggles for the long twelve-hour show on the road to her setting, get up and go. Just like his wife.

Nadiifa! The woman who bore the burden of history like a hump on her back. A patient, loving person, generous and conscientious, who was responsible for building a homestead whose greatness dwarfed all other houses. Such a generous woman she was; she never said one wicked word about his politics in public or private. When she needed help and support, fortunately she had Elmi-Tiir who was ready to provide all assistance required. And she and her brother spoke of the man she never openly said she loved, and they called out his name but pronounced it as "Diiriye": the one who offers warmth. Then he learnt to read and write, and his letters to her from prison began to arrive, bringing with them memories of him she did not think she had. She used to ask Mursal to read out the letters; then she would request that he wrote his father letters giving their latest news: but these letters to him never spoke of a sick child; never of any shortages; never of the absence of anything; never of the fact that he was missed. She dealt with the aspects of life and politics he loved to know about, careful, of course, that the censors would not block them or confiscate them. It was she who had told him of Haji Omer's appointment as a tribal elder and of the hidden wealth he had come out with years later, wealth he had ensconced somewhere when he received the fee in exchange for the information he had extracted from Waris, then barely eight years old. In short, she was the one who introduced to Mursal and later Zeinab their father's life and politics; she was the first who spoke about the betrayals and hopes – topics he had never dealt with directly until much, much later. Nadiifa!

Yet when he met her early this morning in his sleep, when she blessed him and showered upon him praises for what he had done, he was unable to answer most of her questions. He couldn't remember whether or not Elmi-Tiir had aged well, whether or not he was a grizzled old man supporting himself on a walking-stick; how his daughter Dahaba and her children Kemaal and Mohammed and his sons were; how bad his diabetes was. She asked questions whose answers he would never have sought from anyone; questions which did not allow the cutting of corners but which needed to be faced and responded to. Mild reproof from her: "All life is not politics, Deeriye," and she left it at that. Then she inquired about Natasha and Samawade; about Zeinab and Cantar and Sheherezade. He fared better here, could supply responses to elementary questions concerning movements. And his health? He complained of his asthma, of his legs which, because he walked less and less, were becoming heavier with the water in them; he also complained about the frequent cat-naps which, on occasion, rendered living with different realities difficult for him. He did not know how to distinguish the things in real life from what he saw during those brief naps, he said. The impressions, the visions one had during these *submerged but real times* were, he believed, more real, on occasion, than those one had when one *re-surfaced*.

"There you go again," she said in her teasing, most friendly voice. "Politics and philosophy as usual." And she disappeared as if she were someone a magician had conjured up, taking with her her perfume, her xinna'ed small hands very like a shaman's – and his strength! For a while, he felt as a hairless Samson. Then she reappeared, raised her hands in prayer, her posture solemn. And what about Mahad, Mursal, Mukhtaar and that man Jibriil? Did any of these young men indicate any interest whatsoever in "either of the twin Islamic blessings" of which the Prophet spoke: *victory or martyrdom?* Deeriye reflected for a long time. He searched for clues in the numerous folds of veiled suggestions and innuendos two of these young men had uttered and he resolved that he would find one if he looked a little harder. Which he did. His answer: Victory against the General was far beyond the seven horizons; martyrdom was, in its religious sense, a concept for which these young men had little sympathy. "What about the burial? Are you going to take part in Mukhtaar's burial? Is Mursal?" He replied that he did not know if there would be any burial. This produced an unexpected result for she condemned it harshly and said that every Muslim must be given good burial. "But then Mukhtaar isn't the only person not to have a decent Islamic burial. I can think of a number of other martyrs and great men who did not have any. The Sayyid, for instance, had no known tomb; the Sudanese Mahdi's tomb was desecrated by the British who dug it open and presented the skull – for disposal! – to that lunatic who went by the name of Lord Kitchener. Neither did Corfield, a major casualty of the Sayyid's, have any burial so far as we know; nor did General Gordon. Such is life. There are hundreds and hundreds of men and women whose burial places are not known; except to Allah. And that, in my humble opinion," she said, "is what matters. Mahad and Mukhtaar are both martyrs in that they believe in the cause they are fighting for; Mursal is their friend and has faith in them and the cause, and I respect his unchallenged moratorium on his activities – for which he has the absolute right; Rooble: a man seamed with torrents of trust in the rightness of those he loves: patient as Ayuub and lovable as ever. And there is Elmi-Tiir, whom you know."

She wished him good luck; but before she vanished into memory, to make sure perhaps that he distinguished this from any other morning, she made a gift of the morning to him, a gift which he should open once she had disappeared. And he opened his eyes.

• • • • • • • • • • •

The living-room was chatty with the rivalry of children, each competing to get as much of Zeinab, Dahaba (Elmi-Tiir's daughter) and Deeriye's attention as possible: they fought, they wrestled, they outshouted one another. Samawade, however, alone sat in a corner, engaged in sulky thought; the others, namely Cantar, Sheherezade, Jamaal, Kemaal and Mohamed (the latter three were Dahaba's), were jumpy with playfulness.

Zeinab said something two, three times, something that neither

Deeriye nor Dahaba could hear. She then cried, "Children, quiet and out." The remains of the banter spread lightly and into mumbles and grumbles, then total cessation; and out they went.

"So how are you, Dahaba and how are the children?" said Deeriye. "I haven't seen you, them or your husband for. . . . I can't for the life of me remember how many years now."

"Before you served your last spell of detention period, I think."

"Now, when was that?"

"We had only one child; now, thank Allah, we have three and I had three miscarriages and I am pregnant with another and pray to Allah no complications. For those of us who stay out of prison, time passes fast enough."

"And you reproduce one another," he said. "Or at least your kind."

"I am sorry?"

"Don't mind him. He is being nasty as usual," said Zeinab.

Dahaba was short and bouncy, did not look in the least her father's daughter, was not at all interested in politics. She had married badly: three divorces and maybe a fourth before long, the third having been so far her most stable marriage. She did not show the scars of these broken marriages or seem at all demolished by her miscarriages.

"All is well with you these days?" he asked not too indifferently.

"Yes, yes, thanks to Allah."

"And the children are all right? Doing well at school?"

As though to answer that, Kemaal came in and said, "Did somebody call my name? If so, I am here." He went to Deeriye whom he called "Grandfather" and he took his hand in both his, introduced himself as "Kemaal Ataturk," and said, imitating some cheap spaghetti-western he had seen, "*Agli ordini, Signore.*"

Deeriye, although he had read a biography of Ataturk, was never sure how to interpret the man. Ataturk contained many contradictions, which perhaps made him all the greater. He learnt from him the political choice of inventing dates: did Ataturk invent the 19th of May as his birthday, that being the day when his troops landed at Samsun at the start of a resistance movement against the British? But then he found him a Muslim revisionist; a good man for Turkey, definitely the Kurd's greatest foe indubitably, but a deviant Muslim.

"Kemaal," said Deeriye, "do you know who Ataturk was?"

"A great national figure of Turkey," said the young boy just eleven. "And I have a picture of him on one of our walls in Baidoa. Do you know who gave me the picture, Grandfather?"

"No. Tell me."

"Uncle Mursal."

Then as if on cue Jamaal entered, tall for his ten years, a black moustache painted on his upper lip. He took his grandfather's hand and shook it. "My name is Jamaal and I am named after Cabdunnaasir. You know his history so I won't bother you with details."

And he bowed out, giving the place of prominence to the youngest who called himself "Sayyid Mohammed Abdulle Hassan," and added: "You know me better than I know myself. And my nickname is Shaka. Shaka Zulu. You know who that is too: a great warrior nationalist, another Sayyid."

"Are you not impressed?" Zeinab wanted to know, after a pause.

"I am. Congratulations, Dahaba," he said.

Then Zeinab's "All right now; game is over," disbanded them and brought the chatter to a sudden end. A little later Dahaba, too, found a good reason to leave so Deeriye and Zeinab could have time to talk.

Deeriye asked, "So you are not gone after all?"

"No point in my going if you are not coming," Zeinab said.

"I was made to understand you were going to Hargeisa on government business. Why didn't you go? Was it simply to test me, see how far I would go?"

"Someone else went."

"I wouldn't have come."

"I know. But it wasn't a ploy to test you. Someone who wanted to visit his own family, a man from the North, went in my place. When you insisted you didn't want to go and this doctor from the North insisted he wanted to go, I thought, well, why not!"

Deeriye believed her.

"I understand that you went with Mursal to Mukhtaar's burial?"

"There was no burial."

"But there was."

"Not yesterday. We were given contradictory information: someone volunteered the information and said when he would be buried and at what cemetery; we went there and discovered they had changed their mind so we returned to Sheikh Ibrahim's house and learnt that everything had been postponed."

"There was a burial."

"When?"

"Early this morning."

"How do you know?"

"The radio," Deeriye said.

"Where was he buried?"

"The radio didn't say. But it said that a post-mortem done under the supervision of Dr Ahmed-Wellie clearly indicated that it was suicide."

"Final, isn't it? Once Dr Ahmed-Wellie signs the document."

"I should think so." There was nothing more worth saying.

Cantar and Sheherezade came, stood in the doorway and were frightened away by the deep silence which they found.

"Tough days ahead," Zeinab said, her voice a little flippant.

"Tough, no. Difficult to come through triumphantly, yes," he said. "My friends are my friends, my politics mine. I won't let the clan or a self-appointed group from the clan dictate what I do."

"It's the second time in your life that an ultimatum is served by the governing authority of the country and, it appears, this must be history's joke, for the same reason: hand over *'an assassin'* (in 1934: Mahad's father; now Mahad himself); disclaim all nationalist allegiances; dissociate yourself from a friend of yours whom this authority wishes to punish; and take a position of neutrality."

"Not neutrality. In politics, there is no such thing."

"What?"

"Compromise. In politics, there is no neutrality."

"All right. Compromise."

Deeriye's eyes regained their glitter. He saw Zeinab wanted to say something. "Continue."

"The punitive expedition the Italians sent against the clan of which you were the Sultan claimed hundreds and hundreds of cattle and in the process created a famine which you didn't yourself have to face, since you were taken into detention. This was 1934. The culprit the Italians were after was Mahad's father: Mahad was then in his mother's stomach. You believed, as did your own father and Rooble's, in a brotherhood of Somalis, a brotherhood of Sayyidism, a brotherhood defined only in your head."

"That's not quite right. But go on."

"This is 1981. And Mahad, the son of the man whom the Italians were after, is the burning issue: he started this spreading fire which has so far taken in Mukhtaar and roasted him alive; the flames of his fire have also trapped Rooble; a fire that is famished and, like the hell of Jehenna, needs more persons to keep it going; like a hole which becomes larger the more you take out of it. The only difference, *if there is a difference*, is that in 1934 the enemy and the famine-creating power was colonial and foreign; and now it is neo-colonial and local. Have you not learnt your lesson? Which reminds me of something you used to say: that the history worth studying is one of resistance, not capitulation; and that all great men – Shaka Zulu, Ataturk, Nkrumah, Cabral, Garibaldi, Lenin, Cabdunnaasir, Gandhi, the Sayyid – have one thing in common: the shaping force of their lives has been resistance."

"Hold your horses, please!"

"Yes, Father."

"Between national and colonial governments there is this major difference: the enemy is obvious, the nation's priorities clear on one hand; on the other hand, with national governments, things become unclear, priorities are confused. The enemy is within: a cankerous tumour. You die of it gradually; bloodless, pale and unmourned."

She appeared to disagree but she said, "Right. Let's continue.

"It is not heads of cattle but of people that will be rolling this time – the General's ultimatum appears to imply. And the General means business. No unnatural droughts to be created, for the natural famine claims lives daily and a nationalist war in the Ogaden. It is human heads that will be rolling: this is what the General's ultimatum says in language of terrifying horror. 'You stay out of this,' he says, 'you and your son . . .'."

"' . . . so I can isolate and identify each of you separately, hunt you down and kill you,'" interrupted Deeriye. "Yes. So he can identify this resistance against his tyrannical régime as originating from a clannish source. Whereas, if Mukhtaar, Jibriil, Mursal and myself are members of the same movement, if you can call it that, and if hypothetically

Rooble and Mahad are also members, then the General will be confronted with a nationalist and not a clannish group. . . . "

The children, chattery and noisy, rushed in and wouldn't let them continue despite Zeinab's efforts at insisting that they did. Deeriye told her to leave them be, let them stay, play where they wanted. (She thought she should perhaps point out to him that he had counted himself as a member of Mursal and Mahad's movement. Was he aware of this?) With Zeinab, Samawade, Dahaba, Mursal (who came up rubbing his eyes sleepily) and Deeriye as audience, the five children improvised themselves into a small group of marionette-players whose talented puppetry could have earned anybody's admiration.

After lunch, Mursal said he would take Deeriye to the meeting of the tribal council convened by the General under the chairmanship of Elmi-Tiir.

"Pray for me," he said to Zeinab and Dahaba as he was being driven away. "This is just like the colloquium of 1897 to which the Sayyid was called by an assembly of the elders of the city of Berbera. Pray for us all. And if you don't see me, that means I've been detained or swept into prison with the others – just like Rooble."

• • • • • • • • • • •

No major upsets were to come out of the inquisition. This became obvious as a number of the elders took the floor in turn and each painted it with slogans and symbols of brotherhood, as each opened his speech with a *Faatixa,* as each rambled on and quoted proverbs and the Prophet's tradition. It was a meeting short of any brilliant fires of controversy. When talking about Deeriye, they referred to him in the third person, as though he weren't there or couldn't hear or understand what was being said. Nor did they address him; they addressed Elmi-Tiir who was in the chair. This differed markedly from what everybody had expected since all assumed (wrongly) that to have invited Haji Omer's son who had been the spearhead of the anti-Deeriyists on the one hand, and on the other to have asked Waris to come was tantamount to asking for trouble when Deeriye was there too.

Deeriye was so bored with these protracted speeches that he fell asleep twice, had two most enjoyable naps during one of which (or was it really after he had resurfaced from the tunnel of drowsiness?) someone said something about the General saying that he was going to visit Deeriye and even enter into a discussion with him if necessary; visit him since Deeriye, the General was reported to have said, "turned down many of my invitations to call on me. If Deeriye wishes to call," said the General's message, "let him get in touch." Deeriye was outwardly calm now but was burning inside with the urgent need to find out whether he had heard this *after, during* or *before* his nap. He looked around for someone to ask to confirm or unconfirm the gist of what he had heard. He decided that he wasn't going to make fool of himself by raising his hand and inquiring if this were true. No. He tried to get Elmi-Tiir to look in his direction. Nothing doing, either. So he did all he could: he listened.

Haji Omer's son was speaking, a younger man than most of those present in the room (which had been lent by a clanswoman to the meeting), a man who inherited his father's stipended – but not clan-recognized – chieftaincy. (The clan in the countryside, having learnt years later that Haji Omer was a traitor, resolved to excommunicate him – but the Italians and subsequent national governments kept him on the payroll until his death and then his son took over the office, continuing to serve the exploitative nature of governmental and clan politics.) And what was he saying? Nothing that would make Deeriye lose his peaceful posture. They were seated in a circle, some seventeen to twenty men, all members of the same *dia*-paying community, all but one (Haji Omer's son) more than fifty years old: the elders of the clan. They were seated on the floor, on mats provided by the hostess (women were not invited to important meetings where decisions affecting the clan were made, although Deeriye held the progressive view they should be for it might make some of these stupid idiots talk less, since mixed company would most probably have made them feel ashamed of themselves. He would definitely have loved Nadiifa to be here sitting beside him; she would know whether or not the General had invited himself to speak with Deeriye, or the name and telephone number of the Inspector he was supposed to get in touch with if he wished to see or talk to the General in person).

Haji Omer's son was now saying: "Have you, Deeriye, no conscience and no understanding of the situation? Have you no feeling for the political implications of your activities? Do you never care what happens to our clan? We must not allow one man to drag us all into a controversy and certain disaster. We must not. Just before I was born, there was the massacre in which hundreds and hundreds of cattle lost their lives in the unnatural drought brought about by Deeriye. . . . "

Suddenly a flame as someone said: "Shame on you!"

"What?" someone asked.

Elmi-Tiir intervened, "Please. Calm."

"Shame on you and on your father," said the fiery voice which when Deeriye's eyes followed he could identify as having been Waris's. "Traitor, the son of a traitor! What do we expect from the likes of you?"

Elmi-Tiir again: "Calm down, brothers. Calm down, brothers."

Waris was up on his feet and shouting curses, a man unburdening himself after years of silence. The curse of the clan, he once said to Deeriye, had shaped his life "out of the painful postures of guilt: my eyes were for years downcast, I could never look anyone in the eyes. For years, when the women of the clan refused to speak to me, I thought they knew I was the young boy who would never amount to anything, the young boy who had failed his community. The ways of the traitor are mysterious. When I saw Haji Omer and he asked me where I was running to and what message I was carrying, it didn't occur to me that he hadn't known. So when later it became clear that somebody had talked, sold information to the Italians and that it was Haji Omer, well, there was enough evidence: the stipended chieftaincy et cetera, but . . . by then I was, what? . . . twenty, I think. . . . I confessed to having been the one who told him . . . but the thought of killing him first and then killing myself crossed my mind more than once; take my revenge and kill; although that wouldn't have compensated for the community's loss if I killed myself or him. I believed the curse would hang above my head like a sword in any case and it would fall sooner or later. I went and spoke to Elmi-Tiir and he calmed me down and said he would see to it that the curse was lifted. So he called a meeting and explained to the gathering what had happened, what I had said. The meeting ended with a salvo of *Faatixa* absolving me, and blessing me too. The curse was transferred from my head to Haji Omer's. He was called to another meeting a few days later. A miracle, indeed. For it was during a paroxysmal fit of defending himself that he was struck with a cataclysmic seizure; and he became and finally died a paralytic. Curse the traitor!"

Elmi-Tiir was now saying, "Calm down, please. All will be clear in no time. We are not talking of things which happened years ago, we are addressing ourselves specifically to the General's ultimatum; and this is no colonial government but a national one; and Deeriye is not on trial. This meeting has been called to talk about the ultimatum."

Waris was gently asked to sit down and remain quiet: Haji Omer's son, at any rate, it was apparent, hadn't the support of anyone except two men whom he had brought with him, so he was made to sit and to shut his mouth. Then, sudden as flames, Waris shot up and said,

"I request Elmi-Tiir to please ask the traitor's son, himself a traitor, to leave this room instantly. Else we are not going to continue divulging our secrets openly for we have not only him as a spy but two others. Kindly ask them to leave."

There was confusion. People took the floor although they were not given it by the chairman, with Waris still standing, Deeriye not saying anything and Elmi-Tiir shouting: "Point of order, point of order!"

Then someone said, "But Waris, you cannot tell a clansman to leave."

"I was invited to this meeting. Were you?"

"Yes," said one of the two men who had supported Haji Omer's son.

"Who invited you here?"

"Elmi-Tiir."

"Let's ask Elmi-Tiir if he invited these two men or Haji Omer's son?"

Haji Omer's son shouted, "My name is Mohammed. Why don't you call me by my name? Why do you always refer to me as 'Haji Omer's son'?"

"Your name cannot be Mohammed. Your name is Evil, traitor!" shouted Waris. "Mohammed is the name of the Prophet, God bless him."

The chaos wouldn't die down until the hostess pushed open the door, bringing trays of tea and with her her daughters and a young boy. The hostess's appearance on the scene silenced everybody. When a cup had been placed in front of each person and calm reigned, someone asked Elmi-Tiir: "Did you or did you not invite Haji Omer's son here?"

"No, I did not," said Elmi-Tiir.

"But you invited everybody else?"

"Not everyone else. There are two others here whom I did not invite."

"Is it unfair to ask the gathering whether or not those who were not invited by the chairman should leave the room?" said Waris, his voice triumphant.

"Is that a motion?" asked Elmi-Tiir.

"Yes, it is."

"A vote, then, is that what you're suggesting?"

"No. They should leave. No vote. Shame on traitors."

"Why?" retorted Haji Omer's son. "This is a meeting of the clan."

"Traitors are not members of their communities; nor are sons of traitors. Your father brought disaster and drought upon our community and you will do just the same."

"It was Deeriye brought disasters and unnatural droughts."

Elmi-Tiir took things into his hands and said, "You must leave, whatever-your-name-is, and so must your two friends. Traitors are not welcome in our midst."

Haji Omer's son and his two friends (rumour had it they were in the Secret Service of the Generalissimo) left the room. There was a very heavy moment or so. Then the door opened on its own. More suspense. The sun's rays fell directly on Deeriye's face. No one rose to close the door; everybody sat in mesmerized silence. Deeriye wished Haji Omer's son and his friends had not been turned away. Why? Because dissidence makes people think better and livelier. Now look! They did not know where to start once Haji Omer's son and friends had been expelled; Waris hadn't the vitality to stand up and defend something else in the way he had done before. Meanwhile, with the door still open, Deeriye watched a gust of wind perform a miraculous feat: it spread the sand first (in the courtyard), then sifted it, whirled it upwards like a spiral of smoke. Waris got up and closed the door.

Returning, he said, "We can continue," and sat down.

One of the nameless elders (his name could have been Ali, Ahmed, Abdulle, or anything; he didn't matter, nor would his ideas amount to anything: he was a stipended chieftain and a change of name or title wouldn't have improved anything) said:

"I know that Deeriye has nothing but scorn and contempt for the likes of Haji Omer and his son. I know also that although his rationale may be as incomprehensible to us as a madman's, he has stayed by and walked the same determined road these past forty-odd years. Never has he wavered; never have his actions demonstrated a moment's indecision or hesitation. People like myself have done so. We've been used time and again by whoever headed the government of the country. We have done many things of which Deeriye doesn't approve; he has done a number of things of which I do not approve. But this doesn't mean that I will present a motion to excommunicate him, isolate him or dissociate myself from everything he does in the same way as Rooble's clan have done."

Waris, like a few others, was suddenly interested. "Wait, wait, what did you say? Rooble has been excommunicated from his clan? When did this happen? What is this?"

"A meeting was called and was attended only by the stipended tribal chieftains of Rooble's yesterday afternoon, and those present decided to dissociate themselves from anything he does, has done or stands for."

Waris wanted to know more; whereas all Deeriye wanted was to know the name of this man, who couldn't remain a nameless tribal elder but had to be given a name so that he would be checked on, his identity scrutinized, his background as well. The man sitting next to him said the man's name: Abshir.

"And what did the tribal elders say about Mahad?" Waris again.

"Mahad too. The stipended chieftains were made to put their thumbs to a document in which they supported without reservation anything the General does; fully and absolutely accepted his authority."

Someone said, "Isolate and rule, isolate each community, keep them divided, call the nationalist tribalist and the tribalist nationalist and use them. But rule them."

"Yes. Isolate and rule," another repeated. "Isolate the target and then and only then can you hit your target with any accuracy if you are a good marksman."

And Deeriye lost interest in the speeches that followed this, with each speaker saying more or less the same thing. It did seem that there was nothing to worry about; it appeared very unlikely that anyone would suggest excommunicating him from the clan. In any case, Deeriye didn't much care if they did, though naturally he would feel isolated and would have no base to fight from; as a matter of fact, in a country like Somalia, he wouldn't have a following if his own kith and kin isolated him. It was altogether another matter being clannish or tribalist in the Somali sense, he thought. He now remembered that he had mistakenly, when talking with Zeinab, compared this tribal gathering with the colloquium the Sayyid had with the learned men of the city of Berbera in 1897. The Sayyid, then young, with hardly any experience in clan politics, and full of the vision he had seen; the Sayyid, who hadn't assumed any title, then or later was called before an assembly of learned elders including Sheikh Madar, a learned and most respected man, and was asked in the boldest and plainest of terms to explain himself; to share with the others in the room the visions he claimed to have seen, and to tell the assembled crowd what promises and religious fulfilments these visions held not only for himself (the Sayyid) but for all those he wished to follow the order of which he said he was a spokesman. The main point of the inquisition rested on the question: could the solid structures of the city of Berbera withstand and survive the propensities of the Sayyid's vision and learned thought? The subject of today's colloquy, if one could call it that, was: could the weak structures of the nation-state bear the weight of the constitutional responsibility clearly outlined therein? For one thing must not be missed. *The General uses the authority of a nation-state, of which he is now head in view of his military take-over, and lays this belabouredly on the structures of a clannishly ruled state.*

Then it occurred to Deeriye that he had come round to the same conclusion as Mahad and Mukhtaar: the formula of the *lex talionis:* oh, save us, Lord, what a mess!

Half an hour or so later, Deeriye awoke to his name being called. He looked around him; all the chatter-boxes were silent. Then he heard Elmi-Tiir say something and therefore was able to conclude that he hadn't seen one of his daylight visions, but was still at the meeting.

"We've decided to appoint three persons who will stay on here and talk further and see how best to convince the General of the clan's decision. The three are myself," said Elmi, "Waris and Abshir."

"And the decision?" someone asked.

"The decision will be worded something like this: since Deeriye holds no titular position in the clan's hierarchy, no gathering of the clan can tell him what to do or what principles to hold. The General can seek him out as any citizen, bring a case against him in a court of justice but if he's sought out unjustly then we, the clan, will stand behind him as we would stand behind any other Somali in the same position, whether or not he or she is a member of our clan. What do you think?" Elmi-Tiir asked, soliciting a comment from Deeriye.

He had nothing to say; if anything, he would have said that he was very glad that this acrimonious meeting had come to an end. He now remembered the question he had been meaning to ask: Did the General say he wished to speak with me person to person, face to face? And would someone be so kind as to tell me the name of the man and telephone number I'm supposed to call if I wish to speak with him? But no. He was too tired. He would pray, then take a nap.

He asked, "How do we go home?"

"We don't. You can," said Elmi-Tiir. "Mursal has sent word that he is waiting with transport outside. I will probably come and see you later if we finish early enough and if there is any transport."

Deeriye looked at Elmi-Tiir and saw him with fresh eyes of total and undivided admiration: he envied him his physical and moral strength.

• • • • • • • • • • •

Mursal said, "Yes, yes, I know. Don't tell me."

"What do you know?" asked Deeriye, as they entered their house.

"That three men, including the son of Haji Omer, were thrown out of the meeting."

"And how do you know that?"

"That Elmi-Tiir chaired the session and handled it very well."

"Yes, yes, but how do you know?"

"We have our means of gathering information," boasted Mursal.

"How?"

"One of Dahaba's sons, young Ataturk, was sitting outside, listening to everything that was said and reporting it to Jamaal who in turn reported it to Samawade. A network of informants, as innocent-looking as carrier pigeons: no one would think of stopping Samawade if anyone saw him running homewards."

"But why all the fuss? Why this network of child-informants?"

Deeriye and Mursal were in the living-room. Stripes of darkness and sunlight. Both sat outside these, Deeriye on a prayer-rug having just said several prayers, and Mursal not very far, legs crossed, and back from telephoning a friend.

"You know what happened at the meeting yesterday?"

"Remind me. Please."

"As the meeting was under way . . . "

"Ours or another meeting, which one?"

"The one Rooble attended. As it was under way, there came a knock on the door and two men asked to be let in. No one seemed to know who they were or what they had come for. Then they explained themselves. They said that everyone in that room was under arrest for violating the law of the country in which it was universally known that citizens had no right of free assembly, that is to say no more than five persons are allowed to meet anywhere except in a mosque or when they have come together to celebrate the names of the General."

"Then what happened? And when was this?"

"They negotiated. This is yesterday."

"Is this a new version based on the latest rumour? I am sure I've heard another version."

"Yes, Security officials – hear me to the end, Father – empowered to negotiate with men who had been given encouragement by the inside group of the régime to meet and consider as *deero* – excommunicated – both Mahad and Rooble. But remember the persons who had given this encouragement were different from the Security officers who turned up. The meeting was stopped. Two men were asked to go out and talk to the newly arrived Security officers. But once they went out, they found themselves talking to yet a different set of men (these were self-appointed security officials – actually tribal upstarts). It was suggested that only if they promised to condemn Mahad's action and consider Rooble as *deero* would they not be taken into detention one and all. It transpired that no one was willing to risk being spotted as being anti-Generalissimo, especially since everyone knew there were spies among them."

"But that is political coercion of the vilest kind. And madness!"

"You can call it what you like," said Mursal.

They indulged themselves with a long, relaxed silence in which their minds travelled in all sorts of directions before each found, like a restless hawk, where to alight. Deeriye thought about this madness and political coercion. He thought about the one and only election the General had organized recently to try to legitimize his régime in the eyes of peace-&-stability aid donors, i.e. the western European so-called democracies, who had to be appeased before their governments would step in and replace *the other donors of coercive aid* (who had in their period of conspiratorial mastery insisted that a nominal political party of the socialist brand be given birth – which he did) so a general election was called in which there was only one candidate: *him!* This was no strange thing, perhaps, since many governments, many régimes in Eastern Europe, Latin America, Africa and Asia do this; but they do not paint one ballot box (for Yes) with the flag of the country and under it pen a clear message ("Here put in their votes the persons who love their country and work for her prosperity") and position this ballot box (for Yes) at the most convenient spot so that the voter does not have to walk a few metres up a curtained dark place to find the other ballot box (for No) with no national flag painted on its side but some writing ("This is used by the enemy of the Somali people"), there for the benefit of those who could read, and who dared expose themselves to interrogation later on. Rigging an election is one thing; being loved and elected another.

"And do you want to know why that did not happen at your meeting?" said Mursal. "I mean why they did not remind you of some law which denies the citizenry the right of freedom of assembly?"

"Yes. I know."

"But let me tell you anyway. They took it for granted that Haji Omer's son and his two escorts would know how to deal with it; also they thought you would be considered as *deero* by the council yourself."

"How can one describe all this?"

"Madness."

"A sore forcefully and inexpertly dealt with: this is what we are dealing with. One thing after another, each sillier and madder than the previous ones."

"Madness!"

There was a long silence.

Then he remembered *hearing* (had he heard it or *seen* it during one of his naps during the meeting?) that the General had invited himself to speak to Deeriye or asked that Deeriye contact him by activating a secret telephone line. Did Mursal know anything?

"I've been given the number you can call if you wish to see him. An inspector, namely Keynaan."

"That is weird. I thought I had misheard something. What if he does invite himself here to your house?"

"Alla cena dei poveri vengono senza invito i potenti," Mursal quoted an Italian proverb.

"Listen to my question, Mursal. What if he invites himself here? Would you rather I met him somewhere else? Because if he wishes to see me, I will. I have nothing to lose."

"You can have visitors here, Father. This is as much your house as it is mine. I cannot decide for you who you talk to and who you don't while you live here."

"I just wanted to make sure we are in agreement on this."

Deeriye, getting up to go to his room, said, "I'm going to retire early. It seems we have a long day ahead of us tomorrow."

"But you will see him?" said Mursal.

"What do you think?"

"I am asking, will you see him if he wants you to?"

"You sound like a jealous woman asking, whether her husband intends to meet and talk to his former wife; or a jealous husband asking the same of a woman who wants to see her former husband. I will see him of course. As I said, I've nothing to lose."

"I thought you would," he said, displaying signs of unhappiness.

Deeriye pretended not to hear that.

Then Mursal asked, "You used to say that you wouldn't negotiate with a tyrant like him."

"I must have been younger and less politically experienced. If I ever said any such thing."

"Why do it now then?"

Deeriye put on a smile of dignity. He turned and looked at the setting sun whose light had begun to fade, the sun which was not young any more. He said, "I am a little exhausted, I said."

Mursal finally threw a ball of sarcasm, said, "When one is tired, one does things one regrets later."

"I am not young any more, Mursal," said Deeriye, "and the little fight I have in me I reserve for the worst. If the opportunity presents itself, I shall negotiate with the devil to have Rooble released from detention. No shift of position, no compromise, of course. You are young, strong-willed. Fight for us. I did the fighting when you were small, a mere child. Then I was young, strong-willed and obstinate and fought to change the destiny and history of this country. If you don't mind, I shall retire now. No meals for me tonight. Only prayers of meditation."

He went up the stairs, footsteps soft as the light of the setting sun.

NINE

Raking of the Earth's Dust

Towards early morning, while he was asleep, his head became a condominium of visions and dreams, nightmares and cat-naps; a compendium of thoughts, prophecies and predictions; and talking in conundrums: Nadiifa, Natasha, Zeinab, Elmi-Tiir, and Rooble in that order, each blaming the other for what *had* taken place. *But there was no Mursal*. Why did Mursal not show up? Where was he? Where had he disappeared? No one would tell Deeriye. Not even Samawade who arrived, carrying messages, sharing the latest gossip about Khaliif's reappearance in the village in which they had lived, although he spoke of strange movements occurring right in front of the house, plain-clothesmen and plain-clotheswomen hanging about the area with the irregular line they made serving as a security cordon.

Deeriye woke up feverish, running a high temperature and shouting, "The madness! The madness!" He was markedly disturbed by what he saw. Was he dreaming? Was he awake? Or had he gone mad like Mukhtaar or Khaliif? What kind of visions were these? Then he dropped on his knees, held his open palms out and fell into a solemn prayer: *peace!* And it was! He saw, as would a sufi, the retreating mysterious formlessness of the divine and he contemplated this image of exceptional handsomeness, an image peace-producing as the soul's reunion with God. There came a heavy, profane knocking on the door. When the knocking wouldn't stop, he *awoke* and answered, "Who is it?"

"It's Natasha."

No fever, no temperature, no "divine sighting," no horror and no madness. And no cat-nap, too. He would have to get up, he told himself; something drastic must have taken place for Natasha to knock on his door. What? He asked her in Italian to give him a minute: he would come down to the living-room in a moment or so.

"It is about Mursal," she said.

"What about him?"

"He's disappeared."

To himself: horror and madness, all right! To her, "I will come down shortly. Meanwhile, please call Zeinab, tell her to come here; tell her to drop whatever she's doing."

"All right. You needn't hurry," she said as she went down the stairway.

So he didn't. He lay in bed and thought to himself that Natasha's calling him away from his communion with the Divine Being made his life resplendent with contradictions: it pained him to think (when at his lowest and weakest) that Satan employed the services of a woman (the daughter of Eve), who was a non-Muslim to achieve this separation: this was what crossed his mind long before he was able to condemn his wicked reasoning, long before he regretted his failure to admit the sinfulness of his logic. Yes, how he could think so evilly of her whom he loved as he loved his son? He thought: *But she is part and parcel of invented history;* and the vision had been the source of a divine dream! He remembered how Nadiifa never attempted whether delicately or diplomatically to interfere with his understanding and distinguishing of the real and conceived cosmos (invented histories, imagined divine revelations), although she said that she had at times her reservations about the appropriateness and the sanctity of his politics. Zeinab insisted on his laying aside and curtailing the importance he gave to his imagined world in which Nadiifa and other visions appeared before him. Whereas if asked, he might have explained that his duality (as the dreamer of a dream, as the sleeper astraddle the real and the dreamed world) gave charge to the tension of a complicated set of polarities: the saint-in-satan; the vision, once the tunnel of the nap was illumined with the dawns of a dream.

"She said she will be here in a little while," Natasha shouted up.

"Grazie."

"Would you like some tea?"

"Yes, please."

"Would you like me to bring it up?"

"No. I will come down myself."

"All right."

"I will be down shortly."

But he had no energy to get up, no strength – no willingness to speak a small prayer before he went down to the kitchen. Affected with an enormous ennui, flooded with an avalanche of torrential worries, predictions and prophecies: he wondered would he survive it all? Would dawn break and would Mursal walk out of it: as did that person who (at the first instant and perhaps the second too) looked like Mukhtaar who walked in the centre of Deeriye's dream, only to be struck dead by a man who looked like his father; to be laid out in state; to die struggling, legs moving, hands tied together, mouth gagged with cotton. But the dream in which he saw this happen had been substantially different from all others because death occurred in it: he had never *seen* death before in his conjured up visions: had seen only alternatives to the dreariness of the real life one lived. And why visions and conjured up dreams and invented life? Why follow Ataturk in making up birthdays as significant as the history which gave birth to an idea? These visions guided him through a forest of contradictory pathways, led him to a clearing in which he stood, a man above the squabbles and quagmires of inter-clan rivalries and disputes; led him away from the political amalgams of irreconcilable views; they took him to a place of quiet peace where there lived, together with him, others who were always in agreement and where there existed a loving understanding between the ruler and the ruled – for he, Deeriye, was a member of the ruled! Visions moulded him; these visions gave him, his thoughts, his ideas and his prophecies a recognizable shape and gave his soul the inner peace which the conquering colonials and the national despots had either denied him or could not afford to offer. He believed in the truth of the visions and never doubted or questioned them. The visions it was that riveted him to the paths he took, determined for him which way he went; they held him by the hand as if he were an innocent child and showed him the things he ought to see; they oiled his tongue so he could say what was proper. These visions and dreams had been his companions during the most arduous years of his imprisonment: they had kept him company; they had told him stories; they had brought him news of what Mursal and Zeinab had been doing. Whereas years of imprisonment (and later death) separated him and his Nadiifa, whereas the prison walls had held him and Zeinab and Mursal apart, nothing, other than sinfulness or sleeplessness, could separate him from his dreams and visions. They came clothed in human form; his wife appeared to him smelling of sweet perfume, her body fresh from smoke-bath and her breath from the fresh milk she had drunk. In these visions, these dreams, Mursal and Zeinab remained small, innocent as their infant days, toothless; he never saw them as adults in any of his dreams before this day – which constituted a frightening departure for him. Mursal's familiar handwriting, a child's scrawling pen, dancing to the rhythm of a child's emphasis that everything is clear, beautiful and readable: this writing appeared on the screen on the wall a second or so before Natasha called him away. But Mursal wasn't there in Deeriye's vision today, either as a child or an adult, although Zeinab was – as an adult.

And the photographs: another departure from the usual. The image which used to be in Deeriye's mind was the photograph he had of the three of them, Mursal, Zeinab and Nadiifa – and no one else. But in the one he saw, he himself was there too. His height and size and smile dominated everything, the others looked small: dwarfed; they were, after all, the children and wife of a giant.

"Aren't you coming down?" from Natasha prompted him to say that he had been preparing to join her. Apparently, Zeinab hadn't arrived.

He hastily put on something, carefully went down the stairs and entered the kitchen. *How ugly the unhappy,* thought Deeriye to himself. She was in tears, her hair reduced to strands of disorder, her blue beautiful eyes red from crying. She was not disrespectful, but neither was she generous in her welcoming movements, nor polite as she indicated the chair he should sit on. Then, saying nothing, she walked out. Where had she gone? Perhaps he knew where. To talk to each other without the constant breaking down of conversation (and also because it is not easy to speak a language you do not know well with somebody you hold in deserved reverence; or when you are tired; or wrapped in rags of tears) only one course was available to them: Samawade as interpreter. Deeriye chuckled to himself as he remembered that Mursal's literacy as a youngster had been made use of by Nadiifa: and so he had been introduced to politics at the age of ten or even earlier; which was what was happening right now with Samawade. And Deeriye was impressed to see Samawade up, awake, and adult-like in his reactions, asking no questions other than to elucidate what his mother wanted him to interpret; he behaved like a professional. He interpreted:

"When I went to bed in the small hours of the night," she said, "Mursal had been in his study working. I woke up a couple of times. I saw him working or making himself a cup of tea or mixing himself a drink; but he didn't look nervous, nor did he act at all strangely. Then *someone* came." She stopped, waiting maybe to be asked a question, which Deeriye did.

"Who?"

She did not know, she answered. Although she had the weird sensation that the window which overlooked the street opened (which is why she thought *someone* came), and she could hear Mursal talking to a person whose voice sounded familiar, in the way a voice you've heard on the radio sounds familiar, but definitely not someone she had ever met. And they spoke English, Mursal and this other person.

Deeriye asked: "What did Mursal and this other person speak about?"

Natasha explained that she was only able to catch the occasional word or phrase, but not much.

"And then what happened?"

The window closed: she knew this because that window made a specific noise when being shut. A few minutes passed. Then the typewriter began to go and stop, the noise of paper being crumpled and dropped into the wastepaper basket, again and again. The telephone rang: only once. Mursal answered it immediately, spoke not more than one word and hung up. She knew this because she picked up the phone in the room and heard him say just this: "Right." She thought she should go and show herself to him, as if to say: Here I am, a part of you, an integral part of the painful history of your family and the country's, but for the sake of our love, for the sake of Samawade please do not do anything stupid without consulting me. "Then I remembered what my father, a Jew in Nazi Germany, told me and how the action of only one young man saved hundreds of lives when this young man blew himself up along with his German jailers and the wing of their camp; he died on the spot but enabled the others to escape. A wife, a child, a parent has no business in matters such as this."

"And then?"

A long, long silence. She thought Mursal had gone to sleep on the couch or something (the lights had been switched off, she saw when she went to the bathroom) and she did not go into the study. She closed her eyes for half an hour or so, couldn't go to sleep, and finally resolved to see him and speak with him. He was not there. But he had left something on the cleared desk.

"What?"

"Typewritten notes which were begun . . . begun with my name . . . loving phrases . . . notes ripped out of the machine although not thrown into the waste-paper basket. One of the notes starts: 'My darlingest Natasha, We (and by this I mean my friends and I) . . . ' and then trails off; another: 'My dearest, My love for you is . . . ' then nothing."

Deeriye looked at Natasha, then at Samawade, then at the electric stove, at the fridge whose buzzing sound irritated him: like a helicopter which never took off. He reminded himself that the house in which he woke up was unlike many in the neighbourhood: in the other houses, live coals were preserved in a bed of ashes; in this, Natasha switched the electricity on and off, made coffee or tea standing. He watched her pour herself a cup and offer one to Samawade who shook his head but went to the fridge for a bottle of soda of which he had a sip.

"Do you know who it was that called Mursal?" asked Deeriye.

Samawade translated.

"The voice was familiar but I don't know the man. I've spoken to this voice a number of times on the phone and know he is a good friend of Mursal's."

"Would you by any chance be able to put a name to the voice?"

"Somali. Jibriil Mohamed-Somali, I think."

She took the chair nearest Samawade, placed her hand on his head and played with his hair. He moved away slightly.

"Maybe there is nothing to worry about," said Deeriye through

Samawade who, it turned out, spoke for much longer, perhaps embellishing the translation.

"What worries me is . . . ," and she was silent.

"Yes?"

She indicated Samawade with her chin and said in Italian, which the child did not understand: *"Non siamo soli; c'é lui!'*

Whereupon Samawade requested she finish the sentence. "What is it that worries you? Come on."

But she wouldn't; not until Deeriye said that Samawade was old enough to understand. And then it came in stammered half-phrases: "You see, Mursal is . . . er . . . the only link . . . I am sorry . . . the most significant link I have with . . . this land; if it weren't for him, I would not have come here; if it weren't for him, I wouldn't have a child nor would I have left the profession . . . the career . . . the university teaching career I had been groomed for."

A pause. Then an argument ensued between her and Samawade, an argument which was conducted in English and which excluded Deeriye. There was pain on their faces: the child's and the mother's. And Deeriye so much wished he could reassure her that were Mursal to come to a disastrous end she would be cared for in the same loving manner as Mursal had done. Something else needed to be said, too, although this might have been what she and Samawade had argued about: that she had more links with the land than that. She had Samawade, a loving father-in-law, a loving sister-in-law.

Presently, he decided he was not going to make any more use of Samawade's translating capabilities; this was too complex for him. He wished Zeinab were here. . . . And lo and behold! In the doorway.

Chairs were abandoned, tensions melted, Samawade felt redundant and excluded as the two women hugged, whispered endearments to each other, indifferent to who else was there. Then they fell apart. Tea was offered to Zeinab: she accepted, took a chair, did not look at her father until much much later and when she did her look said something like: "Did I not always tell you this would happen?"

After a while, speaking to Deeriye, she continued accusingly: "Did you not hear him leave?"

He shook his head, no.

"Would you have done anything if you had?"

"No."

"You see!"

Silence. And there they were, thought Deeriye, a foursome together and healthy: thank God! There they were talking about *him* whose relationship with each reflected a fabric of dynamism. They were not now talking about Deeriye in the third person but Mursal who took the limelight: son in place of father; in the way Nadiifa had sought Mursal's assistance in reading and writing letters to him, Nadiifa a woman who did not know how to read or write but knew how to speak and Mursal who knew how to read and write and also how to understand her speech; and Natasha who could read and write but who to communicate with Deeriye had had to resort to using Samawade who spoke her language, she who didn't speak Somali well and therefore needed help. Is this not the dynamics of history?

"I was stopped a couple of times," said Zeinab, first in English then in Somali. Samawade decided that he was redundant and that his presence was not needed.

"Who stopped you?"

"Security, police – I don't know."

"Where?"

"At the entrance of the street leading here."

"What did they ask?"

"They flagged me down, asked me to get out of the car, show my ID, open my car-boot, declare if I was carrying any weapons; things like that. Then they let me leave."

"Do you think they know you are Mursal's sister?"

"I couldn't say."

Natasha appeared much more relaxed now that she had found Zeinab, to whom she could speak directly without being translated by her own child. Meanwhile, they heard the muezzin call all Muslims to prayer.

"Excuse me," said Deeriye. "I'll see you later."

"The muezzin calls," said Zeinab, "and you cannot *not* answer."

"Earnest praying is a vocation, my father used to say," Deeriye said.

"And is that what *my father* says?" she said.

He did not rise to her challenge. He said, "I will see you later, Natasha."

• • • • • • • • • • •

A long, solemn prayer was in order, he told himself.

So he said the Islamic transcendental unity a hundred thousand times, repeated the venerations and the professions of the faith again and again until he became one with the revealed word. And the fever was gone: he no longer saw fireflies of vertiginous pain in front of him.

He thanked God for the day's gifts, the evening's blessings, the morning's sunshine, dawn's greyness, the afternoon's long shadow: gifts from Him which the living must use sensibly. "Every breathing moment is a gift from you, o God, so is the thinking light which illumines the pathways a mind walks, a mind that wouldn't see anything if it weren't for you, o Lord, a mind that wouldn't understand or decipher anything unless You helped, o God! You, o God, are the creator of the night's darkness, who makes possible the nocturnal traffic which takes place, with angels appearing in one's dream, or Satan luring one away, You are the creator of the jinn in human form, speaking to one about lust and similar mortal desires. You are, o God, the convenor of the souls' meetings, and the angels and visions and the reflections which one's uncensored tongue speaks; forgive us our weaknesses, show them to us, o God, so that we may comprehend our strength. At the soul's meetings, o God, the pondering of such verbal baroque: these are but praises, they are but Your names, all ninety-nine of them. The souls rest during the night, thanks to You, o Lord, and they go to an assembly of souls, each of them joining her kind, the good ones keeping Your company, o Virtuous One, and the wicked ones Satan's, *acuudu billaah*! They converse as they praise You, the souls exchange notes and experiences with other souls from distant places who dwell in persons of different backgrounds, different races and cast of mind: but what are these to You, o God! Help us cope with our weaknesses, show Yourself to us every now and then, forgive us if, when feverish, we conjure up nebulous visions: when these cause us some disquiet, when these cause disturbances in our minds and lead us astray, help us, o God. The ways of the soul are mysterious and so are Yours. Make us wiser, make us understand, o God, the contradictions in which we find ourselves. We pray for Mahad, for Mukhtaar's soul, for Jibriil and for Mursal. Mahad: mad as a saint, blinded by the vision he saw; Mukhtaar: the epitome of self-sacrifice; Jibriil: a mysterious angel, conveying the Sacred Word; and Mursal (with whom he communicated by telephone): the Messenger, the one whose self-appointment as the Messenger is in no doubt."

Suddenly he stopped praying, for there was a great deal of activity and noise taking place in the kitchen and the rooms below. It seemed more children had arrived, perhaps Zeinab's and Dahaba's as well. In fact he could hear Dahaba telling Ataturk to stay quiet. Realizing he wouldn't be able to indulge himself in further prayers in tranquillity once they came up, he folded up his prayer-rug, hung it on the wall by the portrait-photographs none of which was his. Then he went and got the radio-cassette player and inserted a cassette: a Koranic recitation chanted by an Egyptian sheikh. He made himself as comfortable as he could and listened. A little later, despite not wanting to, he was thinking about politics, about Mursal's predicament, about the days and years he himself had spent in detention.

The road to prison, he thought, although arduous and trying, was not one he walked alone; nor did he feel lonely when walking it, for there remained with him such sweet thoughts of Nadiifa's companionship. Then many years later the full support of the people came in the form of messages he received in prison. The years preceding political Independence were hard to live through and Deeriye's prison-memoirs if ever written might have been described as "desolate," after Independence . . . with the new generation of young people, historical events were re-interpreted: it was only then that the significance of his deed became clear and his struggle and defiance became interpreted as of national importance. The (Italian) prison experience did not lock him away from the world, did not build fortified walls around him, did not insulate him, nor did detention make it difficult for him to get in touch with the *outside* world like the potential which is one's ambition once in prison, once it is dreamt, once it is envisioned, once it is imagined, the ambition which reflects or rather manifests itself in the actions of those *outside*, actions undertaken in solidarity with the heroes *inside*. It was prison which opened up a world which had been closed to him by virtue of his background and which might have remained unavailable to him were he to stay and live in the encampment in which he was born. The mere giving of a specific date and meaning to the year in which he was born forced upon him the need to understand and cope with the logic of *others*. He could still remember being asked three times the question: "What year were you born?" His answering that he was twenty-two or that he was born in 1351 of the hejira did not satisfy the questioner. Later, he learnt the importance of the year in which he was supposed to have been born: 1912. Corfield was killed, the Dervish movement was at the apex of its success; another important historical event (one wished the movements in the south, north and east of the continent were in touch with one another) was the birth of the African National Congress. The year 1909: Haji Omer, the Traitor, was born; and it was in this year that Abdullahi Shaxaari betrayed the cause of the Dervish by falsely producing a letter by which the Sayyid's mentor was supposed to have condemned the Sayyid's Jihaad as extremist terrorism. Which now reminded Deeriye of Napoleon's encounter with the learned men of Al-Azhar, who seemed mesmerized by Napoleon's immodest display of a warm reverence towards the Koran: first, the hard distrust in the stomachs of the Cairene melted; and once this happened, Napoleon could rule the country through a modicum of learned men and sheikhs who toed his political line. Is there no avoiding that one should belong in one camp or another? Is there no avoiding belonging on the *inside* or *outside* of this camp? And would Mursal go to prison if he were caught in the act of throwing grenades or whatever? And Mahad? Deeriye appreciated the essential difference between his own and, say, Mahad's detention: whereas Deeriye had had a new world made available to him, a world of international and national contradictions, Mahad and his friends had known and lived in this world – and therefore would feel isolated if thrown into detention and denied contact with the *outside* world, if denied the right to receive reading materials and so on.

But he did not *know* what Mursal had been up to, did he? He had suspicions – although one couldn't speak of these speculative suspicions as "true knowledge." Indeed it was he who didn't *really* want to know, lest the weight of this knowledge lay a heavier responsibility on his conscience. It was he who had accepted Mursal's moratorium on his underground activities; and when Zeinab insisted that Mursal spoke to them it was he who had encouraged Mursal not to divulge the dangerous secrets confided in him by, say, the movement if he were a member of such an organization. He didn't *know* what Mursal had been up to but his own conjecture was as good as having "true knowledge." Did he, Deeriye, know what he would do, if his son were hurt or caught planting a bomb? Would he, Deeriye, take revenge, would he kill? He was surprised to hear his own answer: "Yes." It almost frightened him and he was startled. Would he really? A voice in him said, "Why not!" He clocked his heart-beat. He timed the breathing-in and the breathing-out of his lungs: all normal. He concluded what had preceded with the saying thrice of the Islamic transcendental unity. He thanked God for the inner peace obtained along with the *modus vivendi* of his own condition. And. . . .

Then he started hearing the noise of the cassette being ejected. As he got up to change it, he heard Zeinab call out that she was coming up with a cup of something. He replaced the cassette but did not press the "play" button. He returned to his armchair by the window. He could see Yassin, the young miscreant, gathering pebbles. Would he cast them at him? Would he pelt him with pebbles? Deeriye moved away from the window and waited for Zeinab.

• • • • • • • • • • •

He had had a fear that Zeinab would bring with her not only a cup of something but some mind-shattering news. But he was determined he would demonstrate his strength not his weakness this time, he would display his total belief in his visions and in the visions Mursal and Mahad and Mukhtaar had also seen and for which they were ready to die.

Zeinab was in the room, having brought two cups and an assortment of cakes. Serving him graciously, she said, "How many spoons of sugar?" This told Deeriye who made the tea: Natasha. The maid, Dahaba, or even Zeinab would have made it the Somali way: the tea would be boiled together with the sugar. She stirred for him, passed a cup to him. "Cake?"

"Yes, please."

Someone had been to one of those Italian places to get this assortment of cakes. He chose a lemon-cake. But what if it contained a dash of liquor? It didn't matter. No amount of liquor mattered unless it made one feel drunk, one of the sheikhs he knew used to say. "Thanks."

She settled into position; he, likewise. They each sipped in silence. The noise downstairs was less chaotic: the children had gone outside to play, and Yassin, Deeriye could see when he craned his neck from where he was sitting, had re-entered their house.

"I've asked Samawade to go and get today's paper if it's out," she said.

"You mean it didn't come out this morning as usual?"

"Yes. And that's what happens whenever something important in the life of the nation takes place. The paper is held from distribution, the General's counsel is sought and he gives directions, instructions and editorial advice. Always."

Zeinab's sweeping hands, a gesture out of tune with what she was saying: there was something about the way she talked, careful, slow, as though she was too mean to invest in her thoughts.

"How is Natasha taking it?"

"She is in tears. She feels very isolated, excluded; feels, rightly, that no one tells her enough – not in any case when things are happening."

"But we know nothing, do we?"

"We know more than she does."

"Yes, yes, but . . . . "

"She understands things late, she confessed to me; with her extra senses, understands, for instance, that every Italian, since he or she does not believe in the state as an institution, becomes a paying member of a secret society or a Mafia fraternity; the Somali doesn't believe in the logic of the state working justly for all, regardless of clan, and therefore the Somali becomes a *dia*-paying member of his or her own clan. She argues thus: one is secret although universally known (the Italians' membership of secret societies); the other (the Somalis' *dia*-paying membership) is something universally accepted but which nobody nowadays is willing to support *officially:* it's never done."

"Does she know what she wants to do?"

"You mean if something dreadful were to happen to Mursal? She would love to *save* Samawade, if that is the word, *save* him by taking him away: rather in the way Muslims believe that Christ was *saved* by the divine hand before he was crucified."

"I see."

"I wouldn't know what to do if I were her."

"From what I understand," said Deeriye, "her love resides in Mursal, and his going away creates in her a certain emptiness which not even her son let alone you or myself can fill; but if she were to go home, if she were to be with her own parents, her own society, her own kind . . . well, she might fill the emptiness of her life. It hurts me to think what will become of her without Mursal if she decides to stay here. *I wouldn't know what to do with her. Or with myself.* Love her, yes. But . . . !"

It amazed him how confident he appeared in the face of the whirlwinds of disaster about to sweep them off their feet; it amazed him all the more that the thought of Natasha without Mursal frightened him so: he didn't know how he would react if confronted with that prospect. The tension would in the end destroy him. Perhaps he would be able to cope. Certainly life wouldn't be the same. But he did not seem worried about what Zeinab might say or do; he didn't think she would feel as shattered as he. She was saying now:

"I saw Uncle Elmi-Tiir yesterday evening and asked him about his and the clansmen's calling on the General. He said that all is well so far as one can tell and the General suggested either of the following: that he will come and see you himself or that you use a telephone number which he says you have been given; also that Rooble will be freed as soon as the noise has died down."

"I wonder why he wants to visit me. Or why I should telephone him. What do you think?"

"It gives him power over you. Either you telephone and go or else he'll call on you."

"Power, what power?"

"You do not know how or when he will come and that keeps you in suspense, keeps you wondering if it will be tonight or tomorrow or the next morning – and the anxiety will worsen your asthmatic condition. Unless you call him and he decides whether to see you or not."

"But I am not going to wait for him."

"That is not true and you know it. I remember – when was it? – a couple of days ago when you and Mursal were arguing about it all day and when you said you would see the devil to get your friend Rooble released from prison."

"Did I really say that?"

"Yes."

"Twin tensions were behind this perhaps."

"Twin tensions?"

"The fact that I wanted to defend a position however infantile and that I wanted at any cost to have Rooble released. After all, Mursal would do anything to free his friend, anything, even endanger his own life to achieve this end: which is what he's done now; although it does sound as though I did not want him to do this . . . I mean there is something selfish in each of us and we hold those we love close to our own hearts, afraid that if we let them go we may never see them again. Do you understand what I mean?"

"I think I do," said Zeinab.

"And the twin tensions in turn become twin necessities."

"In particular when a third party is introduced," said Zeinab.

"I don't think I understand," said Deeriye.

"Love and power: for instance. You need someone to receive your love; you need someone to show your power to. In most situations, the two never coexist. In other words, you cannot love those upon whom you exercise full power, nor can you use all the power you have upon those whom you love. You need a third party. Hence, the tensions that Natasha feels towards us, the fact that Mursal's absence severs the link she has with us, with Somalia, and this forces her to come to the insane decision that she can *save* the whole thing by taking Samawade away. Do you understand what I am saying?"

He was impressed, and so was she. Theories, philosophical and political theories. His daughter was the one person who usually never listened to his "invented nonsense": was the one to put his life before ideas, whereas she was one who immediately she entered asked: "How are you?" meaning: "How is your asthmatic condition?" meaning: "Have you taken the tablets? Have you followed your doctor's instructions?" He used to say that Mursal's cosmetic politics was preferable to

Zeinab's: "Pulse, give it here." Not today. She heard him out, patient, calm, and did not play the role of doctor or daughter; did not, except when they were in the kitchen just after she had walked in, let it be known that she had been right all along about Mursal's moratorium on his secret activities, right about what would happen if he wasn't kept in constant check.

"I was thinking on the way here that something dreadful must have happened. You see, it was Natasha who called and she just kept repeating Mursal's name again and again, inarticulate, saying nothing else," said Zeinab.

"What did you think?" said Deeriye.

"I thought, God forbid, but I thought . . . well . . . there is a precedent, isn't there? A father who kills his son for not listening to the patriarchical advice of his parent. Mukhtaar . . . I thought . . . and Sheikh-Ibrahim . . . my God!"

"You disappoint me," he said.

And she went on, "I thought, what am I going to do if the old man has gone mad and said that he'll activate the telephone made available to him? I didn't think for an instant that Mursal had disappeared."

Deeriye repeated what he had said before, "You disappoint me."

Then something untoward, something unbargained for, occurred: she went and kissed him on the forehead, placed her hands on his knees and sought his forgiveness. Silence: weighty and unbreakable, with tears welling in his eyes, about to overflow like tributaries during a tropical downpour. He looked away, wiped away the trickle which had wet his cheeks but held his breath in check, feeling that something was coming: perhaps an attack. Nothing came. And he heard her say:

"Natasha has apologized to me for something she said to you this morning. She said she didn't mean it and she wanted you to know that."

"I can't remember her saying anything worth apologizing for."

"She wants you to know that Mursal is not her only link with this country and its people and that all the links will not be severed completely if something were to happen to him. It won't be the same. But there is a link. There is you, she says. There's Samawade. There is me," said Zeinab.

The sun erected a construction of rays reminiscent of a scaffolding, and the framework of the dark and white stripes engulfed them both as she reached him the tray. She smiled.

"Did you see anything in your . . . er . . . vision, dream?" she asked.

He pretended not to have heard what she said; he wanted her to repeat it so he would sense if there was a tinge of sarcasm in her voice. She repeated it. He was pleased there was no sarcasm in it. He answered, "There were enough hints to suggest something had been afoot but I did not *see* Mursal's disappearance."

"Enough hints? What hints?"

"I won't go into them now if you don't mind," he said. He might have told her what he had seen if he was certain she was honest and sincere in wanting to know. What would her reaction be if he told her she had been in his dream, an adult – a departure from the usual, for he used to see her as a child. She would think he was mad.

"Aunt Zeinab?" It was Samawade.

"Come up, come," Zeinab shouted.

Not only Samawade but all the other children arrived, chattery, and also pompous. They attacked the cakes and each took away one and there was nothing left. Zeinab opened her mouth to say something but Deeriye raised his hand and told her no. She said to Samawade, drowning the banter of the other children: "Where is the newspaper?"

"It is not on the stands yet. Maybe in an hour or two, the shopkeeper said. I'll go back later if you want me to."

"I'll go myself," she said, adding: "Locusts, not children. Look at that. And you let them do what they please," she said to Deeriye. "They have no discipline, these children." She went out, leaving behind her the cups and the trays she had brought up.

• • • • • • • • • • •

Samawade sat, propped up on the floor against the armchair, patient, waiting, pleading with the others to be quiet and listen to the story Grandfather Deeriye was about to tell. "Go on, Grandfather," he encouraged. Samawade did not appear perturbed by his father's disappearance and now Deeriye recalled that Samawade had said, "He will be with us sooner or later. Just like you. Some of us have to go to prison or die for a principle or a cause so that others, whether they are aware of it now or not, whether they are grateful for it or not, can live a decent life. Don't worry, he will come home again. And who knows, his soul may enter and give life to a warrior in Zululand or Palestine." It was incredible how one could indoctrinate a child into thinking what one liked, make a Mursal out of a Samawade; it was unbelievable how one could burden a child with the weight of history, garland them with the fruits of this or that past, show how they should take the side of the injured, the humiliated and the oppressed. Was this what Mursal was like as a young boy? Was this what he used to say, looking serious and politically minded when the other children of his own age played *dhundhuumashaw* or *shanlax* or other games? Samawade when Yassin had struck Deeriye said, incensed, that he would kill him (Yassin), Yassin who was himself the product of another political thinking: that of the tribalist, a thinking that was antagonistic to Deeriye's and Mursal's mature philosophies.

"Go on, Grandfather."

"Please," said Deeriye. "Not now. Not today."

"Don't tell us you can't think of any!" said Ataturk sarcastically.

"Now, now," said Jamaal, "be careful how you speak to Grandfather."

"What is it to you, anyway?" said Ataturk.

Cantar and Sheherezade intervened. They were both harsh like their mother, they shouted at Jamaal and Kemaal, one at a time, and then suggested that if they wanted to fight it out, they should go out and let Grandfather tell them the story in peace.

"Why don't you tell us one, Sheherezade?" said Ataturk.

"Quiet, now, quiet," said Samawade.

And they fell quiet. They moved around for a while, took a long time to settle. The sun, young and powerful, was in Deeriye's eyes and he used his right hand as a shield as he watched each find himself or herself a place. How he loved them! Lovely children! It was sad they did not figure in the inventory of his visions. But they were part of a future he didn't think he would live into and he couldn't imagine what their lives would be like. Would they, twenty to twenty-five years from now, resort to the same tactics as Mursal: kill a tyrant or be killed?

"Go on with the story, Grandfather," said Samawade.

Sheherezade said, "Samawade once told me one in which there is a blind old man who is wise." She turned to Samawade and asked him if he could remember. He nodded. "Shall we ask Grandfather to tell us that then?" she inquired. Samawade said, yes. But Ataturk wanted another. He did not like blind old men and their stories.

Now Cantar, his voice firm and strong, said, getting up, "You shut up or else. . . . "

Deeriye intervened. He would tell the story, he would tell the story.

Silent, he was slightly touched with the feverish mood of speech although his lips did not move; and Samawade, Cantar and Sheherezade's eyes, eager and innocent and beautiful, were preciously untouched with any tinge of memories other than that of what they thought at that instant. When Deeriye had told him the story the first time, Samawade confessed that he identified the wise old man in the tale with him, the things he spoke of in the tale as the very things which seemed to engage his grandfather's mind all the time; the things the old man in the story touched were those Deeriye's body came into tactile relationship with when he emerged from one of those feverish attacks or from one of his naps. Such a wise little man, had thought Deeriye. And not blind, thank God. He wondered, seeing the innocence in their eyes, if it crossed their minds that Mursal might be in some kind of trouble; that he might have created a political upheaval in having disappeared. But they were children; they lived their lives, and not history.

"Will you tell the story?" said Ataturk's impatient voice.

"Right this moment," said Deeriye, and. . . .

• • • • • • • • • • •

Once upon a time, there was an old man who was blind and who, while travelling one day, sat down to make water; but when he got up could not find his walking-stick anywhere. He thought that perhaps the devil had come and taken it away to tempt him and so he continued his journey without a walking-stick to guide him or tell him where not to tread or which side of the road was bushy, which thorny and which was clear and safe. To his enormous disappointment, he discovered that it was not easy to walk now that the device by which he knew his moves was no longer available to him. But never mind. He walked and walked and walked, stumbling on a bushy shrub now and again, tripping upon a low shrub every now and then, he walked until he came to a dwelling. However, just before he managed to stop with a view to taking a break, now that there were human beings in the vicinity and since he was very exhausted, he stumbled on something: now he might never have touched this thing with his own hands if he had the walking-stick to hand. And he was so surprised he shouted excitedly and said to a passer-by to please stop, stop and tell him something.

"What is your question, Old Man?" said the passer-by.

"What, in the name of Allah, is this thing that I have stumbled upon? It seems to me like a mound of dirt or earth but it feels different when I touch it with my bare hands."

"It is an ant-hill," said the passer-by.

"An ant-hill, indeed," said the blind old man and reached out to make sure it was still there. He took a handful from the mound of earth, turned it in his hand, squeezed it until his closed fists spurted sand at either side and at the knuckles, felt it as best he could with a blind man's sensitivity and was silent for a long time. Then he said, "And pray do answer my stupid question, if I may be so indiscreet, and please forgive."

"What is your question?"

The blind old man touched the ant-hill again. He did not immediately ask a question but repeated to himself, "It is a marvel indeed. A marvel of marvels. It is very large, many thanks be to He Who is a lot bigger and larger than all we know, have touched or ever set eyes on. Pardon, pardon, I am being very indiscreet. I am sorry."

"Your question, what is your question?"

"My question? I've clean forgotten. Now I was saying it is a wonder of wonders, a real wonder of wonders: this life. But what was my question?"

Whereupon, the passer-by volunteered some information, basing his answer upon imaginary questions he thought the blind old man might have asked. He said, "Do you know who raises this mound of earth?"

"Allah, of course."

"Allah, of course, for Allah is the creator of all," stammered the passer-by. "But I meant . . . ," and his voice trailed off.

"I am sorry. Tell me who makes it," said the blind man.

"Speaking in a commonplace, trivial sense, of course. . . . "

"Speaking thus, who makes it? We know that the Almighty is the only

Creator in the . . . er . . . most accomplished sense of the term. But who makes this mound in the trivial, everyday sense?"

"An insect called aboor!"

"Aboor, *did you say?"*

"An insect small as any member of the ant family."

"And it has made a mound this size? A wonder, a marvel, may God be thanked for that. A small insect which constructs a mound this big."

"And do you know what with?"

"I suspect the information you are about to give me will startle me as has the rest of the new discovery. Let me sit down for it. There. Pray tell me, I am ready. What with?"

"Sand and saliva, her own saliva."

"Sand and saliva indeed! Now if that is not a marvel worth hearing about I don't know any other as marvellous, save God's and the Prophet's names to which we pay due reverence. May His name be blessed. Amen!"

"Amen!"

"A marvel of marvels, indeed," the blind old man repeated.

"And do you know when?"

"When?"

"After nightfall."

"Now that is the greatest wonder I have heard in a long, long time. I, a blind man, large as the mound which is raised by an ant out of her saliva mixed with sand; and she sees at night, works after nightfall and builds this impossible structure. That is a marvel of marvels indeed."

And the man who told the blind man the story of how the aboor *constructs an ant-hill from her own saliva after nightfall helped him find a walking-stick. The blind man thanked him and went on his way, saying that the greatest wonders of the world is God himself – only the second greatest miracle was man!*

• • • • • • • • • • •

Later. Zeinab had returned with the daily newspaper. By then, the tension in the house had reached its highest crescendo, with Natasha losing her temper once or twice as she shouted at the children for making unnecessary noise. Zeinab. Natasha. Deeriye. Amina. Medina. Dahaba.

Sagal. Ladan. Ebla. These were in the kitchen. The children had been sent out to play. The day outside was sunny bright. The newspaper made the rounds, each read it in silence and then passed it on to the person seated next: anti-clockwise. Until it reached Natasha. She said she didn't know enough Somali to understand what it said. Would somebody kindly translate for her? The others looked at each other.

"This is the government's version of what has occurred," Zeinab said.

"Yes, yes, but what is the government's version?" asked Natasha.

Zeinab looked about her, looked in the faces of those whose eyes were trained on her, sought encouragement and help, although she didn't get either. She drew on the store of her own strength, careful to say nothing that might disturb Natasha. Deeriye was thinking: was this a perverted image his own mind and eye screened upon a reality so familiar by now: women with no men; and behind them, dependent upon them for provender, for fodder: the elderly and children? With Soyaan dead and Loyaan exiled; Koschin reduced to a vegetable; Samater in detention; with Mahad mysteriously held in one of those underground prisons, perhaps the same prison where Ibrahim Siciliano was being kept; with Mukhtaar killed; Mursal vanished and Jibriil. . . .

"The paper says that the Security Services came upon and surprised a man who was trying to plant a time-bomb not far from the residence of the General. The man was told to drop everything and to raise his hands above his head. But the man, mad that he was (I am translating the text directly), attempted to pull a revolver out of one of his pockets. Before he managed that, the man was hit in the stomach and he collapsed and fell and pretended he was dead. When one of the security officials went to check, the man pulled the trigger and shot the official. Whereupon, the other security official showered him with so many shots it became impossible to determine what the body's sex had been or whether it was human in the first place."

Natasha's eyes: watchful and fixed and waiting. Zeinab continued:

"The incident was reported to the Security Services HQ. An ambulance was sent to take the dead bodies to hospital for identification. It was not difficult to determine who the martyred Security official was (a special burial ceremony will be held in his honour the day after tomorrow, to be attended by the General himself) but who *the other* was no one has any idea."

"Someone said, "Come. Tell her the end of the piece."

Zeinab said, "I am trying to translate. Which is why it is taking me a long time to read it. Or does someone else wish to try it?"

Sagal said, "Just tell her it is not Mursal."

At the mention of Mursal's name, sharp swords of silence assailed all those present: most of them shifted in their seats as though after all this time something began to prick just then. Natasha finally said, "Do continue, please," the tone of her voice level, her expression almost religiously solemn.

"The *other* was named a few hours later. (On his body they found a letter addressed to someone whose name began with the initial M, like the letter of evidence a suicide plants in the vicinity of his corpse.) His name is Jibriil Mohamed-Somali. To all those who knew him he was a good-for-nothing man," she continued reading, "a man who had once been a most trusted army officer, with the rank of major but had been dismissed from the service because of his excessive drinking. So far, it is believed he was working alone and not in collaboration with any dissident group either inside or outside of the country."

Cold sweat had broken on Natasha's face. Her hand made as though to wipe it away, but fell short; or rather, hung in mid-air. "Nothing about Mursal?" she asked.

They all started at the shrill of the telephone. Natasha jumped up to answer it. But it stopped ringing. Before she managed to return to her chair, it rang again. Then it stopped after two rings. A little later, it rang: three rings. She *knew* who it was: Mursal. Where was he? How could she get rid of all these people? She would very much like to have a private talk with him. Where was he?

Deeriye said he would go: it was time for one of his solemn prayers. The others, save Medina who stayed by Natasha and Dahaba who had made it her job to keep Zeinab company, left.

TEN

What's Your Name, Jaalle?

The telephone rang five minutes to the hour four times. Every time Natasha picked it up, it went dead. It rang precisely an hour later, three rings then dead on being answered. Natasha was going insane; Zeinab was censorious, saying: "If he is afraid to go ahead, why doesn't he simply come home, good little boy that he is? Why doesn't he?" The others had gone; the children out of the way like any discomfort. And Deeriye alone, in his room, was frightened.

Fear was the no-man's-land his thoughts had led him to. He was afraid of his own reactions: and that worried him greatly. He was a star made pale by the brightness of a twelve-day-old moon – or like a moon grazing with a herd of clouds in broad daylight, lustreless. It dawned on him (and not for the first time) that he was in no danger any more, that he was not worth arresting, not worth reckoning with. After all, he was sick, with his condition worsening; it had been predicted more than once by rumour-mongers like Cigaal that he would die any day soon. He was a man already in his tomb, a tomb of indifference which needn't be dug up to find out if its occupant was still breathing. Was it not high time he did something heroic to prove them wrong? Disorder. Discredit. Disclaim. Dissociate. Disown. Disband. Divide. Disunite. Do everything by a designed order. Rooble and Mahad disowned by their clan, clan members who were tracked down and told they violated the no-right-of-assembly degree. Mukhtaar dead: murdered. Jibriil: dead body discovered. Mursal?

He remembered he had been to Mursal's study to tidy it – just in case of a raid, in the event of a purge; he had ransacked the drawers, hidden some of the documents he thought the Security would be after, found and read in haste Soyaan's only surviving Memorandum (Mursal had written *"Per un eventuale distribuzione/pubblicazione"*). Then the list of the members of the organization, the names of those who belonged to the movement ten young men and one woman had founded together. In alphabetical order, the list read: Ahmed-Wellie; Jibriil; Koschin; Mahad; Medina; Mukhtaar; Mursal; Samater; Siciliano and Soyaan. Deeriye knew them all except Jibriil and Siciliano, knew them personally, knew how they thought, had dialogued with each of them separately and had known, in one way or another, what phase they were going through: but he had never imagined they were an organized group as such. (Neither did all the members know of one another. Each person knew the one other person who was in the same cell. Although two of them knew who the others were and these two, namely Soyaan and after his death Medina, took assigned jobs and was a de facto head.) He did not find it hard to recall that Soyaan, Jibriil and Mukhtaar had shaken hands with death heroically. Was it not high time he himself did something *heroic* to prove them wrong? Then he choked on a thought which crossed his mind, a thought which surprised and at the same time frightened him: that he should look for the service revolver he once saw hidden in Mursal's study and, if necessary, use it to "vindicate justice," not his son or friends – yes, vindicate justice. Immediately he realized the seriousness of "Satan's" suggestion, Deeriye sought refuge in the name of God although this didn't last long. Expletives. Imperatives. Don't *they* create a disorder, don't *they* discredit, don't *they* make others disclaim, disown and dissociate from those one feels closest to? Don't *they* disband, disunite and divide? Don't *they?* Samater, Siciliano (the former once a minister of state) and now Mahad were being held in detention; Medina and Koschin were in varying degrees rendered disabled: Koschin half-paralysed and Medina (rumour had it) affected with insomnia which was a result of a self-afflicted paranoia – but to Deeriye, she looked well, level-headed and a very likable person as always; and now Mursal? Fate still unknown and dependent on what? Not those telephone calls, he hoped. For those suggested nervousness of a kind he didn't wish to associate with Mursal; telephone calls which appeared to originate from someone desperate to get a message through but frightened to deliver the very message. Which was why Deeriye himself was frightened; of his own reactions.

Frightened? But why? And why of his own reactions? Whenever the telephone rang and then stopped, Deeriye came closer to having one of those wicked seizures. What he was frightened of was that he would eventually come round to the decision to answer the telephone himself, make contact with Mursal and say, "Come, my son. You've done your share. Let me take over. Just come home, come back to your Samawade and your Natasha, let me deal with it." Did that mean that the son couldn't and wouldn't go all the way, as far as the father had? Why, for example, would he be tempted to answer the telephone now when he had never viewed the apparatus which conveyed *messages* and *voices* from distant places with anything short of suspicion and disrespect? (He remembered the day he answered the telephone: a message for Mursal from Mukhtaar, a message about Mahad's failed assassination attempt.) Mursal never could bear any physical pain; had carried around a dead tooth in his mouth for months on end when a child, afraid to show it to an adult and have it pulled out: he talked about the day he had been beaten by his teacher as the day on which he became certain he was definitely against corporal punishment of any kind. All that philosophical talk about private and public justice! What could happen if Deeriye made contact and said, "Mursal, my son, come and mind your wife and child and leave politics to us . . . ?" Then what? Did Deeriye not always believe that Mursal, by virtue of his marriage to a foreign woman, was the last person a movement would field? Rightly or wrongly, this was definitely a wise position to take in the circumstances: otherwise, Natasha's name was likely to attract or give adverse publicity to the motives of a movement. In other words, the General's régime would bank on that and conclude that because Natasha was who she was (an American and a Jew), the Americans and Israelis were behind Mursal's move. Deeriye, however, could bring all that to an end. He could pick up the telephone, make contact with Mursal, help him through his coming-home-as-a-good-boy steps. Then, he could hang up and dial the General and request to be received as soon as possible. And then what? Then with the service revolver hidden, go, meet the General: and kill. What? "Yes, kill," said a voice inside of him. "Yes, kill not to avenge his son but to vindicate justice." Aaah! That tranquillity came in the nature of a whisper with the divine and a short but solemn prayer. But the thought of killing and vindicating justice wouldn't leave him alone.

What immodest proposals!

Now he was overrun by a torrent of worries and what-ifs. . . . What if the person phoning was not Mursal but somebody else whose intention was to set in motion a series of suspicions and activities so as to bring forth all clues which might eventually lead to Natasha's (or Deeriye's?) trying to make contact? Then under safe-conduct of this contact, the Security would discover what he might be up to. What if Mursal were trying to distract everybody by somehow attracting this excessive attention? What if he had already left the country? What if it were somebody else trying to communicate the sad news that Mursal had died in the explosion which had disfigured Jibriil's corpse? Yes, what if he were dead? Or what if . . . ? What if . . . ?! Nervous, agitated, frightened: he decided to go down to Mursal's study to save the salvageable. Should he call Natasha, consult Zeinab, and seek their advice as to what should be hidden away from the eyes of the curious, the suspicious, what should be destroyed, what papers or photographs should be torn to shreds and thrown into the waste-paper basket or burnt? Or should he consult someone else, say Medina? What if, indifferent as he should be to relations of blood or marriage, he were to solicit Medina's comment on all this, Medina (Deeriye saw the list) who had belonged to the same underground movement as he, the only woman and *(therefore?)* the only person whom the General wouldn't condescend to taking seriously – yes, what if . . . ?!

Mursal! Dearest Mursal! What must I do?

Deeriye wished he could communicate to him his willingness to do anything to alleviate his pain – pain being what Mursal feared most; Deeriye wished he could tell him somehow that although he wasn't present when Mursal lost his first tooth, or when he was being circumcised or subjected to any of those painful operations – he was there today, the day of decision-making, the day Mursal tried to cap his life with the heroic star of having done as much for the nation as his father had done. . . .

He got up. He was decided now. He would go, steal his way to Mursal's study and do what he must do: alone.

Once inside the study, he went about his business quietly. He opened and closed drawers, selected documents and put a pile of them to one side. Photographs: many of them, portraits of Mursal, Natasha, Zeinab, Samawade, each of the other children, and one large print of a photograph of Nadiifa taken a year before her death; and a group photograph in which a few members of the movement appeared holding hands; and a larger print of Deeriye's portrait dated 24 November 1977 and with the inscription: *The day Jigjiga fell!* He took the group photograph, he recognized Mursal, Medina and Samater but before he had given himself time to study it, his eyes fell on the service revolver. He picked it up: the weapon felt so heavy Deeriye thought it would kill, he who had never shot a weapon. He walked to the standing mirror and was studying himself in it, now he was potentially armed, when another face, alive, half-smiling, half-querying, appeared there as well. The face became Zeinab's voice: but not before Deeriye had given himself time to steel himself against her sharpened tongue. Trembling a little, behaving as though innocent of any crime, furtive of gesture, quiet of voice, he pretended he didn't hear her. He said, "What are you doing here?"

Deeriye went and stood by the swivel-chair with which he played: the squeak could be heard in this tense situation. He neither hid nor unnecessarily showed off the service revolver which he now wore in the same way as a Yemeni bedouin is arrayed in daggers. Were they both there for the same reason? Did each come to look for an heirloom of viewpoints, profligate opinions which once belonged to the secret life of Mursal? Had they better not wait until they knew what had become of him? But anyway what was *she* doing there?

"I'm looking for one or two documents," she said.

"Documents, what documents?"

She closed the door behind her and said: "An inventory of names of the members of an underground organization, an organization with no name. Mursal was a member of that organization. Medina. Soyaan. Samater. Siciliano. Mukhtaar."

"Was or is? Did you say Mursal is or was?"

She corrected herself. "I am sorry, I meant is."

"Right. And how do you know about this document?" he said, holding the documents he had selected in one hand and the service revolver in the other – hiding neither.

The door opened, and, before she had answered his question, another face appeared in the mirror, this time a startled face: Natasha's. Her presence, in effect, decided for Deeriye and Zeinab: they made up a story to explain why they were in Mursal's study, a story which they suspected Natasha wouldn't believe. Then Zeinab, perhaps because she could think of nothing to do or say, suggested they had afternoon tea together. Deeriye said he would join them in the kitchen once he had put the revolver away in a safe place and had locked Mursal's study.

Poised to the puzzled look on Zeinab and Deeriye's faces, Natasha spoke at length and in fury about the fact that she felt excluded from the plots and conspiracies taking place right in "her" own house, plots and conspiracies which concerned her as much as the rest of the family. Why, she said, addressing Deeriye, did they both fight day in day out, year in and year out, against being moved around like pieces of furniture: he, an old man, reduced to being dependent on others, virtually homeless but for his children's; a man who had spoken contemptuously of "cosmetic politics;" who didn't want obstacles removed from his way but wished to confront them, deal with them himself, come to terms with Yassin's rascality, Cigaal's unneighbourliness; a man who dissociated himself from the treacherous perfidies of his peers, stipended chieftains toeing the line of the authorities that paid them a monthly pittance as "peace-keepers;" a man who said proudly again and again that he loved his daughter-in-law, a white Jew, just as he would love her if she were a Somali Muslim, and who drew a distinction between Jews anywhere and Jews in Israel – as if it mattered! Then she spoke directly, without need of an interpreter, to Zeinab.

Yes. Was Zeinab not a woman who understood and who behaved lovingly and demonstrated her affectionate sympathy and love: by a single gesture, a mere touch! A feminist, full of an extraordinary enthusiasm for women's causes. But was it possible for Natasha ever to become the cornerstone of her adopted family, into which she had married and whose son she loved? Now, now, calm down, please.

What was her complaint? She believed she received pompous civilities, a great many of these, but when it came to deciding on her and

Mursal's life together and in the family bosom, there was a retreat, a withdrawal of affections; Zeinab and Deeriye would whisper in corners, speak softly about her (in the same manner that Zeinab and Mursal spoke about Deeriye when he had a bad night: in the third person, as though he were deaf; to him: as though he were a child, that's it, a *child!*). "But I am not a child," she finally shouted, feeling she had not, after all, expressed herself as well as she had thought "I'm not an outsider."

"No one said you are," said Zeinab.

"You don't have to say it. It's clear," said Natasha.

"It's the tension, Natasha. Everything will be all right, said Zeinab. "You will see. It's the tension we all feel, what with everything that's happening here."

"There," she pointed an accusing finger rising, a gesture which puzzled Deeriye for he didn't quite understand all that was being said, and Samawade looked upset to see them shout at each other like that. "It will be all right?" challenged Natasha. "You think I am a child? Mursal said precisely that and used the same sort of tone one employs when addressing a child. 'It will be all right.' Deeriye used to say that when he heard someone speak about *peace,* he was tempted to reach for a gun. When I hear 'It will be all right' spoken in that tone of condescension, I feel like reaching for one myself."

Deeriye, having asked Samawade to translate what she had said, was shocked beyond repair. He wished he could extinguish the fire of hate before it drew on Satan's and became the fire the sparrow picked up and took into its hut, the fire which burnt everything in sight, killed everyone and created a famine worse than the one the Italians had decreed should be the lot of their Somali subjects during the colonial era. But what could he do? He had Natasha and Zeinab's chatter in the background, their voices alternating in unceasing argument.He hadn't the language to speak to Natasha directly; he had to use an interpreter, there was no avoiding that. He wished he had learnt the language so he could make her understand what was on his mind.

He tried to say something.

But Zeinab and Natasha would hear nothing aside from what they were saying to each other, the verbal crescendo of their irrationality too deafening, too loathsome to bear. His left hand went to his throat: he thought perhaps an attack, perhaps not; the other hand he placed on his chest. The fear was like a shadow passing overhead. He saw Natasha rise, gesticulate, heard her speak with a vehemence he had never associated with her. She towered above them all, they were the rubble upon which her angry words trampled.

Deeriye rose slowly, moved in her direction, his stride slow and deliberate, and when Natasha's voice fell to a mesmerizing diminuendo, he suddenly surprised everybody, including himself, by taking both her hands in his and planting kisses on them; then he grabbed her by the knees and said in the most humble tone: *"Ti chiediamo perdono, ti chiediamo!"* For a long, long time no one moved or said anything. Deeriye rose only when Natasha helped him to. Then they hugged. He felt like one who had said a most divine prayer.

• • • • • • • • • • •

Dusk. The sun, red like the blood of sacrifice, hung in the heavens but darkness hadn't descended yet. Deeriye was sitting up in his favourite armchair, suspended between sleep and wakefulness. He could hear things, sense movements, feel if someone came up into his room, could register any change however small. Now he could hear a man and a woman talking on the landing of the stairway. The man's voice suggested that of Elmi-Tiir, the woman's Zeinab; and the man was saying, "He is a saint, he really is." This made Deeriye open his eyes in wonder and ask himself who "the saint" was. But he did not get up, nor did he call to Elmi-Tiir or Zeinab. He listened and was surprised to hear this: "A saint among mortals." No name; this saint could have been anybody: Mursal, Mahad, Rooble, Khaliif the madman. . . . Then Zeinab described at length what Deeriye had done, how humble he looked when he fell on his knees in supplication today, how she (Zeinab) was not at first sure of her own reactions to this but later resolved, "Yes, this was *saintly,* after all."

It was curious Deeriye felt so embarrassed he wanted to call Elmi-Tiir away so he would bring this ridiculous talk to an end. However, he was in no mood to do so; moreover, he had not the energy. And Elmi-Tiir was saying before long that he could not think of any of Deeriye's peers who would do anything as saintly as that; that no one among them was humble enough to bow and "hold the knees" of a woman, let alone seek forgiveness of a woman – who was white and a Jew at that. "But he does not think it is below him. Nadiifa, your mother – God bless her soul – used to tell me how he would spend nights on end by her bed as she slept, seated by her bed in postures of prayer, for her, for himself, for the country. And he would wash her feet and wipe them dry. She used to be frightened someone would walk in on them and find them thus. 'What would people think?' she asked. A saint, I said, no doubt about it!"

As Deeriye readied himself to shout to Elmi-Tiir, fortunately someone else – Samawade, it transpired later – interrupted the conversation and wondered if they knew whether or not Deeriye had woken up. Elmi-Tiir said he would go and find out.

"I am up and awake, Elmi. Greetings. Enter. Welcome."

"Do not rise, please do not rise," he said, coming to the door.

Elmi-Tiir moved about purposefully: he put his armchair where he could avoid looking at the setting sun. But before that, he brought the radio and said he had heard it play the *Samadiidow* song, a song Radio Mogadiscio generally played whenever somebody was about to be executed. Elmi-Tiir appeared conscious of possible reactions this might draw from Deeriye but he provided the information with such calm he was not surprised his brother-in-law did not show how upset he was by the news. Although in the end there was a shortlived shudder in the air.

"And who was it for, do you think?" asked Deeriye.

"I don't know."

"You haven't heard anything, have you?"

"There are rumours and rumours, nothing but rumours."

"Have you been to Baar Novecento?"

"Afrah was there, so were the others, wondering how you were. No one outside this house, as far as I can tell, knows anything about Mursal. I hadn't heard about his disappearance until I came here."

"What did Afrah say? Did he offer you some *misinformation?*"

"Now that I think of it, yes."

"What? Misinform me."

"The General is ill."

"They always say that about dictators, don't they? The Spanish made similar wishes when Franco did not die, Ethiopians prayed for Haile Selassie's death, and now Somalis for the General's; if I remember correctly, they've been saying the same things the past five or so years. They say: he doesn't sleep and suffers from incurable insomnia; he has cancer; he has syphilis; he has VD; and he will die soon. Everybody makes that mad wish. I don't. I wish him the best of health. I wish him a long life. But . . . ," and his index finger was out, challengingly.

"Yes?"

"I do not spare those who do not spare my life and those of my children and my friend. Although it must be said that I have less respect for those who have served *him* and allowed him to humiliate them by humouring him, by clapping applauses of praises and by hiding in the safety of a clowning crowd."

"I know. You've said that before."

"I am afraid I may say it again."

The evening's shadows created a semblance of dawn: and Deeriye yawned. Was it evening or was it early morning?

"And there was something else," said Elmi-Tiir.

"What?"

"Rooble and Mahad have both been moved to Laanta Buur. How Afrah came by that information, I haven't the slightest idea."

"I wonder why they are playing the *Samadiidow* song then? Wasn't it first played on the morning when Gaveyre, Dheel and Caynaanshe were publicly executed, the first time in this nation's history anyone was publicly executed? I was shocked. I trembled the whole day. I prayed and prayed and prayed: too late. I was in a bus when I heard, coming back from Afgoi, I remember. I had asked for an appointment to speak to him, I mean the General. My request for an audience was granted but it was made to coincide with another event, totally unrelated, that was to occur a few days later. What was I going to say to him if I met him? Oh, I was going to tell him it was beastly to kill anyone for his or her opinions and we Somalis were known for tolerance of the ideas of others. Yes, I was going to tell him that it was these alien advisers he encircled himself with who heavy-handedly were trying to make him appear a fool in the eyes of *his* and not *their* people. I was to say that later anyway. And he threw me into prison. As if I had never been through it. I had been through it all. '*The worst prison is the shackles your own fear fetters you with,'* I told him that. Yes, yes. I told him that and more. What could he do? I was a sick man, it was universally known that I was asthmatic; it was also universally accepted that I had fought for the liberation of the country. I am not boasting, am I?"

"No, no. God forbid."

"Anyway. Another spell in prison. No books; on his instructions. I had requested that the Holy Book be provided and that reading material sent by Mursal and Natasha be sent in as well. No books, the warden repeated. 'Not even the Holy Book?' I asked. No. I could have killed that warden. But then he wasn't the General and I wouldn't have gained anything by killing him. That was the only day I thought I should kill, the day I was denied free access to the word of God. I have never spoken about this before. never told anyone this. I reminded the prison officer that it was only during the fascist era that I was not allowed to be issued books, mainly biographical works on the lives of the Sudanese Mahdi, Shaka Zulu, Ataturk, Garibaldi, or Napoleon. I was allowed, I said to the (General's prison's) warden condescendingly, nigger that I was, a low-breed of no high IQ, I was allowed a copy of the Koran and the writings and speeches of the Duce. Do you know what the prison officer said to me in 1972 in a Somalia ruled supposedly by a national government? He said: 'No Koran. You are a low-breed, not entitled to touch the Holy Book. All you will get is *The Collected Wisdom of the General, Volumes I & II; you* can choose what language you want to read *The Wisdom* in: English, Italian, Arabic or Somali,' he said. I could've killed him."

"I am glad you didn't."

"Twenty-eight years later, would you believe it?"

"I do, I do."

"Well, I will tell you something I've never told anyone before this evening," he said, looking at his watch. Just as he did that the muezzin called. "The evening prayer," he said.

"Later," said Elmi-Tiir. "Go on with the story. I want you to tell me what you've never before told a living soul. Come on. It is not every day I hear you speak with such openness."

"I am curious," said Elmi-Tiir.

Deeriye felt teased by his brother-in-law in a way he had never known and he liked what he found, saw and heard. The sky was an umbrella of indigo, calm and cloudless. Deeriye continued, "Whereas I pored over every line Mussolini had written, since it was the only book I had access to, I did not open the General's *Collected Wisdom*. Not for one instant did it enter my head to open it."

"Why?"

Deeriye said: "I pored over the Duce for two main reasons. One: I wanted to know what he thought about his own people and about Somalia; I also needed something to practise my reading on since I had just then learnt to read and write."

"I see."

"Whereas I thought I knew what the General thought and, as Somalis might say, one couldn't read about a goat that bleats only to the tune of its own boastful cry. Also, whereas I got the scripture delivered to my cell during the fascist era, I was denied access to the Holy Book until after the General had made a public show of coming to ask me and the other prisoners what we needed most and granting it so we would be grateful to him 'for saving our souls and making our bodies suffer' – a phrase he used when he paid us a visit in prison – a week before the Red Cross representatives came to inspect the prison. And what a sinful fool I was. I did not open the Holy Book which was delivered to my cell for a day or so. May the Lord forgive me for my arrogance."

He got up, having made it obvious that he had said all he intended to say. He rubbed his hands together and asked if Elmi-Tiir would like to use the bathroom for the ritual of ablution.

"I don't need to," came Elmi-Tiir's response.

"In a minute you will lead the prayer," Deeriye said respectfully, pleased to hear the telephone ringing: which meant Mursal was still *there,* outside of prison and alive. Or was he?

• • • • • • • • • • •

Nervous movements here and there: as at a wake. Children's voices climbed a crescendo of self-importance when they were told they should stay in the living-room on the ground floor. The adult community moved about with the quiet that was necessary not to get on each other's nerves. Tea was made and drunk; stories were told; visitors were received but no one was consulted on what to do – not even Medina. Things in the end fell to an acceptable rhythm: the women downstairs, the men (Deeriye, Elmi-Tiir and Samawade) in Deeriye's room.

The telephone did not ring for two hours. Natasha and Zeinab complained to Deeriye as though he could do something about it. Five minutes before the third hour, Natasha and Zeinab went to his room seeking his counsel as to what to do if *he* did not ring. Thank God, the telephone rang before he had time to answer their question.

He was alive, thank God, said Natasha and added: "And not yet in prison. Who knows, he may be here any time." *He* became someone whose progress you could follow and study on a computer-screen in front of you, only you had to imagine where *he* was and *who he was.*

Then Zeinab said something very strange indeed. She said, "*He* is beyond blame. *He* is a madman with no audience to perform to, a Khaliif hiding from his potential audience: us!"

And this made Deeriye wonder if it wasn't they who were mad. How could they tell it was Mursal ringing? Natasha and Zeinab went out.

Deeriye then said, "We are in a house, Mursal's, that is quarantined, cordoned off by a fearsome secret nobody outside shares: save *him,* if it is *him.*"

"Do you think it is him?" asked Elmi-Tiir.

"I cannot say."

"It is very absurd."

"Somalia has become a stage where the Grandest Actor performs in front of an applauding audience that should be booing him. Anyone who wishes to share the spotlight either goes mad or in the end is imprisoned. Otherwise, everyone is made to join the crowd and applaud with it," Deeriye said.

Elmi-Tiir patiently listened as Deeriye went on:

"I could never have predicted the country would go this way, never. It is not true that the concept of state is new here, or that it was introduced here by Europeans intent upon civilizing the native. Islam and contact with Persia, Turkey and Arabia took care of that. What I could never have predicted (and many Somalis are likewise surprised by this phenomenon) is how easily governable we are."

Out of the darkness: an owl's hooting cry, portending, as Somalis say, death and disaster in the air. Deeriye looked out at the night and his eyes fell on the hole, small as a cat-door, that Yassin's flung pebble-stones had made in the window. He told himself he had survived many other disasters and deaths and would survive this too, would survive it so that he could take good and loving care of Samawade and Natasha if they chose to stay, chose to be with him – in the way Elmi-Tiir, sitting here, had taken loving care of Nadiifa, Mursal and Zeinab. Which brought to Deeriye's mind the question he wanted to ask Elmi-Tiir: what was Mursal like as a child? Was he aware of the politics and controversies his father Deeriye had been involved in? How much was the young boy told? What did he used to say? What were his dreams as a small boy?

Elmi-Tiir said, "He was very intelligent, he seemed to understand what was going on. Later, as a matter of fact, he told me that he had reshaped his mother's ideas when she dictated them by translating them the way he wanted; in other words, most of the things you read in those letters you received in prison were either made up by him or twisted in such a way you got the impression he intended for you to."

"How old was he when he started writing letters for Nadiifa?"

"How old is Samawade?" Samawade answered, "Eleven."

"I think he was either ten or eleven."

"Anything else you remember?"

"He couldn't bear the sight of blood," said Elmi-Tiir. "He cried for days every time he saw blood. He had a terrible month when he was circumcised. And to pull his teeth one had to do so much plotting. One day, one of his aunts hit him unconscious and pulled out two teeth: he didn't mind that. We did. She was a relative who had come to Mogadiscio and had nowhere to go to and that was why she was with us."

"What else?"

"Zeinab, on the other hand, did not need anyone to nurse her wounds or pull out one of her teeth. And she used to fight a lot; Mursal, hardly. He was too adult-like compared with others his own age."

"Yes, yes. What else – about Mursal?"

"We're talking about him as though he were dead, do you realize that? Talking about Mursal as though he were no longer going to be with us?" said Elmi-Tiir.

"Are we? It hadn't occurred to me. It's no business of ours anyway, it is God's, the giver and the taker away of life, the decider of our and other peoples' destinies," said Deeriye.

"Anyway . . . ," began Elmi-Tiir but trailed off as Deeriye went on.

"I have buried Nadiifa, buried, in a manner of speaking, the massacred cattle and many other men and women. There is Mahad; there is Rooble; there is Mukhtaar whose body was lowered into its resting place uncleansed because someone said he was a suicide and therefore did not deserve the company of the Holy Word; there is Jibriil who hasn't received his due burial. Mursal's destiny is tied with the others' fate; and the nation's, for that matter. There were ten of them in an underground movement (I read this in a document I found in Mursal's study). And he is the last on the list. Two-thirds of the members of that organization have met with violent deaths or have vanished mysteriously. Nine men and one woman who took an oath to do anything in their power to overthrow the General's tyrannical régime. So as far as I am concerned, Mursal is no longer with us; he may be here a few more days, we may hear a few telephone rings before the apparatus ceases to sound his alarm. That is why it doesn't bother me much to speak about him as though he were dead."

"What would you do if he walked in through that door?"

"Do you want my honest answer?"

"I do."

"I say this because you are a friend and I trust you with my inner secrets. You are his maternal uncle, and among Somalis this is considered of the highest honour and importance. And you are also his father in the sense that you formed him, shaped his mind much more than I have."

"You provided the myth. You were the father who was doing well, out there in a dungeon somewhere, being tortured, being tormented. Yes, Deeriye, you provided the myth."

"A myth is but a backdrop. It is not the painting."

"But it was very important," said Elmi-Tiir.

"You were the painter; I, the backdrop: the myth."

Elmi-Tiir would not allow his brother-in-law to be evasive. He wanted an answer. What would Deeriye do if Mursal returned now?

"I would be terribly disappointed in him."

"Disappointed in him?"

"Yes. We cannot afford to harbour traitors, withdrawers at the last minute, non-finishers of projects begun and non-deliverers of promises made, I would tell him. I would ask him, 'Where are your friends?' I would say to him: 'Whatever has become of the other nine members of the underground organization'?"

"Would you really?" Deeriye nodded.

"I believe you."

"Thank you."

They fell silent. Not that there was nothing to say but a great deal one could say but wouldn't. Deeriye remembered where it all began: a stone flung by man's primitive instinct at the sight of an owl or something which frightened him (man), in his aggressiveness, a lesser, an inferior being; man, in his primitive state, using a stone before catapults and other contrivances enabled him to strike a target with any measure of accuracy. And Deeriye had been moved, his life managed by others – "like mine now," as Natasha said this morning. This and other mad activities culminated in Samawade's determined wish to use the cassette on which the Sayyid's "Death of Corfield" had been recorded and the Holy Book as weapons in order to chase Khaliif who had referred to Mursal's (and Deeriye, Samawade and Natasha's) house as the betrayer's home. Meanwhile: discussions. Yaziid; Mucaawiya; Ali's death; the Islamic controversy which resulted in breakaway factions like the *Shi'ites* Mahad off the board. Rooble too. Mukhtaar forced off it. Jibriil blown up in an explosion. And now Mursal?

"You haven't answered my question, Elmi-Tiir," Deeriye suddenly said.

"Which one?"

"Special things you remember about Mursal's growing up under your patronage. Let us say you were to dictate to a journalist an epitaph for Mursal. Or should I have to unsay that? Anyway, what other things do you recall as special?"

"He knew how to keep a secret. . . . There you are, Deeriye. You've made me say 'he knew' as though he were dead and no longer with us. 'He knows.' Yes. He knows."

"Does it matter what tense you use? To you, I suspect it does. I have had to re-invent my tenses. Because when in prison for a long, long time you don't know what tense to use and whether or not others are still there outside of it, if you know what I mean. Time assumes, and so does tense, a different coating altogether: it rusts, it rigidifies into a kind of pattern which makes you believe nothing else exists outside of it. We are quarantined with the cordons of fear around us. I suspect he is now in another square, spotlit, never out of the eye of the marksman."

"How cold you can be!"

"Warm. It is fear that induces cold. I am not afraid any more. Yes. Not afraid. Could kill. If I had a gun, a revolver, any weapon. I could kill to vindicate not my son but justice."

They enjoyed the silences which separated them and which made it possible for each to find the area in which his thoughts were weakest, in order to polish them, strengthen them, stand them up for full display: like the bust of a dead hero! But was Mursal a hero? He was definitely different from the hero manufactured to order, a hero who died under the name of Soyaan – no street named after him, after all the fuss, after all the publicity. What if he died unmourned and unburied like Mukhtaar and Jibriil Mohamed-Somali? Or taken prisoner like Mahad, an unsuccessful kamikaze? Samawade, Cantar, Sheherezade, Ataturk, Jamaal and Shaka were named, anointed thus so they would continue the struggle others had begun, and Mursal was there only to keep the flames going, keep the live coals under a bed of ashes so that when they reached the age where they could handle things on their own, they would find the fire buried under the ground: and like one of those instant cameras already adjusted: click! With button pressed, the printed photograph would unroll: a family-portrait with a healthy background, grandfathers and fathers and uncles dedicated to a struggle, amen!, the liberation of Africa!

Elmi-Tiir was saying, "I remember a few interesting anecdotes about Mursal's following the codes of secrecy about anything. At age nine, before he became his mother's scribe, there occurred an incident which has remained in my memory. He arranged, and did it marvellously, the marriage between two adults neither of whom had the intention of contracting matrimony. He plotted, carried messages back and forth, invented most of these messages himself. It was only after they had become husband and wife that the two realized he had done it all."

"Someone told me that."

And his nickname was *'Oge'*. What he didn't know didn't exist, Nadiifa used to say. He knew where things were hidden, where his mother kept her money and all that. Zeinab, however, was less practical. Once a thief came to the house when all the adults and Mursal were away. The thief asked if anyone was home, and not only did she say that no adult was home but she told him where her mother had gone, where she had hidden her jewellery, when she was likely to return. The thief asked her for a glass of water. While she was gone, he went into the house and took everything away."

"Thank you for all that. I don't know what they would've done without you. I don't know what Rooble's family could have done without you. The saint is you, my friend."

"We won't argue about that."

"Of course, we won't," said Deeriye.

"Although I wonder what secrets he has taken away with him. I mean Mursal, for he always had many. He was a bank of secrets. Mahad wasn't. Mahad would say, 'Tell me nothing of your secrets; I am bound to blabber, to forget where I am and to speak.' It should've been the other way round – what with Mahad's father betrayed because of an intercepted message that Waris, an eight-year-old, had been trusted with. But things don't work like that, do they?"

"Incidentally. . . . Did you deliver the message to the General before the deadline of his ultimatum?"

"We are not sure of that," Elmi-Tiir said.

"How do you mean?"

"We did not deliver it to him personally. But we were promised he would receive it in time."

"And you remember the telephone number I'm supposed to call if I wish to see or speak with him?"

"Yes."

"Please give me the number again."

Elmi-Tiir obliged. Deeriye wrote the number down and put the paper in his breast pocket. He smiled: a mischievous smile, thought

Elmi-Tiir. But why? Elmi-Tiir did not have the chance to ask, for they were joined by Natasha and Zeinab; Natasha in a state of total shock, looking lost in the maze of the sorrows and complications she had been thrown into by one single event: the disappearance of Mursal. She said to Zeinab: "He hasn't telephoned. Tell this to your father."

"What could he do anyway?" Zeinab said.

"He should be told." Then turning to Samawade, "Tell him."

Samawade did so.

"Tell her that Somalis say that when one loses a camel one desperately, if searching for it, might put one's hand in the milk-container to see if it is there. But tell her we are not desperate," said Elmi-Tiir.

Samawade sought Zeinab's help in rendering the proverb adequately in English. Natasha turned that over in her head, then said, "Why are we not desperate?"

"Because we know where he is," volunteered Elmi-Tiir.

No one said anything for a while. She requested, "Translation, please." And when given, she said, "Where is *he?*" Why isn't *he* telephoning? Why isn't *he* making us share his progress?"

"Only God knows," said Deeriye.

Her eyes flashing with the madness of the desperate, she half-shouted: *"Someone else must know."*

"Who?" asked Zeinab.

And the ringing voice of Khaliif tolled a doom: he cursed those who kill, who never resign themselves to the will of the divine; he cursed those who never accept His word as the Sacred Message but who force people to go to Orientation Centres instead of mosques and who ask to be worshipped in His place. They all craned to see, in such uncontrolled graceless haste that Zeinab and Natasha knocked into each other and Samawade climbed over his grandfather Elmi-Tiir: they forgot to be courteous, they did not apologize to one another but listened to Khaliif, waiting to hear if this madman knew anything. He appeared like a saxifrage out of the stony greyness of the dark night, a flower in a desert. He was doing the unusual thing, he was talking to himself: he had no crowd to address himself to, no audience.

"May God bless the martyrs, may He grant them peace, may He make things easy for those who survive: a saintly father, a wife from beyond the sea's ladders-of-seven and child. And let me say this. They began as a community, a community of ten, and worked together as a community and suffered as a community of brotherhood. Can you think of anything better to say about a group of young people, ten of them, and among them the betrayers: they suffered on behalf of the suffering humanity." He was silent. He looked about him: no audience. But that did not worry him today. He continued speaking: "Contact will be made again; from the void will come the voice, his voice: a pious Muslim dies twice: a martyr thrice. Yes: listen to his voice from the void."

Then Natasha said: "He is wearing Mursal's shirt and trousers. How very weird." She got up to go and speak with him, ask him to tell her when and where he had last seen Mursal, her husband, her love; *tell her something since no one else will tell her anything.*

"Are you mad?" said Zeinab.

Natasha was held until Khaliif's voice faded into the distance. Deeriye sensed the tension in the room rise. He reached for the radio and switched it on. He turned to Elmi-Tiir and asked on what shortwave frequencies one might get the BBC Arabic Service.

"Put that thing away," said Elmi-Tiir. "How would they know what is happening here in Mogadiscio at this time of night?"

"He spoke of Orientation Centres, Khaliif did. Was the General likely to be speaking at one of the Orientation Centres tonight? And where? Why not try Radio Mogadiscio: it is nearly midnight. The midnight news, perhaps," said Zeinab; then she translated that for Natasha.

Deeriye tried Radio Mogadiscio. And the announcer:

"News is just reaching us concerning a bomb explosion at Hodan Orientation Centre where the General and Head of State was speaking. We will tell you more when we have received the details." This was the single news item and no more.

Deeriye and the others sat by the radio. "Either the phone will ring (and this means he is still alive) or it won't and the radio will play that accursed song *'Samadiidow'* in a short while," said Elmi-Tiir.

"Samadiidow" was played. Only Natasha cried. The others sat in mournful silence: waiting. Their angry eyes converged on the radio. A little later, Elmi-Tiir switched it off.

Deeriye said, "A prayer for the soul of the martyred is in order.

Please take Natasha to one of the rooms downstairs and comfort her. And you, Samawade, can join us in prayer if you wish."

"Yes, Grandfather."

As the women went downstairs, he asked, "But we don't know anything for sure, do we? We don't know if he's survived the explosion, do we? Or if it is *he* – our Mursal – in the first place?"

"No, we do not know," said Elmi-Tiir.

"Only God knows," said Deeriye.

And they prepared to pray for the soul of the martyred. But then:

"Can you remember where I put the telephone number of the Security inspector I was to contact were I of a mind to see the General in person?" asked Deeriye. "The name of the Security Inspector . . . ?"

"Keynaan, and his number is 123456. Why?"

Deeriye excused himself, went down and telephoned Keynaan and said that he wished to see the General first thing in the morning. Having fixed that appointment, he came back, said nothing but joined Elmi-Tiir and Samawade in prayer, without having taken the proper ablutionary purification.

PART FOUR

Could you be in two times at once? Certainly your mind could be in one time and your body in another. . . . Somebody might come to you out of *his* time into yours. You might, for instance, come face to face with your father as he was when he was a boy. Of course, you wouldn't *know* each other; still you might meet and become friends, the way you do with people in dreams.

–Forrester Reid

Ill at ease in tyranny
Ill at ease in the Republic
In the one I longed for freedom
In the other for the end of corruption.

–Czeslaw Milosz

E P I L O G U E

With Death Only a Whisper Away

No day is a replica of any other day, thought Deeriye, *nobody's personal or political history can ever be the same as anyone else's.* He was seated in the living-room, with Samawade within arm's reach, concentrating on changing the reels of the tape-recorder so that his two grandfathers could listen to Sheikh Abdulqawi recite selected verses from the Holy Book. On Deeriye's lap, inactive, lay the headphones. Samawade coughed now and then, but did not lose his concentration: he would wipe his running nose and stained cheeks with the back of his hand, sniff, bite his lower lip harder, squint like a marksman aiming at a dangerous target, position the reel, roll it forward with his hands, lose patience and take it off. You wouldn't think, looking at him, that he was only eleven. He tried again. Now the spools made the lip-lip-lapping sound indicating that he had pressed the wrong button.

"Do you want me to try it myself?" asked Deeriye.

"No. No. Just one more try. Please," said Samawade.

"We've been waiting for nearly an hour," said Elmi-Tiir.

"That's not true," protested Samawade.

"Samawade!" said Deeriye; and Samawade knew what that meant. He apologized to Elmi-Tiir, "I'm sorry."

They had been up all night. Perhaps that was why Samawade was nervous. Had it been Mursal's wake? Agitated activity here and there, with Natasha trying to telephone the States; Samawade saying he wouldn't sleep; and Zeinab insisting that she go and find out what had been happening outside. Dahaba and her children camped in the living-room whereas Elmi-Tiir had had a camp-bed brought into

Deeriye's room and the two lay side by side, neither able to sleep. But when they were silent for a long time and once they had switched off the lights and darkened the room like a photographer's, Nadiifa came to him and blamed him for his part in "leading astray" a young mind – that of their son Mursal. And she added,

"Whereas Sheikh Ibrahim cut the flowering tree that was Mukhtaar, cut it stem, root and all and got away scot-free because he was the one who had planted it in the first place, you, Deeriye, may be accused of having *imagined* a jungle of ideas in which our son Mursal has lost his way. I am partly responsible for this, in the sense that it was I who had trusted him with adults' political secrets when he was ten or eleven; but I didn't know any better. I was young and uninitiated, I was inexperienced and being a woman hadn't the chance to be heard, to be taken seriously. Anyway: I, too, was lost in your jungle of ideas and visions. The question now is, will you avenge our son?"

Deeriye, as usual, defended himself saying, "The maker of a map isn't responsible if the person who has acquired it does not know how to read it properly."

She said that this didn't convince her and went on: "I am the sharer of your secrets, I am in a manner of speaking the provider of your visions – *indeed, I am your visions*. Since I am your double (or am I your secret-sharer), let me remind you that you know that I know that you've given one thing a thought yourself; yes, let me finish. I know you've hidden a revolver somewhere; I know you've activated the line of communication between yourself and the Inspector, the General's uncle on his mother's side, who's accepted to take up your request for an audience with the General today and I know, naive that you are, that you will go to meet the General armed with the standard revolver which once belonged to a Jibriil Mohamed-Somali! You may as well ask me why you've had this change of heart, you, Deeriye, who always spoke violently against the use of violence. It seems you cannot envisage being on your knees all the time, seeking Natasha's pardon day in and day out. It is as simple as that. The point is, you ask yourself, how you can make allies of all those who should've been your enemies when you are on your knees – in need of being given a pardon. Your body is weak, you have asthma, your lung is your soul, you are a burden to yourself, and Natasha and Samawade, because of Mursal's death, have become a heavy weight on your conscience. The duellists are your two selves, your two souls; and you are not sure of anything any more. If only you were sure of your own station in life, of the position you've carved for yourself – and of your own sanity! What was the question you asked yourself just before my coming to you: will I give way, like a falling star, will I be on my knees all my life – if not in prostration before the General then with weak knees in front of Natasha's gigantic need for help? If you ask my opinion, I say, why not do it, yes, why not finish the job your son couldn't? Yes, my love. Avenge your son. Let the powerful heat of anger persuade you, don't wait until it cools. *Then come and join me,"* she concluded. *"I am here, awaiting your arrival, I am the* houri *assigned to you – on earth as well as in paradise."*

"Are you all right?" Elmi-Tiir was saying to Samawade now.

"He has a weak constitution that plays havoc whenever he stays up past eight in the evening. He is all right, I am sure. Aren't you?"

He sneezed, said *"Alxamdulillaah"* and nodded.

"You go and look for the other headphones for Grandfather Elmi-Tiir while I fix it. I think I can do it better than you today. All right? Go into your father's study and don't disturb him, do you hear me?"

"But he is not there."

"He is not?" he said, obviously taken aback.

"He is not in his study," said Samawade. "Have you forgotten?"

Elmi-Tiir said, "Go and look for the other headphones, anyway. Go."

There he was again, making a fool of himself: confounding things. Nadiifa had gained the body and flesh: and her message stood like a person in front of him. He shook his head, woke to this world's reality and began saying to Elmi-Tiir, "How can I be expected to register all that's happening? How can anyone expect me to remember all that has happened? He was here only yesterday morning."

"You are tired. It's been a long stretch and a hundred and one things have happened. You are right. And we don't know what has taken place, do we?"

"Only God does."

He was decidedly disturbed by his inability to cope with things: either things were too slow or too quick for him to note. He remembered the decision he had made; he remembered the appointment he had made. He would perform a heroic deed just when everybody had written him off as a useless old man; he would vindicate justice. . . . Someone was in the doorway.

"Did you send for something, Father?" said Zeinab, holding Samawade by the wrist.

"We asked him to get some headphones for his grandfather. Why?"

She pushed him in and walked away saying, "Let him tell you."

Samawade stepped in further, walked to where the spools had lain, set to work but with less enthusiasm.

After a while Elmi-Tiir asked, "What did you do?"

"Nothing."

"You must have done something. What did you do?"

"I said, nothing."

"Did you break something, take away something?"

"I wouldn't do any such thing."

Deeriye asked: "What did you do then?"

"I sat in Mursal's swivel chair, put my feet up, held a pipe between my teeth and had two to three books open beside me. I had just done that when she walked in and found me like that," and he demonstrated.

"Just like your father?" said Deeriye.

"Yes."

"What else did you do?"

"Well, I opened a drawer, pretended I had lost something, emptied it and then put everything back in, acted as though I was desperately looking for something and thus created disorder."

"Just like your father?"

"Yes."

Silence. They heard Natasha's sobbing cry, a stifled cry which climbed up the stairs and entered through the door which opened when again Zeinab walked in, bringing with her a set of headphones. "Is this what he was looking for?" she said accusingly.

"Don't you ever know how to let go?" asked Deeriye.

"There was no reason why he should empty the drawer and create such a disorder in his father's study. No reason, you hear me?"

She wouldn't have understood if her father or uncle told her what the boy had said. She had a father who *"imagined things and invented histories and made up tales and conjured up interlocutors.*" She was not ready to have a nephew who would follow in the steps of his grandfather, no.

Deeriye then said, "Zeinab, take a seat, please."

"I must go down and be with Natasha."

"In a while. A nurse who has a number of patients must divide her time justly between them. You can go soon, but do take a seat."

She did so.

"I wanted to tell you a few things and I can't think of a better time than this, since we have your uncle Elmi-Tiir and your nephew Samawade," he said, his voice serious but kind and gentle.

"Yes, Father."

"Did I ever tell you why I conjure up interlocutors, why I have visions, why it is that I invent histories, why I try to create symbolic links between unrelated historical events, why it is that I speak to your mother in my sleep . . . did I ever bother to explain myself?"

"I suppose you have."

"Do you remember what explanations I gave?"

She looked like a pupil faced by a difficult test. "I don't think I can remember the precise woods you used but I am certain I've heard you on the subject before."

Deeriye said, "To speak of that about which others are silent and to remain sane at the same time is a very difficult task. The difficulties I have had to face are enormous. I have been on the fringe of *madness* the past forty years: *the madness* of which I talk is in itself a political statement. What did I invent? Not my date of birth. I was asked what year I was born and I said how old I was. I did not invent the African National Congress of South Africa. I did not invent the death of Corfield: there is enough evidence in literature and history. What did I invent? A link with my wife Nadiifa whom I loved and still love and whose feet I washed and will wash any day in heaven or earth, did I invent that? No, I did not. I made myself available to her and therefore since she loved me too *she* invented me; and I, her. It is the chicken and egg story here. You accuse me of things I have not done, my daughter."

"Father?"

"Quiet, my daughter," said Elmi-Tiir.

"All my mind did not need to manufacture, since there was plenty in me and in the community, was guilt. I was taken away, *saved* – this is the irony of history – by the Italians who threw me into prison and by that action turned me into a hero, something I do not believe I am or will ever be. If the Italians had been wise to their deed, they might have left me there and I would have been devoured alive right there and then by my people, I can tell you that."

"You exaggerate," said Elmi-Tiir.

"I don't think so. With all due respect to you, Elmi-Tiir, I do not think I would have survived in the compound another day. They had the right to tear me to shreds, feed me to their famished beasts or devour me themselves."

"I still think you exaggerate," said Elmi-Tiir.

Deeriye continued: "You remained behind and I did not; you could take their temperature when they were unwell, I could not for I was not there. But I could foresee no future for me there. Years later, I remember replying to someone's question that were it not for that period of detention, I might never have known what it was like being a Sayyidist, a Somali nationalist and a Pan-Africanist all at the same time. I am not saying that the Italians did me a favour by imprisoning me because that taught me who I was – although that's true too. But I am saying that once in prison and alone my mind set to work and I reasoned that I had not been detained to teach me who I was, a low-breed of a black man anywhere – a fact I hadn't known: I had thought I was an aristocrat born and bred, and a Muslim at that: and no son of an infidel could ever think he was superior to me. Am I digressing?"

"You are doing well," said Elmi-Tiir encouragingly.

Zeinab was still behaving like a pupil and Samawade, fascinated by the way the narrative had unfolded, was silent.

"During one of my irreligious fever-ridden bouts – may God forgive us and all Muslims all sins, amen! – I am supposed to have described Nadiifa as an angel; I am supposed to have said that she could come to me at will, any time, any hour she pleased and I would keep myself free for her. Now that, I believe, was an exaggeration on my part and an irreligious thmg to utter. No mortal, not even Nadiifa, should be offered that privilege: only God. But she kept me company, she helped me stay sane, she talked to me when I needed someone to converse with. She? Or my own invention? I would say, she. She was too great to be invented. Too angelic. Like the divine revelation my mortal eyes happened to fall on the dawn Natasha called me away, to tell me that Mursal had disappeared. I could not have invented that. One does not invent God He is there. He blesses those *He* loves, the deserving few, and no amount of overinventiveness can invent Him."

A brief silence.

Then he continued: "I could talk on and on, describing how I came by the thoughts of which I am made, for I am a collage of many notions and some of them are yours and some are Mursal's and some are Nadiifa's and some come from Natasha and some from Rooble; and so someone never goes away for ever – one can always call that part of oneself which is from the vanished person and talk to *it* or *him* or *her*. We are not only ourselves, we are *others* too, those whom we love, those who have influenced our lives, who have made us what we are. Do you understand?"

She did not answer immediately but got up once he stopped talking, as if ready to take leave. Then she spoke: "All I said – I am sorry if you misunderstood me – is that you are in doubt about everything: about what you see, what you touch, whether you heard or saw something during a fever-ridden bout or in a dream or a vision."

"It is the prerogative of God alone to be sure of anything."

"No doubt, no doubt," she said, unwilling to get carried away again.

"I am only a human. And therefore I am in doubt," he said.

She backed out of the room: answering Natasha's call. Right on cue.

• • • • • • • • • • •

Alone, he listened to the beautiful chanting of the Koran, responsive to nothing but the Holy Message, impervious to the outside and profane world, indifferent to the visitors who called, for many persons had heard the midday news which confirmed Mursal's encounter with death. He wasn't going to let anyone spoil the pleasure the reading gave him. He registered every word's rise and fall. The poetry of the Koran had an organic rhythm of its own – rather like water descending from a great height; and the turning of the spools sounded like tyres on tarmac when it had just rained heavily; whereas the quietness inside of him was peaceful like a pool.

"There are visitors, Grandfather," said Samawade, speaking hesitantly. "Grandfather Elmi-Tiir said to come and let you know. What shall I tell him?"

Deeriye appeared not to hear or see; nor did he remove the headphones. What Samawade found strange was that, although for all intents and purposes his eyes were open, Deeriye did not even acknowledge his presence. But he heard, "Leave him be," and turned and saw Cantar, who added, "Can't you see he is not here?"

And Sheherezade said, "Where do you think he is, Fool?"

"In the heavens, can't you see?" Cantar said.

Samawade pushed them away and said, "Shut up, you."

An umbrella of shade advanced on the room and Deeriye was covered half in shadow. He sat as though posing for a portrait: not a movement in his body, nor a flicker of his eyes.

Visibly worried, Cantar said, "Do you think he is all right?"

"What do you mean?" challenged Samawade. "Of course he is. And shut up, both of you, anyway. Go away. Go and play somewhere else."

Sheherezade said, "I'll call Aunt Zeinab."

In less than a minute, Zeinab was pressing forward to enter: Deeriye was now partly in shade and partly in the sun's light, quiet and motionless, his shoulders stooped, his eyes stationary. Her hand reached out and switched off the tape-recorder, thus cutting the flow. Deeriye started. Before he managed to say anything, Zeinab: "You had us frightened."

"What's happened?" he said, removing his headphones.

She was uncertain what to say, how to apologize.

"The children came down running and said Grandfather was in the heavens, silent and unmoving. I thought. . . . "

He nodded his head. He registered the noises that were coming from below. He repeated his question without changing emphasis or tone: "What's happened?"

"Oh, a group of sheikhs have arrived, many of whom you know. Uncle Elmi-Tiir is with them. They have come to give their blessing. They say they heard the sad news on the radio: the midday news."

Suddenly, he was fully alive to what was taking place. He wanted to know, "Did the midday news say how he met his death?"

"No, it didn't."

He got up, and as he did so yawned: during the brief pause, he managed to say a small prayer in which he sought divine guidance. He looked around him. By then Cantar and Sheherezade had lost interest and had gone down. But Samawade stayed. Deeriye, addressing Zeinab, asked, "Have we the right to bury him?"

"The midday news didn't elaborate."

He moved about putting things in order: the tape-recorder, which he patted as if it were his favourite horse; the window, which he closed. He turned and said, "Was Natasha consulted about the sheikhs' arrival?"

"There was no time. They arrived without announcing themselves."

Deeriye shook his head disapprovingly. "And how is she?"

"She is in no state to speak well of."

"Understandable, understandable."

"She is in the bedroom with friends. Medina. Sagal. And others."

He had many, many questions. But did she know the answers? Mursal's body – whatever had become of it? He would have loved to know if Mursal died well; if the thought of *regret* had crossed his mind before he gasped his last; if dying *pained* and how much; if . . . ! He would have many questions to answer himself: when he finally met his friend Rooble; when and if Mahad was ever released; when Samawade grew up. In a flash of visions, as though in a pocket of memories, these names, these concepts came to him: Yaziid; Mucaawiya; the Constitution of the City of Medina; Mina and the act of stoning; the Minaret which was of concrete: stone; Satan's *rajiim;* the blessing of the martyred ones beginning in this case with Mukhtaar and Jibriil Mohamed-Somali; and finally Mursal: all carriers of the message, the irony being they didn't see themselves as conveyers of the Message of the Living One; the mad discourse of the sane; the saintly discourse of the sufi.

And Sheherezade ran up and half panting said, "He has come, he just walked in like that," she demonstrated, "and without bothering to say anything entered the sheikhs' room and seated himself. Like that."

Who? Had the General come? Zeinab, who was certain it was the General (he engaged people's thoughts all the time, day and night, this General), ran down the flight of stairs at frightening speed.

"Who has come?" he said to Sheherezade. "Who is this person?"

"Khaliif the madman," she said when she was panting no more

"How is he dressed?" asked Deeriye, displaying a little amusement.

"He is in military uniform, Khaliif is, his chest decked with ribbons of honour and medallions, walking like this, acting big and very important. You wouldn't think he was mad," she said.

He gave her a hand and gave the other to Samawade and said, "Shall we go down and meet him?"

On the way down they met Cantar, who was just as excited, saying, "Grandfather, you wouldn't think he was at all mad, the way he carries himself, the way he carries on."

"Would you like to join us? We are meeting the General," said Deeriye.

With Cantar in front and the other three following, they went down, step by step, prepared for anything, four persons – one very old and three very young, four men and one woman: ready, as a delegation from the world of the mad, to meet the sane.

• • • • • • • • • • •

Just before nightfall, after a day spent in prayers, consultations with the divine guidance, Deeriye got up, went to Mursal's study, opened a drawer, took out the standard revolver and, hiding it in his pocket, said that he would go out for a walk. Zeinab offered to walk with him. He assured her that he wasn't afraid of Yassin, whom they could see standing in front of them, and believed that it would do him a lot of good to go alone. He did not tell anyone what he intended to do; Nadiifa would be his only secret-sharer, Nadiifa who was out of harm's way, Nadiifa: the reward his martyrdom would gain him in the form of her companionship.

Once out, his right hand's finger busy counting the steps of the prayer-beads which would lead him eventually to the palace of heaven and to an appointment with Nadiifa and, given the time and logic of it, to a meeting with Mursal, Mukhtaar, Soyaan and the others. The evening breeze blew about him. He walked straight, neither looking back nor to the sides, his right hand clutching the beads while his left held on to the bulge which was the revolver. He wondered if he would be searched before he was let into the room where the General was waiting for bim. Somehow, he was sure he would reach the General without the least hindrance; and he would kill him. Nadiifa would have warned him of impending danger. And since she didn't – well? He turned left, he turned right, he was certain he would get to the appointment in time.

Then a sudden thought came to him as he walked, without looking to see if he was being followed. The thought held him hostage for a long time. It made him slow down a little and in less than a minute he was saying loudly to himself, his voice not very different from Khaliif's: "All our lives, mortals that we are, we misname things and objects, we misdefine, we misdescribe illnesses and misuse metaphors. Why, it is not my lungs: my face! Why, this suggests the loss of face, the loss of reputation, and nothing more than that! Why, this doesn't suggest the loss of faith, the spiritual loss, the spiritual famine which envelops one – right from the moment hundreds of heads of cattle rolled. I didn't lose face: I lost faith, yes, faith, in my own capability, faith in my people." A face, if lost, can be recovered; a reputation can be padded like the reprinted photograph which can be re-touched, and on which a line can be added, a wrinkle removed. "Nadiifa," he said to himself silently now, "spoke of my lungs as my soul: she didn't speak of my lungs as though they were my face. Which perhaps means she believes that my soul is struggling, has been struggling to free itself and join its Creator from the day the Italians made the cattle's heads roll. Why has this never occurred to me? In my lungs is my soul, struggling to be free from this body so it can join Nadiifa's and prepare for the eventual roll-call of names of the pious when these souls will be one with their Creator."

He finally halted in front of a door. There was no movement in the street. Night had fallen, dark but starry, with cloudy patches creating something of the effect of exits in the sky.

He stood before the closed door and looked up at the openings in the heavens, wondering if his soul, when it parted with his body, would enter by one of them. He put his rosary in the pocket where the revolver had been and said a brief but elaborate prayer. He felt light, as if any stirring in the air might blow him away at any time. But he didn't feel tense. His chest didn't contract, his lungs, it appeared, wouldn't explode; there was no fear of that. If his attempt failed, people would say he had gone mad, he thought to himself as he readied himself to

press the doorbell, and if he succeeded he would be made a hero.
And he pressed the doorbell.

• • • • • • • • • • •

No one could account for Deeriye's movements for three solid days. And it took the best part of the fourth day to piece together stories stranded with gaps nobody could fill. Was he the old man all in white (as though adorned in Archangel Azraail's shroud) who was seen, three nights previously, walking away in haste from a house in which a bell rang and the bell's ringing set into motion a series of explosions – a house in which a dozen men and women, believed to be plotting the overthrow of the General's régime, met with violent death? Had he been seen in the company of Khaliif – were they the two old men who were overheard engaged in a discourse so without grammar it was incomprehensible to the sane? Did Deeriye go into a retreat, spending a couple of days in prayer, seeking divine guidance? Did he spend a day or two learning how to march to a drill-sergeant's instructions and how, with a certain margin of efficiency, to pull a revolver's trigger? Into what dark hole of mystery did he disappear between being seen with Khaliif and turning up, arrayed in army uniform, marching in rhythm with the other soldiers – and, standing at attention before the General who was awarding medals to heroes of the land, pulling out, by mistake, prayer-beads instead of a revolver to shoot the General dead? (Another version told how the prayer-beads, like a boa-constrictor, entwined themselves around the muzzle of the revolver – and Deeriye could not disentangle it in time.) He was an easy target, now that he hadn't hit his. And the General's bodyguards emptied into him cartridges of machine-gun fire until his body was cut nearly in half.

When they searched his body, they found the following: a tattered copy of the Koranic chapter *Ya-sin,* notes on the Sayyid's "Death of Corfield," a pamphlet on the underground activities of the ANC, Nadiifa's photoraph, Deeriye's own ID card, a couple of inhalers to forestall an attack, and a standard revolver. His corpse, the story goes, lay inert, clumsily spread precisely where it fell (a journalist took a photograph of it). It lay soulless, shrouded in blood, alive with tropical insects, it lay untouched until the medal-awarding ceremony ended and the General's entourage left the scene. Deeriye would have been the first to appreciate the irony here, thought Zeinab, as she sorted out his and Mursal's belongings before a certain Security raid. If only he had pulled out the revolver in good time, she thought, if only . . . ! But perhaps he had looked forward to . . . dying; perhaps he had looked forward to being with Nadiifa for ever, never to be separated again from his soul-mate; perhaps this was his way of bidding farewell to a life crowded with ironies. His epitaph: "Here lies dead a hero whose vision and faith in Africa remained unshaken," Zeinab said to herself, not shedding a single tear.

Would his body be given to her for burial? she wondered to herself, as she cringed, for she now heard Natasha and Samawade crying to each other in another room. Would Mursal's corpse be handed over too so she could have them buried side by side in the same tomb – so they could continue uninterrupted the dialogue they had begun? At least, she thought, looking up and seeing Natasha and Samawade in the doorway, sobbing in chorus, at least neither died an anonymous death – and that was heroic.

Author's Note

I served as Guest Professor in the department of Comparative Literature's Africana Section, University of Bayreuth, during the period it took me to write this novel: I find it appropriate to address a word of thanks to the secretarial and teaching staff of the department as well as the librarians who were all friendly and generous with their time; my gratitude also to the President of the University, who took personal interest in my well-being.

Of the many books I read for this novel, the following have been very useful: Lane & Storr: *Asthma: The Facts,* OUP 1979; I.M. Lewis: *A Modern History of Somalia,* Longman Pb 1980; *Somali Poetry* edited by B.W. Andrzejewski & I.M. Lewis, OUP 1964; *Islamic Political Thought,* W.M. Watt, Edinburgh University Press 1968; David Cooper: *The Language of Madness,* Penguin Books 1980; Angelo del Boca: *Gli Italiani in Africa Orientale, La Conquista dell' Impero,* Vol. II, Editori Laterza 1979; Margaret Laurence: *A Tree of Poverty,* Irish University Press 1970 (although being a Somali myself, I've had to depend more on the resources of my own memory than on Laurence's).

On occasions, I did not hesitate to borrow the skeleton of a notion or phrases but have had to cover this body of information with flesh and skin of my own manufacture. Many thanks: my acknowledgement.

One last word. *Close Sesame* is the third part of a trilogy which began with *Sweet & Sour Milk* (1979) and whose second part is *Sardines* (1981). The overall title for the trilogy is: *Variations on the Theme of an African Dictatorship.*

N.F.

About the Author

Nuruddin Farah is an internationally recognized author. He was born in 1945 in Baidoa, in what is now the Republic of Somalia. In 1991, he received the Swedish Tucholsky Literary Award, given to literary exiles, and he was the recipient of the German DAAD fellowship in 1990. *Sweet and Sour Milk* won the English-Speaking Union Literary Award of 1980.

This book was designed by

April Leidig-Higgins.

It is set in Berkeley Old Style Book

type by The Typeworks and

manufactured by Edwards Brothers

on acid-free paper.